THEIR SUMMER RESCUE

SERA TAÍNO

Harlequin

SPECIAL EDITION

Harlequin® SPECIAL EDITION™

Recycling programs for this product may not exist in your area.

ISBN-13: 978-1-335-18047-6

Their Summer Rescue

Copyright © 2026 by Sera Taíno

Harlequin Enterprises ULC
22 Adelaide St. West, 41st Floor
Toronto, Ontario M5H 4E3, Canada
www.Harlequin.com

HarperCollins Publishers
Macken House, 39/40 Mayor Street Upper,
Dublin 1, D01 C9W8, Ireland
www.HarperCollins.com

Printed in Lithuania

1 2 3 4 5 6 7 8 9 10 LIT 28 27 26 25

Sera Taíno writes Latinx romances exploring love in the context of family and community. She is the 2019–2020 recipient of the Harlequin Romance Includes You Mentorship, resulting in the publication of her debut contemporary romance, *A Delicious Dilemma*. When she's not writing, she can be found teaching her high school literature class, crafting, and wrangling her husband and two children.

Books by Sera Taíno

Harlequin Special Edition

The Navarros

A Delicious Dilemma
The Best Man's Problem

Soledad Bay

Their Summer Rescue
A Summer to Start Over

Visit the Author Profile page
at Harlequin.com for more titles.

For my late mother-in-law, who loved without limits, met hardship with humor and taught us what resilience looks like in every obstacle she overcame. *Ci manchi così tanto.*

Chapter One

Nyla

The conference room of the Sea Turtle Research and Education Center smelled faintly of salt and disinfectants. The blinds were half drawn against the afternoon sun, slicing the gulf light into strips across the long table where laptops hummed and wires draped like seagrass over the floor. Traces of the turtle pools still clung to Dr. Nyla Dávila's skin even after she'd scrubbed her hands. The sea-colored hues of the center's conference room usually calmed her. Today, they did nothing. Panic gripped her by the throat, flashing through her in waves.

Dr. Anuar Jimenez, their in-house marine veterinarian, sat stiffly to her left, knee bouncing so hard, his chair vibrated. He hadn't cracked a joke in hours, which unsettled Nyla more than the scrolling lines of red-jay-colored code flashing on the laptop screen before her. He was pure sunshine in person, but after he'd brought her news of the ransomware attack on the center's systems the day before, he hadn't smiled since.

Dr. Dionne Sommers, the state's university liaison, sat on Nyla's right, calm as ever in her crisp maroon suit. Her friend's stillness cocooned her like armor against the chaos that had decimated their operating systems and crippled the lab Nyla had established after she graduated with her PhD in marine biology nine years earlier. She knew things were grim when their in-house network manager, Yasmin Acosta, didn't seem to blink as she sat hunched over her laptop, fingers stabbing at the keyboard like she was trying to spear sea eels with a blunt stick.

And then there was the stranger.

Olivia Navarro, founder of CyberHunters, the organization contracted by the state to deal with the attack, sat at the head of the table, her posture easy but not relaxed, as if the chair was forced to curve around her body against its will, and not the other way around. The dark line of her bob framed a face sharpened by focus, the coiled silver snake necklace around her slim neck glinting each time she moved. Through the glass wall behind her, Nyla caught glimpses of Olivia's team working in the adjacent conference room, monitors alive with the same red cascading numbers that she'd learned was the trademark of the malware that now held the center's systems hostage. They hardly seemed real compared with the sharp focus of the woman in front of her, whom, in any other context, Nyla would have described as strikingly beautiful.

Now, all Nyla could see was her hijacked data, and the intense woman who had the power to pull her life's work out of the clutches of renegade programmers.

"You're telling me my data is locked, and the only option is to either give up my passwords or pay these hackers?" Nyla spoke, her voice cracking across the table, sharper than she intended.

Olivia didn't flinch. "Dr. Dávila, your servers are fully compromised. To contain the damage, we need full access to your research files. Otherwise—" her tone was maddeningly casual "—pay the ransom and be done with it, if you can afford it."

The audacity.

The clinical dismissal in her tone stung more than the words themselves. Years of hatchling survival records and migration charts had been reduced to nothing but corrupted spreadsheets. All the raw data Nyla had spent her career collecting and protecting, because she had learned her lesson about allowing the wrong people to get close to the things that mattered.

She didn't even know Olivia Navarro existed before today. And despite the side-eye Dionne gave her before returning to her notes, it was a lot to ask to just give up access to her life's work.

Ironic, because she was now protecting data she no longer had control over. Not after the malware had stolen access to it right out from under her nose.

Nyla's jaw tightened, her hands curling around the edge of the table.

Anuar shot her a worried glance, his knee bouncing faster. Dionne, without looking up from her notepad, set a calming hand on Nyla's arm as if to say, *Stand down. She's on your team.*

She knew it wasn't meant as provocation. Olivia Navarro wasn't trying to bait her. Nyla was raging inside in a way she'd rarely experienced in her life, although she was capable of anger. She wasn't a robot, even if that was the first impression she often gave off. Calm and self-assured, the cracks in her professionalism were intentionally kept tightly under control. She was simply…indifferent to anything not related to her work.

Nyla exhaled, her pulse still pounding in her throat. No, this wasn't just about spreadsheets. It was about her turtles. If they didn't resolve this soon, the release schedule would collapse. Kayuga, still healing from a propeller gash to her shell that left her unable to forage. Yuno, recovering from tumor removal. The nests Nyla monitored so hatchlings had a fighting chance. Every one of them depended on careful timing.

The backups had failed at the worst moment. Tanks had spiked in salinity during the attack, forcing her to transfer patients and pray no one was destabilized. And now? Without restored data, she couldn't geotag Kayuga or Yuno before their release window in three weeks. Losing that would mean losing a year of migration data. A year of hard-won progress.

Her life's purpose compromised, all because Dr. Anuar had clicked the wrong link. She knew he felt awful about it. He was the most caring, considerate person she'd ever known. But the damage was done.

Yet here was this woman who had walked in like she owned the place. It felt like the center no longer belonged to Nyla.

How dare those hackers?

How dare she?

Her rage was a blast that barreled outward at a radius of 360 degrees.

Nyla caught herself studying the sharp edges of Olivia's profile. The restless eyes, the silver snake pendant at the base of her throat and the sleek navy suit that seemed designed for command. Astute and calculating, she carried the same kind of focus Nyla recognized in herself. She hated the flicker of reluctant respect toward the person that her anger had inconveniently chosen as its target.

"You'll forgive me if I don't find the choices reassuring," Nyla retorted, forcing her tone to sound cool.

Finally, Olivia's gaze lifted from her laptop, locking with hers. The intensity of it nearly knocked Nyla back in her chair, though she refused to look away.

"I'm not here to reassure you," Olivia said evenly. "I'm here to get your center back online. If you want comfort, talk to your university liaison." Her eyes flew to Dionne, who noticeably straightened in her chair.

"I've researched the kind of attack this center has been subjected to. The first phase of recovery could take anywhere from a few weeks to months. Our center won't survive an extended closure if those are the timelines we're looking at," Nyla said.

Olivia's eyes narrowed briefly, the attention burning through her until Nyla felt an unbearable compulsion to look away. She did not. She wasn't one to wither under anyone's hot glare.

"Whatever timelines your research has revealed, I assure you I can do the job in half the time. That's why CyberHunters was brought on. We're small, but our business rating is nearly perfect. We'll get your data back and your center online in half the estimated time, rest assured."

Yasmin snorted into her coffee and Nyla appreciated the skepticism. Anuar stopped bouncing his knee long enough to whisper a quick prayer under his breath. Dionne's eyes flicked between the two women, exuding the even calm she was known for.

Nyla folded her arms, a move that bought her a moment to steady the flare in her chest. She'd dealt with arrogant consultants before. But arrogance paired with competence? That was dangerous. And if she was being brutally honest with herself, somehow intoxicating. Especially when that competence came in the package of an objectively attractive woman and a fellow Latina, no less.

She forced herself to break eye contact first, hating capitulation, but not too proud to understand that petulance would get her exactly nowhere. She scribbled a series of lines on her legal pad. Her pen trembled slightly, her thoughts going to another time when she'd had to give up access to her data to defend herself against someone whom she'd believed to be her research partner and friend. The center had been Ethan Robles's dream too, but he'd blown his chance to be a part of it because of resentment, greed and simple human jealousy.

"Here are my usernames and passwords. Any required authentications have been included." Nyla tore the page from the pad and held it up. "This is who I am, my life's work." Her hostility drained away. This woman, abrasive and competent, was not her enemy, though she very much wanted to see her that way. "Please be gentle with it."

Olivia stared at the paper for a few beats before sliding it out of Nyla's grasp. Her fingers were slender but strong, much like the woman who sat across from her, whose oversize character compensated for her slim build and average height. "Your system is in good hands. I give you my word on that."

Nyla rose to her feet. "I truly hope so, Ms. Navarro." She turned and made for the door, trying very hard not to let the knot of tears building at the back of her throat burst out in front of everyone. "I'm trusting you with the most important endeavor of my life."

"Olivia."

Nyla paused, turning to look over her shoulder, hoping that the tears that had gathered were not visible to the woman who spoke to her. "What?"

"Call me Olivia."

Nyla nodded once before pulling the door open and escaping as quickly as was dignified.

* * *

"The ransom could cripple the research center, possibly forcing its closure, even with insurance coverage. There's no reason for the amount to be this absurdly high, and negotiations to lower it have so far been unproductive," Dionne said after she'd left the meeting room that had become ground zero for dealing with the ransomware attack and found Nyla in her office in the Nest, the medical laboratory where turtles were taken for care.

"It's only been a few days since the infection," Nyla said, gripping her pen in hand. She'd had to revert to old-school notetaking now that even her iPad had been compromised. "How is the insurance company already on their third and fourth rounds of negotiation?"

"These things move quickly," Dionne answered as she took the seat across from Nyla's desk. "Extreme demands on short timelines are made to frighten institutions into acting quickly, under threat of having their systems corrupted beyond repair. That's why CyberHunters needed to get here, ASAP."

Nyla wanted to cling to any kind of good news, especially from Dionne, whom she could trust to tell her the unvarnished truth. The former computer science fellow at U of M when Nyla was a graduate student now worked for the Board of Governors' Office of Technology and Cybersecurity as a liaison to research institutes receiving state funding. A Black woman in her fifties, the Howard University alum was athletically built, a callback to her days as a high school and university track star. She exuded confidence and equanimity that Nyla desperately wished she possessed at this moment.

"The center was just getting back to normal operations." Nyla reached for her computer keyboard before thinking better of it. "Hurricane Adaliz nearly decimated the town. Soledad Bay was only five miles south of turning into a post-apocalyptic beach town, and now this? I'm angry, Dionne." Soledad Bay was limping toward wholeness again. Nyla had been a part of the community cleanup and recovery efforts. The residents of the seaside enclave had come far in a short period of time. Now the center was being held hostage by a malicious actor, and this time, Nyla's hands were tied.

"This town, this center, deserves better," Dionne said. "But ransomware is often opportunistic. Hackers send out the package and attack wherever it lands. I'm just sorry it happened to be you." She paused. "Yasmin looked rough. How is she holding up?"

Nyla remembered her conversation with her network manager when she first learned about the attack. "In a word? Pissed. At the hackers. At the point of breach, but I suspect, mostly at herself. She sees it as a personal failure."

"Reassure her," Dionne said. "Yasmin is prickly, but I know she works hard. There was only so much she could do. That email shouldn't have made it through our firewalls. All it took was one click, and I know she's trained your staff extensively on what not to click on."

"A conspiracy of carelessness. I know all this, and I suspect she does, as well. But emotions don't require confirmation in the real world to feel true. That's what makes them so treacherous." At Dionne's puzzled expression, Nyla spread her hands in a helpless gesture, refusing to elaborate. That was Nyla's problem, no one else's. "So tell me more about this contractor that I'm entrusting my work to."

Dionne's gaze lingered on Nyla for a few more beats before she relaxed at this line of inquiry. "CyberHunters is a boutique cybersecurity consultant firm specializing in ransomware attacks."

"Shouldn't we have something like that in-house? I don't need the well-being of this institute in the hands of a nepo baby or some politico's bestie."

Dionne tsked. "Feisty. Don't worry, CyberHunters is highly recommended and has an impressive résumé. They've progressed far beyond basic computer programming script. You'll be in good hands, or they'll have to answer to me."

Nyla remembered that she hadn't dabbed Florida water on her pulse points today and worried that her skepticism of that superstitious practice had finally caught up to her. She sternly directed her mind to not lose focus.

Dionne reached a hand across the desk to squeeze Nyla's, pulling her out of her head. "I hear you," Dionne said slowly. "But this company has a good reputation. Their growth has been impressive, and the CEO has a reputation for being brilliant and hands-on. You're getting the best possible team we could find. You just have to trust the process."

"You know how hard that is for me. Contractors are a bad bet. Everyone knows that." Much like mercenaries, they didn't have much more incentive than the payout on a contract to get their work done. "They're not part of the university culture, so they have no stake in ensuring our ultimate well-being." Nyla couldn't help being skeptical. It was as much a part of her DNA as her dark eyes, thick, black hair or the soft brown color of her skin.

"Dr. Dávila," Dionne said sternly, though the firm warmth of her hand radiated through Nyla's. "I was part of the committee that approved the contract. If you can't trust the state, can you at least trust me?"

Nyla raised her free hand, pressing it on her forehead.

"Of course I do, but you can't control everyone, even if you think you can."

Dionne smiled as if conceding to the point, knowing full well that she, like Nyla, was not the kind to relinquish control easily. Dionne had been a part of Nyla's educational and professional life since her graduate school days and was as close to a mentor as Nyla would ever get. She had to trust Dionne's judgment because there was no one she respected more.

"I'll figure myself out." Nyla sighed, resigned. "On to more pleasant topics. How is Harper?"

At the mention of her wife, Dionne smiled. "Happy as a clam, teaching graduate students and writing yet another book." She laughed, but there was nothing but contentment and self-indulgence in the sound and Nyla couldn't help but smile along with her. "Dr. Harper Sommers is never happier than when she's buried elbow-deep in some research library, or on a historical site for one scholarly paper or another, and she's extra happy to share every last detail with me."

Nyla knew Harper well. According to her, there were too many gaps in the US historical record of Black history, and she had committed her life to filling them. Dionne and Harper—two intellectuals with consuming but opposing interests—had somehow made their relationship work and built a beautiful family with two children who were just as accomplished as their parents.

"I'm guessing you don't mind," Nyla said.

"Not at all," Dionne answered fondly. "Her mind is an amazing place to visit."

"You two make me feel more single than I already am." Nyla feigned gagging before grinning at her friend.

Dionne actually giggled, which Nyla found incredibly sweet. "I'm one of the lucky ones." She pursed her lips, giving her a sly smile. "And you will be, too. You'll find a woman who is as passionate about your work as she is about her own. She'll be brilliant and she's going to knock you over and carry you away."

"Don't knock me over! I'm too fragile for that kind of handling." Nyla couldn't help but laugh along with Dionne even as they rose to their feet.

"Now, Nyla, I never took you for a liar. You and I both know you're about as fragile as a storm wall. This company has no choice but to do right by you, because I know you'll blow up my DMs if they don't."

"Yes, ma'am, I will. *A mi no me importa.* I don't play with my center." She walked Dionne to the door, her stomach still twisted in worry despite her friend's efforts to assure her. "Thanks for trying to make this easier," she said.

"You know I'm here for you, sis." Dionne gave Nyla a hug that warmed her all the way through.

As she led the way out of the Nest and to the conference room next to the IT hub where Olivia and her team had set up shop, Nyla couldn't hold back the memories of another time when she'd experienced the same horrible feelings she'd been experiencing since her system had been infected. She was a graduate student all over again, working beside Ethan Robles, once her trusted fellow graduate assistant and, she'd naively believed, her friend. She had shared all the details of her dreams for a sea turtle rescue center, the subject of her doctoral thesis. She had trusted him with her work.

And that had been her fatal error.

Ethan hadn't seen a partner in Nyla. He'd seen an easy mark. He'd copied her data, tried to pass her research off as his own and came close to stealing years of graduate work. Only her meticulous records saved her. That had proved indispensable as a woman of color in a male-dominated field trying to prove that the work was indeed her own. The scandal ended his career, but not the venom he spat at her afterward, as if she owed him her life's work.

Nyla swore that she would never trust so blindly again. She was, at heart, an introvert who preferred the company of her thoughts over interacting with people. But that didn't make her a doormat.

She was reliving yet again her horror and powerlessness at the possibility that she could lose everything she had worked so hard for because of someone else's underhandedness. Except this time, the thief didn't have a face, no university panel was going to judge in favor of her merit, and its resolution was in the hands of someone she wasn't sure she could trust.

This day couldn't end soon enough. Only the promise of her nightly beach rounds, checking in on her nests and the future each turtle egg carried, could restore her faith. She needed a reminder of her purpose, now more than ever.

Chapter Two

The concierge at Alba's Beachside Resort unloaded their bags while Olivia's tech team, Dareen, Alejandro and Feliz, checked in. They'd flown into Tallahassee the day before, had worked nonstop with the state cybercrime office, then woken up early that morning to drive straight to Soledad Bay for the task debrief. When Feliz mentioned the Sea Turtle Research and Education Center, the front-desk manager, an attractive young woman by the name of Jade, seemed to already know why they were there. Despite being peak season, she upgraded them to a four-bedroom beachfront bungalow.

"Y'all take care of Dr. Dávila and the research center," Jade had said while handing over the key cards. "The center does good work."

It was Olivia's first clue: The center wasn't just a lab; it was part of the town's beating heart.

"We'll be sure to do that," Olivia answered sincerely.

They were finally at the end of a grueling few days that had begun before they'd even set out to Soledad Bay, Florida. After the staff debrief of CyberHunters' action plan, followed by a more detailed debrief with Dr. Dionne Sommers, to whom they would be reporting, it would be a relief to finally get to the bungalow, kick off her fabulous shoes and unwind.

Of all the moments that stood out for Olivia, meeting Dr. Nyla Dávila had to be the most interesting. As she moved with her team through the lobby of the hotel, it was only now that Olivia acknowledged that she had been uncharacteristically abrasive with the professor, an action ironically born of a desire to impress the director. Dr. Dávila was attractive—Olivia would give her that—but there was something impenetrable about her that needled at Olivia and drove her desire to provoke the uptight director.

That had been an unprofessional instinct, one she shouldn't have given in to.

She needed to do a better job of compartmentalizing anyone who was connected to her into a strictly professional context and not react to them on such an emotional level. Emotions were a liability that had gotten Olivia into too much trouble in her life already. She could do without them.

"Wait." Dareen picked up the carry-on and computer bag Olivia was dragging behind her and set everything on the luggage cart that was already piled high with everyone's bags. Before Olivia could protest, she said, "Why carry your stuff when you literally have four wheels to do it for you?"

"Good point." Olivia was grateful to her lead programmer. Her brain was running a mile a minute, as it often did, usually on project details, but this time on her interactions with Dr. Dávila, until she was disconnected from her surroundings and moved on autopilot.

"What's gotten into you?" Dareen asked.

"Nothing," Olivia rushed to say, adding, "Just going down my mental list of things to do."

"Aren't you always?" Dareen retorted. Her family had permanently relocated from Puerto Rico during her parents' generation, and she'd grown up in New York and spoke English like an extra from the *Long Island Housewives*. She adjusted her soft-blue shirtdress and looked out toward the atrium that led to the on-site pool and the sea beyond. Her expression grew dreamy at the sight of the crashing waves. "Can't believe we get to work in a beach town. Can we stay on an extra week after we finish up this contract?"

"I guess, if you're into that," Olivia said, drafting a text message to her cousin Val to let her know she'd gotten in, then promptly deciding she'd just call her from her room.

"What do you mean, 'If you're into that'? I'm not asking you to tie me up. Who reacts that way to a week on the beach?"

Olivia's preoccupation with Dr. Davila shriveled up even further at the thought of the environment they'd be living in for at least a month. "Sand."

Dareen's face screwed up in confusion. "There's sand, yes. What's your point?"

"Sand," Olivia sniffed, "belongs in the seventh bolgia of hell."

"Olivia!" Dareen erupted in giggles that she had to smother behind her hand. "Are you alright, *nena*?"

"Perfectly," Olivia said, revving up to give her well-thought-out and incontestable opinion. "I just think sand is a cruel invention of the universe, much like mosquitoes, and both belong in hell, not between my toes or my butt cheeks when I'm trying to enjoy a nice walk in the shallows."

Dareen's green eyes went wide as she covered her mouth with her hand. "If you're walking along the water, why would any get any between your butt cheeks? I'm truly confused."

Olivia knew she had left out critical context that had included the first time she'd made out with her high school girlfriend on a trip to Coney Island and underestimated the utter ubiquity of the substance they'd naively rolled around in, and how it had gotten *everywhere*. She debated sharing this tidbit of information and quickly decided against it. "Never mind. Are we done checking in?"

Dareen shook her head. "Yes, check-in is done." She walked ahead, Olivia following close behind her. "I want to leave my things in our suite, take a hot shower and get cleaned up. I'm grimy from traveling."

"Bungalow," Feliz piped in, catching up to them, her multicolored boho dress swishing around her legs. "We're staying in a bungalow."

She lifted her arms and spun in place, her dress fluffing under her matching peach linen jacket, her attempt at professional dress, despite the braid that wound around her head like a crown above the cascade of her dark hair and the colorful butterfly tattoo that stretched across her chest, accented with rose vines that looped up her shoulders. The twenty-four-year-old transfemme had been headed for a life of crime when she broke into a medium-sized social media platform when she was only a teenager, a crime that company had chosen not to prosecute her for. Olivia had gotten to know her through an online hackers' forum and, after doing her due diligence, offered her a job. Olivia liked to think that she had managed to keep her tiny pixie programming queen out of jail. She truly believed that someone as brilliant as Feliz shouldn't squander her talents in a high-security detention facility when there were far worse criminals, dressed up in corporate respectability, setting the world on fire.

"Everyone gets their own room this time," Olivia announced, heedless of the conversation that had moved on without her.

Dareen frowned but chose not to call her out on the interruption. "You mean we don't have to sleep two to a bed, smashed together like sardines? That last hotel was starting to feel like my parents' house," Feliz said.

"It was a booking mistake. I would never have done that intentionally," Olivia retorted. The four-star hotel in Tallahassee had mixed up their reservation and shoved her team of four into a room with two full-sized beds and a single bathroom. It had been the most uncomfortable two days of Olivia's life. Luckily, they had been too busy working on the early stages of this hack to feel the full inconvenience of the tight accommodations.

"You would be capable of doing it, just for a laugh," Dareen interjected, her eyes twinkling with mirth.

"And be forced to sleep next to Al all over again? I don't think so," Olivia protested. The quiet giant of a man was tapping away on his phone as he walked, pausing only to push the mop of wavy brown hair away from his smooth, olive-tinted forehead and avoid walking into walls or furniture.

"You sound like a dying whale the moment you hit REM sleep, boss," he deadpanned, continuing to type away as if he wasn't having three different conversations on his phone in addition to sassing Olivia.

"Rude!" Olivia protested. "I don't snore." Remembering that she'd woken herself only the night before with a loud wheeze through her nose, she amended, "Not all the time."

"Well, it's better to sound like a dying whale than to smell like one, in my opinion," Feliz countered, coming to Olivia's rescue.

That was her girl. Olivia guffawed and Dareen snorted. Al's only response was the flicker of his amber brown eyes to take in Feliz, lingering a moment before he dropped them again to continue his texting, the ultimate unbothered king, despite Feliz's constant ribbing.

"Now, now, now," Olivia soothed. "We're just not used to the smell of a man in our midst. It's hard on us gay gals."

The corner of Al's lip quirked upward at her comment. "Not appreciating having to carry the flag as the only gay dude in this community. Feeling attacked right now."

"Aw, poor love." Dareen reached out, smoothing her fingers through his hair. "Let's not single out our baby boy for abuse."

"Not an improvement," he retorted as he continued to tap away at his device before tucking it into the inside pocket of his jacket. He pushed a burst of air from between pursed lips. "It's freaking humid. I'm gonna need a bath, and not because I smell like a whale," he quickly amended when Feliz was about to open her mouth.

Olivia looked out toward the Beachwalk, the path that led to the bungalows and the beach beyond, then back to the trifold in her hand. "Map says we're around the bend. We should have followed the bellhop." Olivia led the way down the walk, their luggage no doubt already in their room, thanks to the brisk and efficient concierge, leaving her with map duty. Visually, the sea was stunning, its gorgeous foam-tipped waves washing toward the bleach-white beach with rhythmic inexorability. But Olivia instinctively recoiled at the sight of so much sand. She was a city girl, through and through. She loved her black wardrobe, layered jackets and heavy, thick-soled boots. Cold weather and coffeehouses at off-peak hours (because let's be serious—*people* were as bad as sand) were some of her personal joys, as well as the aesthetics of traffic as she dodged her way on foot throughout the city.

It was all very pretty, but the sounds were all wrong,

nothing like the bustling foot traffic and honking noise of her city. Here EV vehicles packed with people wearing next to nothing zoomed up and down the sand. And talking about sand—had she mentioned that it was *everywhere*?

Olivia found herself breathing in the sea air despite her rejection of it. She figured she could endure the sand for a few weeks, at least until this hacking job was resolved and they got paid. They had other, longer-term projects lined up already. Business was that good, thanks to all the crooks in the world taking a stab at cyber thievery.

Every gig had the potential to become a permanent contract, ensuring the company's sustainability, so she needed—no, *demanded*—things to go flawlessly

As her team took in the spacious bungalow, with all its comforts and amenities, Olivia lingered on the back porch, watching seabirds rustle quietly among the large-leaf plants that clustered like a patchwork quilt outside the sliding glass doors. She shifted back and forth on her Prada brushed-leather wedge cutout pumps, perfect for when she knew she would be on her feet for a long day. But even they were starting to wear on her. She sprawled across the aquamarine-and-white pillows of the chaise lounge and answered several email messages on her phone while she waited for her team to claim their rooms before she took whichever one was left.

Her mind wandered back to when she'd started Cyber-Hunters as a one-woman operation five years earlier. Over time, she had moved the cluster of high-powered servers from her cramped apartment to a growing headquarters, while her staff was made up of talented programmers that she'd handpicked and trained herself. Soon, she'd found herself running a small company, employing a full-time staff with titles and benefits like a fully functioning adult. She still outsourced her payroll—her company was small enough that outsourcing the service was less costly than creating a department in-house. But it was dizzying to look back and see how far she'd come in only a few years, and yet she still felt like she had room to grow.

She'd asked her quirky crew to accompany her down south because they were the best in her company. They knew how to show up and show out in everything they did. Olivia was no stranger to having to prove that she was the best and smartest person in the room. It came with being a queer woman of color in spaces that were not made for her. If she was here, it was because she knew what she was doing. She wasn't going to let herself or her people down anytime soon.

Unprompted, images of her ex crept across her mind like a bad movie. The end of that relationship had definitely been an exercise in Olivia not being enough, and she wasn't in the mood to think about that. It had been a few years since the breakup, yet Aleysha and those negative feelings still showed up in her thoughts like an uninvited guest when her defenses were down.

Dareen thankfully stepped onto the patio at that moment, changed into comfortable shorts and a shirt, forcing Olivia to banish Aleysha from her thoughts. "The three of us were thinking of heading to the beach before dinner. Want to join us?"

Olivia tucked her phone in her pocket before grabbing her carrier bag. "You guys go ahead. I have some paperwork to look at and a couple of phone calls to make before I can call it a day." At Dareen's disappointment, more on Olivia's behalf than her own, she added, "Don't worry. I'll take a walk after dinner." Before Dareen could tease her, she added, "I can enjoy a short walk, that doesn't mean my opinion on sand has changed."

"Who knows, this could be the trip that changes your mind about the beach. You could fall in love with it." Dareen laughed, rolling up the short sleeves of her T-shirt to her shoulders. "You might never go back up north again."

"Banish the thought," Olivia retorted, shivering in horror. "I promised Dr. Dávila I'd do this job in half the time. That's how badly I want to get out of here."

Dr. Nyla Dávila's face flashed like a bolt of lightning across Olivia's mind, and she heard her own brash words echo in her mind. *I'll do it in half the time.*

Her word was her bond. She'd made a promise to Dr. Dávila. Barring a natural disaster, or internal sabotage, Olivia was going to get the job done in record time.

She and the pretty professor with the prickly personality had gotten off to a rough start, and she was certain the woman couldn't stand her, which was fine by Olivia.

"I made a promise and I mean to keep it," Olivia said, almost to herself.

Dareen chuckled. "More like a bet, knowing you."

Her team knew her well. If she made any kind of commitment, she'd move heaven and earth to keep it. It was simply her character, and she didn't know any other way to be. Not in her professional life and certainly not in her personal life. *Especially* in her personal life. Aleysha had known this about her, too. While a commitment wasn't enough to make things go her way, she'd be damned if this was the one time she proved herself a liar.

"Gotta keep business spicy," she quipped, trying with all her might to kick her sudden melancholy to the curb. Damn Aleysha and her freaking memories.

Her crew left soon after. Olivia headed to the bedroom that they'd set aside for her. It was a master bedroom, which she was hoping someone else would take. Just because she was the owner, it didn't mean she felt entitled to special privileges. They all worked hard together.

She shook her head as she unpacked her luggage, fetching a pair of loose pants and a tank top. She saw the brochures for Disney World on the pinewood end table, which complemented the creams and pale blues of the room. There were also advertisements for several events in the Orlando area. She lingered on one of the brochures, thinking about her ex, Aleysha, and how things ended between them.

Now, she was just a stone's throw away from where Olivia was, and she couldn't help spinning schedules and plans, a habit that helped her in her business. She calculated how long it would take to drive out to see her if she were sufficiently motivated to do so, which she wasn't. Still, she couldn't help but feel aware of the short distance, and of the pull of something that felt deceptively like closure.

Instead, she grabbed her phone and hit the quick dial on the single-most-used number in her contacts. She sank down on the edge of the bed as the call rang.

"Olivia!" Her cousin Val's voice barreled cheerfully through the line. "*Prima!* It's been hours! Why didn't you call me when you got to your meeting?"

"We were running behind schedule," Olivia answered, shrinking at her cousin's words. This was on her. Olivia prided herself on always keeping her promises, no matter what, and she'd failed to follow through on calling her cousin when she said she would.

"I'm sorry, Darth Cupcake," she added, using the nickname she'd given Val after a childhood cooking mishap resulted in them both nearly burning down the apartment building they lived in. "I won't let it happen again." She heard a screaming child pierce the conversation, and a male baritone soothing the child. "How is our niece?"

Val's voice came through like a bell, as if she'd leaned in closer to speak. "Loud. She takes after her father."

"Which one?" Olivia said, smiling at the continued ruckus in the background.

"You know there's only one chatterbox between Étienne and Rafi. Zuri looks and acts exactly like Étienne. We've taken to calling her Little E because she's the spitting image of her father." Val's brother and Olivia's cousin, Rafi, married Etienne Galois, a fashion photographer, three years earlier and, with the help of a friend, now had a daughter, Zuri. Val, like the proud *tía* she was, continued to describe Zuri's antics with the tone of someone who lived for the chaos.

Olivia managed to get herself undressed as her cousin spoke, shimmying out of her pants without dropping the phone wedged between her cheek and shoulder. Val loved to chat, especially when it was about their family. And Val was over the moon with her niece, Zuri, since she was postponing having children with her husband, Philip, until her second restaurant was on stable footing. Val was living her dreams, and children simply weren't part of her and her husband's equation at the moment.

"How is your pretty husband?" Olivia continued.

Val sighed. "Managing his workaholism as best he can now that his father is fully retired." Val's husband, Philip Wagner, inherited his father's development corporation, and though his approach to managing the company was far saner than his father's, the apple hadn't fallen too far from the tree. "I make sure to remind him that I'm around, too. Thankfully, I don't have to strong-arm him too much. How's your project going? Have I told you how jealous I am that you're in Florida?"

"At least a hundred times, *prima*. You never miss a chance to remind me. Love you for that." Olivia's sarcasm was dripping like honey as she moved to the sliding glass door and the porch beyond.

"That's because I'm always jealous! I've never been to Florida."

"Because your husband takes you to places like Nice on the Cote D'Azur. You know, in France?"

She could hear the smirk in her cousin's voice. "I never said he didn't take me anywhere. I just haven't been to Florida yet, that's all. I bet it's beautiful."

"There's sand everywhere," Olivia complained, though she couldn't tear her eyes away from the white-tipped blue waves crashing into the shoreline.

Val's laugh came over the phone, clear and full of joy. Olivia liked the sound of it. She was a simp for her family, especially when they were happy. "It's a beach, *tonta*. What did you expect?"

"Nothing. I had zero expectations. I knew exactly what I was getting into." At least when it came to the beach and the sand. Not, it seems, with Dr. Dávila and this project.

"How's the work going, anyway?" Val asked, eerily mirroring Olivia's thoughts.

"Honestly? It just got exponentially more difficult, and that's saying a lot, given the type of virus that infected their systems." She proceeded to fill Val in on the general details of the virus without overwhelming her with technical details. "I've been digging into it since we were called in. It's a sophisticated virus that was launched against a soft target to gain access to the wider university network. Makes sense, because who would go through all that trouble to hit a research institute—no offense to the turtles." Olivia was aware that she was rambling, but her brain had taken off at the mere mention of a problem to be solved.

Val laughed out loud, the sound weaving its way through her runaway thoughts. "I'm sure the turtles don't care."

Olivia barreled on. "The turtles are amazing, no doubt, but that's how we know they were going for bigger fish, no pun intended. The virus is overkill. Like bringing a tank to a knife fight. No, I'm convinced the real target was the university network and the only reason the virus didn't tank their network is because they have dozens of fail-safe security protocols that were not present at the epicenter of infection. They figured a sea turtle research center would be an easier target, and they were right."

"I'm sure you'll figure it out, *prima*," Val said, trying to be encouraging even though Olivia was 100 percent sure that most of what she'd said had flown right over her head.

As if realizing something, Val added, "Wait a second! Sea turtles? *¡Ay Dios mío!*"

Olivia's head spun with the sudden shift in conversation. "Do you have an actual attention span? I'm talking about sophisticated programming code and you're asking about turtles?"

"I love turtles! *Son tan preciosos.* I bet Zuri would love them, too. Now we have to go to the aquarium. Have you seen any yet?"

"It's not like they hang out on Beachside Drive." Did time have any meaning for Val? She'd been in town for barely twenty-four hours, hadn't even stepped outside yet. "I'll keep an eye out. The professor who runs the institute keeps track of them, so I'm bound to see one eventually." Olivia grew sheepish. She got excited about a lot of things, but she usually kept the gushing to herself. "I'm hoping I have a good chance of seeing at least one turtle while I'm here."

"You see? You're not as indifferent as you pretend to be. I hope you sort out their virus situation soon so you can relax and enjoy the scenery." Olivia could almost hear Val shaking her head. "It's a shame a place that is actually doing something useful in the world has to deal with this nonsense."

"When you're greedy, you don't care about who you hurt." Olivia thought about her cousins, how they each in their own way gave something back to the world, and how not-greedy they were. It made her even more determined to get the center back up and running, no matter what she personally thought about the somewhat stuffy professor. Anyone doing that kind of work had redeeming value in her eyes.

And Olivia knew herself. She could forgive many slights when there was a pretty face involved. And Dr. Dávila had one of the prettiest faces she'd ever seen.

"So," Val said, easing quietly into a transition in the conversation. Olivia knew exactly where she was headed. "Have you seen Aleysha yet?"

Olivia growled. "What part of 'I've barely been in town for twenty-four hours' didn't make sense to you?"

"Okay, okay, *calmate*. I was just asking because I know that she lives close to where you are."

Olivia sighed. When it came to Aleysha, her nerves turned razor sharp. It wasn't Val's fault if she was just trying to be supportive. "Sorry, I didn't mean to snap. If you want the truth, I—" She paused, unsure how much to reveal. "I might have been tempted to drive over to Orlando and see her. I don't know what good it will do. It feels like I need something from her, but I'm not sure what it is."

"You know my opinion on this," Val said.

"Yes, dear cousin, you've made it abundantly clear what you think of her."

Val made a sound of frustration. "I have nothing against

Aleysha. She was a lovely woman, and you seemed to be really happy with her. I just don't want you to fall into temptation and get hurt again, that's all."

"I wouldn't go in with any expectations. I don't think she's going to change her mind." In fact, Aleysha was one of the most stubborn people on the planet. It would be inconceivable for her to change her mind about any of this. "I just need to know—"

"If she was honest about breaking up with you? And going to see her is somehow going to make her more honest about it?"

Val had Olivia there. Aleysha's breakup was this open wound still beating under her skin. She wanted to know why, that was all. What had she done to earn it? How could she go into other relationships without knowing what was so fundamentally wrong with her that her long-term girlfriend had been able to break things off so easily, without warning. What if Olivia committed the same unknown mistake and drove away the next person she fell for?

Olivia wasn't going to say all that to Val. She hated feeling this vulnerability, even with her cousin, whom she trusted more than anyone else. "I could give her a chance to be honest with me about what I believed was an important relationship in both our lives."

"We all need people in our lives who are willing to fight for us, or to stand up to others on our behalf. Not people who are quick to shed us like old snakeskin when we become inconvenient," Val said.

"Wow, you really don't like Aleysha," Olivia said simply.

"I *did* like Aleysha, until she walked away from you with that lame-ass excuse." Val's voice grew sharp with anger as the conversation went on. It was something she loved about her cousin—how easy she was to read and understand what she was feeling. She had a hard time lying and Olivia needed people to be as honest and transparent with her as possible.

"If she could drop you so easily and without compromise in a moment when anyone else would have been reaching out to the person they loved for support, then she wasn't the one for you. She wasn't your person. And I really wish you'd focus on finding that person rather than rehashing the past with someone who clearly doesn't deserve you. You are too awesome for that. The woman of your dreams is out there, waiting for you. She might be walking on the beach as we speak."

Olivia was touched by her tirade. "You really think that way about me, *prima*? You think I'm awesome?"

"Now I know I created a monster. You're going to have a fat head now and no one is going to be able to talk to you again. Yes, Olivia, you are awesome. A badass. Go find yourself someone who wants their world rocked by someone like you. Why go after the leftovers of your past? *¡Pa'lante, niña!* Move forward. Life is too short for any of that. Ask me how I know."

Olivia knew that Val was thinking about her ex-boyfriend and how Philip had wiped away every bad memory she'd ever made with him.

She loved her unhinged, adorable cousin. Val had two restaurants, a family, an amazing man and a good life. She wasn't missing out on anything, yet she had a heart as big as the city they'd grown up in. Val was one of the most generous spirits she'd ever known.

"I'll keep all that in mind," she said finally. She could hear Val's exasperation in the sigh she released, but thankfully, she didn't dwell on the issue anymore and changed the conversation. Val shared some little tidbits of news about the family. The Navarros were a dynamic group and East

Ward, for all its size, was always hopping. People getting married, getting divorced, getting pregnant or opening and closing businesses. It was a busy little enclave where everyone knew everyone else. Olivia couldn't imagine anywhere else being quite like East Ward and was grateful that she could call that town her home.

When she hung up the phone, she stared out into the darkening sky. She'd have to head downstairs and squeeze in a walk now if she wanted to beat the night.

She glanced over at the brochures as if they would leap off the nightstand and bite her. Aleysha was there, somewhere between Epic Universe and the Happiest Place on Earth, and it made Olivia restless.

Next to those brochures was one for the Sea Turtle Research and Education Center. Olivia picked it up. Couldn't they have come up with a shorter name? Like Loggerhead Express or Turtle World? The Great Sea Turtle Emporium?

Olivia let the brochures fall and dropped back on the bed, starfish-spread. Val's voice echoed in her ear: *Pa'lante, niña! Move forward.*

Easier said than done. But when she closed her eyes, she didn't see Aleysha—she saw Dr. Nyla Dávila. Smart. Severe. Gorgeous in a way that made Olivia's chest tighten. And dismissive enough to make her want to prove herself twice over.

If she'd been in that meeting room, her cousin would have laughed and whispered, *She didn't even look at you, chica.* But Olivia had caught that flicker in the professor's eyes, quick as lightning, betraying how much she cared about her center. Olivia knew that language. She spoke it fluently every time she thought about her little company.

She pressed her palms over her face and groaned. This

wasn't why she was here. She had a system to rebuild, a team to lead, a promise to keep. That was all.

Pretty people were a problem. They brought out the stupid in her.

Chapter Three

Olivia

By the time her team returned from the beach, Olivia had sorted out her schedule and solidified a game plan for the rest of the week. She and her team had dinner together, where everyone spoke excitedly about their beach walk. Olivia began to feel stripped raw by the endless workday and the togetherness with her team. She resisted the urge to take a shower and give in to exhaustion. It would be a waste to work on the beach and not experience it in some way.

She stepped out onto the patio, locking the sliding glass doors behind her, and headed out onto the boardwalk leading to the beach.

The sight of the water revived her, while the sound of the sea, the smell of salt and the pungent aroma of seaweed soothed something that had grown jagged inside her. She truly believed that if she slowed down, even for one moment, all her insecurities about work and her grief over the end of her relationship with Aleysha would come roaring back to drown her. She didn't have time for that. She needed a win for her company, and closure for her soul. Maybe after that, she might consider a well-earned vacation.

As she made her way down to the shore, the sun began to sink below the horizon, and the sea was slowly being illuminated by the glow of the moon. Aleysha used to tell her about the intense, humid summer heat of her childhood in Florida. Now Olivia was here, in the state Aleysha called home, that same burning heat sweetly tempered by the fresh ocean breeze.

Olivia turned away from the view, tugging on the light sweater she'd grabbed on her way out of the room. The baby-blue-painted wooden path ran parallel to the shore, connecting the resorts, hotels and condo buildings to the beach and each other. It had grown dark, but the lights that lit up as she advanced along the shore were nothing but a dim yellow that barely illuminated the path. Luckily, the moon was rising, but she was a city girl, through and through, and nothing short of bright, electric lights would make her feel entirely comfortable. Her imagination supplied her with scenario after scenario of all the sharp and dangerous things she could step on if she removed her sand-logged sandals. She hated the way the granules lodged in the straps and scraped against the soft skin of her feet, but she wanted to return to the bungalow with all ten of her toes intact.

Comfort finally won out and she hooked a finger through the straps of her sandals, pulling them off. With her free hand, she turned on her cell phone's flashlight and illuminated the path before her. As she walked, thoughts of Aleysha refused to leave her in peace, even as she was confronted with the picture-worthy view of the full moon reflecting off the surface of the ocean.

The rejection still stung after all this time, leaving scars in Olivia's heart that made her gun-shy about relationships. Aleysha had broken things off when she decided to return home to Orlando to help care for her sick mother. Because of the mobile nature of her work, Olivia had the flexibility to work from anywhere and had offered to go down South to help Aleysha. But Aleysha had refused, telling Olivia that she'd only serve as a distraction from caring for her mother.

After three years together, Olivia had been reduced to a *distraction*.

Olivia felt like she spent most of her life proving herself to others, first to her mother, then to her work contacts. She was used to it with her mother, and in a professional sphere it was common, though at times annoying, but she hated that she'd had to do it in an intimate relationship.

She willed her rebellious mind to banish, once and for all, any thoughts of Aleysha and take her cousin's advice. She focused instead on the sea, the way it undulated under the pale moonlight, the water highlighted by its silver glow, shimmering at the edges of each gentle wave. Despite her worries about sharp glass and the alien grittiness of the sand, she rolled up her pants and stepped into the sea. The sensation of waves rushing up to her ankles felt unfamiliar but wonderful against her skin, accustomed as they were to winter boots and closed-toe shoes tapping against unyielding city pavement. She pointed the light toward the water, capturing a shadowy version of the blue she associated with the ocean. Her feet sinking into wet sand was a sensation she refused to call pleasure.

When the water rushed up to lap at her pants, she stepped out, afraid she might drop her phone and lose it in the rising tide. She was so focused on illuminating the sand before her that she didn't see the approaching woman until she was almost in front of her.

The moonlight limned her in an almost surreal halo of shimmering light tempered by the rich, amber lamp that was affixed to what looked like a sand wagon.

But as she grew closer, two things quickly became apparent.

First, she had an incredible figure. Taller than Olivia, the moonlight made her dark skin glow. She had beautiful braids and a swimmer's body—long lines of muscles under a tank top and capri pants that painted her curves in soft, voluptuous lines.

As the woman neared, a second fact became clear. She looked way too familiar. And she was definitely annoyed. Especially when Olivia inadvertently lifted the phone to illuminate the newcomer's face.

"Do you mind?" Nyla yelped, raising an arm to shield her eyes.

"Oh, hey, I'm so sorry!" Olivia hastily dropped the phone onto the sand. She scrambled to pick it up before it got swept out by incoming waves. She straightened to her full height, breathless with shock and embarrassment. "I didn't recognize you."

Nyla lowered her arm, blinking away the last of the glare. "At least I'm not permanently blinded, so there's that." She took a deep breath, her expression relaxing, though the hard edges of her irritation hadn't melted completely away. She pointed at the flashlight. "May I ask you to turn that off?"

Olivia glanced at the phone, which still had clumps of sand stuck to the case. She shook them loose. "Why? It's dark out here."

"There's a full moon. You don't need additional light."

"So say you," Olivia protested. "There could be a poisonous snake in the sand."

Nyla crossed her arms, considering Olivia with an expression that looked like she was one step away from awarding her a failing grade on a final exam. "I assure you, poisonous snakes do not venture this close to the ocean in this climate."

"But they do somewhere in the world, so how do I know they won't get the idea to do it here, too?" She waved toward the knot of sawgrass growing from under the wooden boardwalk. "They might jump out at us if we're completely in the dark."

Nyla's face grew pinched, but Olivia didn't back down. She knew she was being silly—Nyla was the ultimate expert on this beach. But Olivia's fear of losing a body part to a wild animal was winning out over her rational brain.

Nyla raised two fingers. "Only two varieties of native poisonous snakes are nocturnal, and exactly none of them hunt on the beach. So you are not in danger of snakes 'jumping out' at you in the dark." Her air quotes felt dismissive of Olivia's fears, even as she proved them to be unfounded. "In any case, that should be the least of your concerns."

"Poisonous snakes will always top my list of concerns, together with deadly spiders, and monitor lizards," Olivia retorted.

Nyla raised one perfect eyebrow, and Olivia felt her self-respect shrivel up to the size of a raisin. Even she knew those guys weren't on this side of the planet and she sounded absolutely bonkers suggesting that they were. "Maybe not the monitor lizards," Olivia rushed to add.

The pretty professor gave a quick shake of her head, as if to get rid of any sudden, intrusive thoughts like the ones plaguing Olivia now. "As I was saying, that is the least of your concerns. What you should be concerned about is that you are violating the lights out ordinance, which can set you up for a hefty fine if you're caught. And I can almost guarantee that, along this stretch of beach, you will be caught and fined."

Olivia drew herself to her full height, which was still not as tall as Dr. Dávila. "Why is that?"

Dr. Dávila gave her a smile dripping with self-satisfaction.

"Because I will be the first one to report you. And my reputation carries some weight with the local authorities."

"The audacity," Olivia mumbled, glancing up and down the beach. This is why Olivia didn't do people. They were infuriating and intractable and unreasonable. "That's not a very nice thing to do to someone who is not only a guest of your fine state, but also a professional collaborator."

Confusion made a brief appearance on the professor's face, but then she was back to being stern. "Hence the courtesy warning. Under any other circumstance, I wouldn't have bothered with a warning, especially given the number of signs our institute has put in place, warning tourists against the very behavior I'm calling you out for."

Olivia scowled, assessing the beach in each direction. Only now did she see a sign at the nearest entry point from the boardwalk. A glance up and down the buildings along the coast revealed there were very few lights visible from the buildings that loomed like shadows out of the darkness, even though it was not particularly late. Olivia surveyed the surrounding area more closely. In buildings closer to her, all was darkness except for the occasional glow around a curtain or doorframe. She glanced at Nyla, whose expression was as dry and expectant as a parent waiting for a student to comply with her instructions. Olivia was in the wrong here, and as much as she wanted to protest and rail against it, the facts didn't change the outcome, no matter how she felt about it.

Olivia begrudgingly tapped the icon for the flashlight app, shutting it off. Darkness raced in to fill the space left by the light, her eyes struggling to adjust. "What's so special about this beach that you're willing to report me for using my cell phone light?"

"It's not just this beach. All beaches along the Florida

Gulf Coast have local lights out ordinances in place during turtle nesting season." She pointed down the beach at a small yellow flag fixed on top of a sand dune. "You see that right there?"

Olivia squinted, following the direction Nyla indicated. "That hill there?"

Nyla nodded. "That is why you need to turn off all artificial lighting during nesting season. Sea turtles return to the same beaches year after year to lay their eggs before heading back to sea." She pointed up at the sky. "When those eggs hatch, hatchlings follow the moon and stars to get from their nest to the water, especially on nights when the moon is full. When bright lights compete with moonlight, the hatchlings get confused and waste valuable energy following the wrong light source, causing them to die of exhaustion before they can reach the sea."

Poor little guys, Olivia thought, flooded with immediate chagrin. "I wasn't aware of that."

Nyla's posture seemed to soften, no longer looking like tension was forcing her to stand ramrod straight. Olivia was grateful, because she was starting to worry about the well-being of the pretty professor's spinal column.

"It's not good for adult sea turtles, either," Nyla continued. "They can get lost, wander inland and get run over by a car or picked off by predators."

Olivia lifted her head to take in the sea wind. She could be annoyed with Nyla, and claim ignorance, but she hadn't reacted well when the professor had tried to correct her and now she was ashamed of herself.

She spread her hands and spun in a slow circle to indicate the entire beach, attempting humor to cover her bruised ego. "I owe you an apology. Sadly, I am unfamiliar with the way of the turtle, but I promise to do better." She turned to face

Nyla, to see disbelief fixed firmly on her face. Olivia was okay with that. She was used to shocking people. "I hope that you will forgive this oversight."

"Okay." Nyla drew the word out slowly. *"¿Estás bien?"*

"Oh, I'm doing great! This is me all the time, except when I have to lock in for work." Olivia smiled with as much sincerity as she could muster despite the team of bees and butterflies swirling in her belly. "I promise that I will take your word on everything turtle-related from now on. I'm assuming from your title that you are qualified to guide me in their mystical ways."

"I have a literal PhD in the field," Nyla deadpanned. "There's nothing mystical about it. It's just science." She tilted her head, her expression now puzzled. "Are you mocking me?"

Olivia threw up her hands as if warding off a blow. "I promise, I'm not. It's just my sense of humor kicks in when I'm nervous or, in this case, out of my depth." She dropped her hands. "Sometimes science can seem downright magical. I know absolutely nothing about what you do, but you do. That's why I know I'm in the best of hands."

For the first time, Nyla released a huff that almost sounded like laughter. "You are different, Ms. Navarro."

"Olivia, remember? Ms. Navarro has too many syllables." Olivia was unreasonably thrilled that she was able to pull a smile out of the stern director of the Sea Turtle Research and Education Center after her jokes had fallen catastrophically flat. "I'll just keep calling you Nyla."

"Of course," Nyla answered, her lips pursed. She was trying to stop herself from smiling. Olivia felt victorious. Better a smiling collaborator than one who frowned all day. Olivia wanted to ask her more. *Where were her people from? What does her name mean? Was she married or single? Was she queer or straight*? God, she hoped she was queer. But Nyla didn't seem like the type to just spill her private details so easily. Even now, she was the picture of cool, calm and collected. Olivia thought it might be fun to thaw out that icy exterior and see what made Nyla tick. For science, of course.

Olivia brought her attention back to something she knew Nyla wouldn't mind talking about. She pointed at the amber light hanging from Nyla's wagon. "If my cell phone light is so bad, why do you have that lamp?"

Nyla stared at Olivia for several seconds until she tore her gaze away to nod toward the wagon. "Amber is on the red end of the light spectrum, and most animals, including turtles, cannot see it. Therefore, it won't misdirect them. It is far better than the blue light that emanates from mobile phones or electrical lights from streetlamps and homes, which mislead the turtles away from the sea."

"Interesting," Olivia said, genuinely impressed. "I feel like I should have known that. I took an undergraduate course in optics."

"You took optics, but I suspect it was in the context of computer engineering or classical mechanics," Nyla said. "Your application may not prepare you for the effect light will have on living organisms. It's not in the same wheelhouse."

"Okay, Professor. I get it. I'm a noob." Olivia really was leagues and leagues out of her intellectual depth when it came to the way of the turtle. It didn't help that Nyla had the air of someone who could take out a ruler at any given moment and rap her knuckles with it. "Before I expose my ignorance any further, I think I'll salvage whatever is left of my dignity and wish you a good night."

Nyla's lips quirked up at the corner, cracking through her otherwise impassive expression. "All sciences operate from a place of ignorance. Now you know something more than when you stumbled on this beach. I'd consider that a successful outcome."

Olivia wasn't sure why that small praise made her heart race. "I appreciate the time you took to explain things to me instead of reporting me, so thanks for that." Olivia gave her the most winning smile she could muster. She could have sworn Nyla took in a sharp breath, but despite the moonlight, it was easy for the darkness to play tricks with Olivia's eyes. All she could confirm was that Nyla was one gorgeous woman with an intellect that was frankly more than a bit intimidating, even to someone like Olivia, who wasn't impressed by people very often. "I'll see you bright and early tomorrow morning."

Nyla blinked several times, as if clearing her vision. She frowned, and Olivia thought a face like hers should never look so perturbed. "Are you confident that you can decode the encryption quickly enough to avoid having to pay those hackers? My institute can't stay shut down for very long."

That was the rub, wasn't it? The point of all this. "Promised I would," Olivia answered, walking slowly backward toward the resort while praying that neither of the only two specimens of poisonous snake native to Florida decided to change their habits and play under her feet. "And I always do what I say I'm going to do."

Nyla nodded at that.

"Good night, Nyla." With that, Olivia gave her a quick wave before turning around and making her way toward the steps that led to the boardwalk. She made sure to move with confidence, hiding under layers of bravado her almost pathological fear of snakes and creepy-crawlies. Nyla didn't need to know that Olivia was basically a fake-it-till-you-make-it person, leading with confidence even when she was dying of uncertainty inside. She did it with everyone around her, even her family, unless she was really in emotional pieces. Stoicism and snark were the main compositions of her organism, the things people could count on getting from her.

But there was so much more to what she could offer, and one of those was commitment. If she promised she was going to get this thing done, she would, even if a look at the code had been a chilling bucket of ice on her confidence. It was a configuration on an older code that she hadn't seen before, and it seemed custom-made to hit every single one of the institute's architectural weaknesses. The steps her team had taken so far had been by the book, the key to unraveling the code proving elusive.

But Olivia hadn't come this far just to be intimidated by a little custom coding. She had more tricks up her sleeve than this silly virus was equipped to handle. The pretty professor wasn't the only master of her discipline. Olivia had something to prove to Nyla as well and she'd never met a challenge she wasn't 100 percent sure she could overcome. She was looking forward to clocking this victory, as well.

Chapter Four

Nyla

Nyla watched Olivia's retreating figure until she disappeared into the shadows beyond the boardwalk steps, the moonlight catching the pale sweep of her sweater one final time before it melted into the darkness.

She exhaled slowly, a long unwinding that didn't do much to unravel the tightness in her chest.

What had just happened?

Dragging a hand over the crown of her freshly woven braids, Nyla turned back toward the wagon, forcing herself to kneel and double-check the night's data tags. But even as her fingers moved automatically over the clipboard, her mind refused to cooperate. It kept drifting, stubbornly and inexorably, back to Olivia Navarro.

Olivia with her soft feet sinking into the sand, a half-wild grin that was a little too cocky for anyone's good, and the kind of mouth that could get her in trouble if she ended up talking her nonsense in the wrong crowd.

Olivia, who had looked at her, not past her, not through her, but *at* her, with open curiosity. Nyla couldn't remember the last time anyone had been interested in what she was thinking outside of a professional context.

Maybe it was the sheer surprise of it that had left her so

off-balance. Or maybe it was the memory of Olivia saying her name, not Dr. Dávila, not Professor, but *Nyla*, soft and low, like she might actually want to taste it.

Nyla frowned, shaking her head. Ridiculous.

She had more important things to do than indulge the sudden, absurd tightness curling under her ribs. She had hatchlings to protect, a research center to resurrect, a career that could shatter if they didn't find the breach and fix it fast.

A cybersecurity expert who couldn't keep her lights off on a beach during turtle nesting season was not exactly what Nyla would have called a comforting solution to her problems.

And yet.

Olivia had apologized without being cornered into it. And there was an earnestness beneath all that bravado, a kind of bright, stubborn optimism that collided almost violently against Nyla's natural skepticism. She was a scientist, after all, and was trained to ask all the questions.

But that wasn't what bothered Nyla.

What bothered her was the way Olivia smiled like rules were only suggestions and consequences were things that happened to other people.

She hated how much she noticed about Olivia.

Hated even more that a part of her didn't want to stop noticing.

Nyla reached into the wagon to knot the garbage bag she'd been slowly filling up on her walk. She stood and glanced once more at the path Olivia had taken, imagining scenarios about a woman she'd barely met. She placed her hands on her hips, giving herself a firm, mental side-eye. Who was she kidding? Olivia probably had a cute, indulgent boyfriend at home, waiting for her to come back from saving the world. Why was she throwing away mental energy on someone she should be working with?

The night pressed close and thick around her, the endless hush of the sea stitching itself into the spaces between her breathing. It was usually soothing, but now tension ramped through her at a frequency that hummed under her skin.

The hack had been unexpected and brought with it a woman with laughing dark eyes and a smart mouth that most likely had a hundred more comebacks lined up, just waiting for the perfect moment to unleash them.

A headache throbbed behind her right eye, the familiar kind, born of too little sleep, too many responsibilities, and now the unexpected complication of one Olivia Navarro. She slung a bag over her shoulder and headed back toward the main path, the soft swoosh of sand under her wagon wheels the only sound accompanying her.

She would not let the wild gleam in a stranger's smile distract her from the work she had spent a lifetime building.

Still, as she reached the edge of the boardwalk, she found herself murmuring under her breath, not a prayer or a plea, but a warning to herself.

She had fought too hard to build this life, to claw her way into a world that didn't make room for women like her, let alone hand them anything freely.

She wasn't about to let herself get distracted now. Not when the center was under an almost existential threat.

Squaring her shoulders, Nyla set off across the sand toward her Jeep. The tide whispered in and out, the stars burned cold overhead and the future, ever since the attack, had become shrouded and uncertain.

The next morning, Nyla stood in the staff kitchen, listening to the coffee burble in the pot. The smell of oatmeal wound around her, intoxicating her with its cinnamon-and-honey aroma. She couldn't have breakfast at five o'clock in the morning, when she woke up and headed to the beach to check on turtle nests before sunrise. She always waited until after she'd written her notes, then checked the turtles in the enclosure before she went to the center to brew her second cup of coffee and have her standard breakfast of warmed-up overnight oats, a banana and a hard-boiled egg. She debated on calling her mother—she spoke to her at least once per day—but considered her adjusted schedule and thought better of it. Filomena Dávila, her mother and the principal of Soledad Bay High School, would already be at work and getting the day underway.

She jumped when her cell phone rang, her thoughts flying to her mother. It wouldn't be the first time she manifested her mother's phone call, though it was an inconvenient time given how busy she was at school. A glance at the screen made Nyla nearly drop her phone. She glanced at the clock, surprised that anyone she wasn't related to would be calling her at this time.

"Hello?" she said, the clock on the microwave changing from 6:45 to 6:46.

"Sorry for the early call," came Olivia's rough voice. It didn't belong to the mischievous, defiant woman she'd met on the beach the night before. She sounded like someone who hadn't spoken in ages, but was trying to get their vocal cords to work again. "I've been on-site since early this morning and have reached a bit of an impasse with the data identification. I sent an email with a request but figured I'd try calling you."

Nyla held the phone in a grip that was growing sweatier with every moment that passed. "Good morning to you. How can I help?"

The silence on the other side was hopefully Olivia real-izing that calling anyone at this time of the morning was an absolute brainless move, though Nyla had her doubts that she even cared. Nyla was no stranger to an early wake-up call, but she didn't even call her mother before seven in the morning unless it was an emergency.

Nyla swiped her phone screen to access the alternate email account she'd been assigned until the malware situ-ation was resolved. Olivia's email glared at her from the screen, tiny prickles of heat springing up along her shoul-ders and upper back.

"You sent the email after I saw you on the beach and now it's barely seven in the morning. When would I have been able to answer it?"

Olivia chuckled—actually chuckled—on the other end of the line, and the sound sharpened her annoyance. "I forget that people work at a different speed down South."

Nyla nearly stopped breathing from the audacity. "I beg your pardon?" she shot back, bristling at not only being in-terrupted in the middle of her morning coffee without an apology for the obscene hour, but also the crime of indi-rectly insulting her work ethic. "I have been monitoring my turtle nests since five thirty this morning. I don't know what misinformation you're operating under, but I'd check your sources if I were you."

"Just kidding," Olivia rushed to say, her voice changing. Nyla recognized the tone from the night before. "I quite lit-erally stumbled on you collecting random debris on a clean beach after sundown. I don't think your work ethic can be questioned." The sound of shifting came across the line and Nyla imagined Olivia leaning back in her chair. "I didn't expect an email response in the middle of the night. I saw your car in the parking lot this morning and figured it was okay to call if you were on-site already."

Nyla's suspicions peaked. "How did you know it was my car?"

"I didn't. I took a gamble on the giant turtle magnets, and the Reserved for Director parking spot."

Oh. Why was she so quick to attribute her motivation to something nefarious? Perhaps because there was something about Olivia that unnerved her and threw her off-center.

She clung to her annoyance with both mental hands and held on tight.

"I apologize again for last night," Olivia said at length. "I'm not usually that oblivious to my surroundings. Good thing you were on hand to reel me in."

"You're mocking me again," Nyla said.

"No!" Olivia exclaimed. "Please, I'm being sincere. You took the time to educate me in the way of the turtle, even though I was being a complete pain."

"Again with *the way of the turtle*?" Nyla retorted, settling down into one of the chairs in the break room, her free hand bringing the coffee mug to her lips. Nyla found Olivia both entertaining and annoying. "Now I am sure you're mocking me."

"Never," Olivia said in faux innocence. "But I have no other way of describing what you do."

"Conservation? Marine biology?"

"Maybe, but I wouldn't put that on a T-shirt."

Nyla scoffed. "And you think *The Way of the Turtle* should go on a T-shirt? Is merchandising part of your contract?"

Olivia chuckled. "I'm just saying, it's a great tagline. I wouldn't miss out on the opportunity."

Nyla cleared her throat to quell the urge to laugh and

draw this conversation out. This was starting to feel a little too informal for her taste. She couldn't lose sight of what they were doing here. She'd gotten an apology. It would have to do. "Is that why you called this early? To pimp a T-shirt design?"

"Well, that, and also to gain access to your individual cloud account."

Nyla sat up straighter. "Personal cloud account? Why would you need access to my personal cloud? You already have my work cloud." Much of the data she stored there was used to write grant applications and wasn't connected to the network.

There was a long pause, which was a contrast to Olivia's quick-witted, high-energy responses of only a few moments earlier.

"Do you know what else gets backed up in cloud accounts, even personal ones, Dr. Dávila?" Olivia's voice came slowly and was nothing like the bantering ease of a few moments ago. Again, an image of her face—cool, annoyed, sharp as the edge of a broken seashell—crossed Nyla's mind and sharpened her own irritation in turn.

"I don't know, Ms. Navarro," she subtly mimicked. "Why don't you tell me?"

An exhale, then, "Sleeper ransomware files. The very program that shut your servers down to begin with. And when triggered, they could make scrambled zeros and ones out of your personal data. I know for a fact you don't want more of that in your life."

Nyla felt goose bumps turn into pinpricks of ice as her resistance deflated. Her protectiveness toward her data would be easy for anyone to deduce, based on her work alone. But after Nyla's experience with Ethan's betrayal, she took extra care to document all data exchanges and create paper trails of her interactions with others, sharing only her finished work, and never her raw data, unless it was with a peer-review committee. She was borderline paranoid about it, and now Olivia was pressing down hard on that bruise, asking for something she would normally deny anyone, but couldn't deny her. The idea of surrendering access of those files to a total stranger stole all the air from her lungs, but she had no choice if she didn't want to obstruct the process of reclaiming control from the ransomware.

"Your work won't…alter that data, will it?"

Another pause, then, "As I've said before, I won't alter your data sets. I promise your personal data will not be touched in any way. I'm simply studying files and pathways. I'm not interested in what's inside any of them." The sound of a tapping keyboard filtered through the phone. "I probably wouldn't understand it in any case. Your work is safe with me."

Nyla steeled herself. She had no choice. "I can email the login credentials."

"Absolutely not," Olivia said, her voice suddenly clipped and icy. "Until your system is completely secure, do not send sensitive information in any digital format. I won't have a full assessment of the extent of the compromise until our work is done here." She took an audible breath, as if calming down. "I don't want to start from scratch if there is a reinfection of your systems."

Nyla couldn't begrudge her instincts. "It isn't as simple as giving you a password to get the information you need. There are authentication protocols that will have to be carried out together." She paused, thinking of the best way to do this. "I'll stop by the conference room in a few minutes. Would you… Can I bring you a cup of coffee?"

Olivia didn't waste a second accepting. "I would love a

cup of coffee. My team won't be here for another hour, and I've been waiting for them to resupply me."

Nyla pulled out one of the coffee tumblers she kept in the cupboard of the workroom and set it on the counter. "You don't need to do that. You're not far from the break room and it's fully stocked. You and your team are welcome to all the coffee your systems can handle."

"That's a considerable amount, ma'am," Olivia quipped. "I'm not sure you want to take on the expense of keeping me caffeinated."

"I earned a PhD in less time than the average graduate student. I'm no stranger to living off unhealthy amounts of caffeine. How do you take your coffee?"

Nyla was sure Olivia was holding back a squeal, even if she didn't seem like the type to squeal. "Black, lightly sweetened, please."

"I'm on my way."

Nyla ended the call, staring for a few moments at the phone, wondering at what point her morning veered so far off her usual routine. She prepared the coffee before moving the short distance down the hall. Olivia couldn't have known she was only a corridor away from the kitchenette where Nyla had been taking her breakfast. She balanced the tumbler in her hand as she pushed open the door to the conference room. The quiet hum of Olivia's laptop and portable computer towers was steady and soothing. Olivia sat alone among a clutter of wires and monitors, one leg tucked under her, her dark hair falling in a neat swing toward her keyboard. She looked up when Nyla entered, and the smile that broke across her face was instant and unguarded.

It was such a striking contrast from the no-nonsense Olivia of their first meeting and was more like the smart-ass she'd spoken to on the beach.

"Coffee delivery service? I could get used to this." Olivia sounded far too pleased.

"Least I can do, considering the time of the morning you called," Nyla said, setting the tumbler down beside her.

Olivia gave a mock salute before picking up the hot coffee. "I get it." She slid the cover on the lip of the tumbler, blowing the hot liquid before she said, "No more calls before seven a.m."

"Appreciate that," Nyla said. "Anyway, consider it an investment. You'll work faster with caffeine in your system."

Olivia held the cup with both hands. "You have no idea how motivating that is. Might even shave another half day off the timeline."

Nyla crossed her arms, unwilling to be won over so easily. "You'll forgive me if I don't measure progress in cups of coffee."

"Fair enough. Still, the gesture's been noted." Olivia blew lightly across the lip before taking a noisy sip. Nyla felt her eye twitch from the sound but said nothing about it. Noisy eating and drinking were one of her pet peeves. Olivia paused in her drinking, expression serious for just a beat. She met Nyla's eyes, softer now, less teasing. "Thank you."

The simple sincerity caught Nyla off guard. She shifted her weight, glancing at the monitors where lines of code flickered in red and green. "How's it going?"

Olivia snapped out of her enjoyment of her coffee. "Meh, I don't want to bore you, but essentially, I'm looking for tells that give an indication of which key will unlock the code holding your center hostage. It's a pain." Olivia's mouth curved again. "But that's why I'm here. Because I can handle it."

Nyla huffed, part sigh, part unwilling laugh. "Humility isn't part of your vocabulary, is it?"

"Just stating facts." Olivia set the coffee down as if she were handling fine crystal. She really was serious about her coffee. "How about that login?"

Nyla cleared her throat before pulling out her phone to begin the authentication process to access her files. After a few minutes of answering prompts and punching in one-time codes, Nyla had been able to grant Olivia access to her personal cloud account. Nyla felt a stab of unease. She knew at an intellectual level that Olivia was just doing her job. But her anxiety recalled another time, another place, another consequence of her misplaced trust.

Olivia, as if anticipating her feelings, said, "I just want to check for any sleeper codes that might have been uploaded with your backups. Then you can change the passcode to something inscrutable again." Olivia gave her a winning smirk.

Nyla relaxed, feeling reassured by her confidence. Olivia had a big personality, but Nyla had a feeling it came from the knowledge that she knew exactly what she was doing and wasn't afraid of reminding people of that fact. "You'd better get back to work, Ms. Navarro. I expect results, not charm."

"Charm, huh? Who says I can't deliver both?" Olivia retorted.

Nyla felt a traitorous upward pull at the corner of her lips before she stopped herself. She couldn't believe she'd just said that to Olivia. *Results, not charm*? Way to maintain professional dignity.

Stepping through the open door, she walked away before her mouth could get her into any more trouble.

Chapter Five

Nyla

The rest of the day sped past in a haze of routine tasks. Nyla buried herself in field notes and turtle rounds, anything that didn't require eye contact with the woman still lingering far too sharply in her thoughts, except for an afternoon debrief that brought no new insights into the attack. By the time the sun had set, she had almost convinced herself she was back in control. Almost.

The next morning, she decided that she would focus on her core passion—the care and maintenance of sea turtles. She was ready to engage in something that would keep her mind off the hack and her conversation with Olivia the day before. She accompanied Anuar to the Nest, the lab where surgeries and rescues were conducted, and assisted him in performing a routine surgical intervention to remove plas tic from a rescued turtle's nasal cavity. The process would allow the poor thing to be comfortable and breathe well again when it was fully healed. It was the kind of work they could do as they bided their time until their systems were back online.

The idea that the fate of something as important as her research center was in the hands of an almost-stranger still made Nyla want to crawl out of her skin if she thought too hard about it, so she did everything in her power to not think of it.

Dionne arrived the next afternoon after attending what she'd termed "an infinity of meetings" in Tallahassee. Nyla expected her to take the half-hour drive to check on the research center almost daily until the situation was resolved. She smelled faintly of lavender and printer ink, the familiar smell grounding Nyla in the here and now. Her knee-length floral print dress and blazer were the perfect flirty business outfit that was only one quick wardrobe change away from a barefooted stroll on the beach.

Nyla turned to her friend and hugged her with all the warmth she carried for her, crushing the clipboard she held against her soft-green V-neck T-shirt, a style she often wore to work, paired with jeans or beige cargo pants.

"Going old school, I see." Dionne pointed at the graph paper Nyla was using for manual data collection before leaning against a column supporting one of the large turtle tanks. She crossed her arms, studying her. "How are you holding up?"

With a shrug, Nyla waved the notepad she'd been using to document her latest rescue, a turtle that had been caught in a wire net and sustained cuts as it escaped. "Back to basics, I suppose. Yasmin actually gave the staff flash drives to use on our local devices to back up any data while the team works."

"Paper and thumb drives. That is quite the throwback," Dionne teased. "Now tell me how you really feel."

"Honestly?" Nyla set down the clipboard and pen, pinching the bridge of her nose. "Technology was supposed to make things easier. Now I'm like Darwin on the Galapagos, trying to keep his notebook from falling in the ocean."

Dionne chuckled. "And CyberHunters? How have they been?"

"Competent," Nyla answered a little too quickly. At Dionne's raised eyebrow, she dropped all pretenses and shared her encounter with Olivia on the beach. "You'll never guess what she did the other night."

Dionne pinched her lip. It looked like she was trying not to smile. "What did she do?"

"She was just *walking* around the beach with her flashlight on like it was a damn parking lot."

"Did she apologize? Once you informed her of the lights out ordinance?"

"Not right away. She acted like there weren't signs posted every ten feet."

"Not right away? But she did apologize eventually?" Dionne chuckled, inviting Nyla to take a seat on one of the cushioned benches that were set up throughout the Nest. Gently, she patted Nyla's knee like a sweet aunt might.

"This is her first time in this part of the world, Nyla. Anyone would agree that North Florida is a universe all its own."

"I don't care if it was her *first hour*," Nyla snapped. She immediately recovered at Dionne's shocked expression. "Sorry. I know CyberHunters is your pick—"

"They are not my pick. They are the university's recommended specialist, the best one they could afford." Dionne smiled gently, her voice patient. "But I think you're mad about more than just the flashlight. She's not the first visitor who has been gently corrected on how to behave on our beaches."

Nyla slumped a little farther onto the bench. *"Sinceramente?"*

Dionne smiled. *"Sinceramente."* She didn't speak Spanish, but she'd been around enough Latinos during her tenure in Miami to have picked up a thing or two. "Give me the real talk."

"*Sinceramente*, I don't like feeling out of control. There, I said it." She placed both hands on her knees and leaned on them. "I built the Nest from the ground up. You know that. And now she's here with her tech team and her corporate calm and they literally hold the fate of this center in their hands. And I know it's unfair because she's doing her job, but it's hard to hand my baby over to someone else, even if it is to save it."

Dionne nodded, not rushing her. "I would be pulling my braids out if I were in the same situation. I truly sympathize with you. I also appreciate you recognizing that maybe you are using her as a proxy for your frustrations."

There was no *maybe* about it. Everything about this hack tasted bitter in Nyla's mouth, and that included the company that was being paid to fix the situation. "It's not like she's going to be hired on permanently. But I just… I need a say in what happens here. We only have a short window to geo-tag and release the turtles we've been caring for before captivity becomes detrimental to their health. I just hope she gets the severity of the situation."

"She has been briefed on the priorities of each stakeholder. To be fair, the only thing she is obligated to do here is her job in the best way her skill set allows. Being a team player helps, but you know better than I do that being nice is not mandatory," Dionne said. "But I've seen her type. Someone who wears her expertise like armor because it's the only thing she thinks people will respect. Sound familiar?"

Nyla raised an eyebrow of her own. "You're asking me to give her the benefit of the doubt?"

"I'm asking you," Dionne said, "to play nice. Because

whether you like it or not, you two have a lot more in common than you realize."

"Doubt it," Nyla said.

"You also have to share a sandbox," Dionne continued. "And right now, it's on fire."

Nyla huffed out a sound of disdain. "You don't have to make so much sense."

Dionne placed a hand on her shoulder. "And you need to stop treating the world like there's an Ethan Robles around every corner."

Nyla hissed. "Not pulling any punches either, I see."

"I wouldn't be a good friend if I did." Dionne reached across the desk and tapped Nyla's notebook. "Let Olivia do her job. But don't disappear from the table just because she's at the head of it. There's a reason her company was chosen to do this. You have to trust the process."

Nyla took to her feet when Dionne did. "I want her to be successful more than anyone else. It's my center, after all, and I'll support her in every way I can. But it doesn't mean I have to like it."

"We're professionals, Nyla. We do what we have to do, because it's expected of us. You know that better than anyone." Dionne looked at her cell phone just as Nyla's pinged, as well. "And speak of the devil. We have our daily progress meeting in a few minutes with your favorite person."

Nyla knew. That didn't keep the unsettled feeling from winding its way through Nyla's belly. They'd broken the ice over coffee that morning. So why did she want to hide in the Nest until Olivia was back on her plane home? She recognized how childish that was. Dionne was right, Nyla was a professional, and didn't need to be reminded of her responsibilities, because she lived and breathed them each day. For the sake of her center, she would handle Olivia's temporary presence in her life. After all, in a few weeks, this nightmare would be over. Her network would be back online, the center would be open for business and Olivia would be well on her way back to her headquarters in East Ward, New Jersey. She just had to focus on doing her part until then.

Nyla and Dionne arrived in the conference room just as Olivia was clicking onto a new slide: a visual representation of the center's current network map, pocked with red flags like a board game of Strategy. She wore a black, sleeveless jumper with large lapels, a series of sleek, black buttons bisecting her from the valley of her breasts to her ribs, tied with a satiny black sash that looked like it would feel like silk between Nyla's fingers.

Nyla nearly bit the inside of her cheek at the thought. Where had that come from?

Yasmin leaned over her laptop, nodding along to something Olivia was explaining while Nyla's senior graduate assistant, Jack, looked on. He sometimes helped Yasmin with some of her duties, since he had studied programming and computer science as part of his double major, and appreciated the chance to show off his expertise.

Nyla's eyes flew back to Yasmin and for a brief, petty moment, she experienced a fierce reaction at the sight of her network manager being meek in a way she never was with Nyla and her team. She was one of hers, not part of some flashy imported crew. Even Jack Martin, one of her senior research assistants, was circling around, trying desperately to be useful, was hers, and Olivia had no right to steal them away.

But when she'd pushed her pettiness down, she saw what her knee-jerk reaction to Olivia hadn't allowed her to see:

Yasmin wasn't just nodding along complacently. She was contributing, engaged and confident in the substance of the conversation. It was so different from the harried, ultra-sarcastic vibe she usually possessed in her day-to-day work in the lab. And Jack was in his glory, asked to do things he was convinced he was good at, and basking in the validation.

If Olivia recruited Yasmin away, hands would be thrown.

Olivia noticed Nyla and Dionne standing near the doorway, thankfully oblivious to every one of Nyla's unkind thoughts, and motioned for them to enter.

"Dr. Dávila, Dr. Sommers." Olivia greeted them with a focused, wholly unreadable expression. "Perfect timing."

Nyla stepped inside warily, taking in the controlled activity in the suddenly small space. The man she'd introduced as Alejandro, and the young woman, Feliz, were working away on their laptops, while the tall woman with the long, straight black hair that she thought was Dareen was taking apart a tower. Yasmin loomed over her own computer next to Olivia. Nyla desperately tried to ignore the enticing swell of cleavage that rose and fell with Olivia's every movement and fixed her attention on her face, which didn't improve her focus at all.

"We've blocked the first wave of the attack, but a second one buried itself deeper than we thought. Right now we're making a list of the most important files to recover first."

"You're trying to identify the high-need files," Dionne said approvingly.

Olivia gave a curt nod before gesturing toward the board, where a spreadsheet of file hierarchies scrolled in a steady rain of code. "But here's the problem—I can't tell which of these files are truly essential and which are just clutter. That's where we need your guidance, Dr. Dávila."

The formality, in such contrast to their conversation

earlier that morning, blasted the brain fog that had nearly smothered all her thoughts. "My guidance?"

Olivia didn't miss a beat. "I don't have your expertise on turtle migration data, or which metadata points are linked to grant renewals. There are some criteria for selecting files, but I'm flying blind."

"I offered to help, but I was told they needed your approval, since you're the director," Jack interjected.

"And we appreciate the offer," Olivia answered.

Jack beamed at the praise and went back to hovering near where Yasmin was working. "I told you. I can do this. I have an instinct for this stuff."

"And you've done a great job so far." Yasmin inhaled deeply. "We tried to prioritize by size and frequency of use, but that can only get us so far."

Nyla stepped forward slowly. The room shifted with her. She felt eyes following her every move.

Her fingers brushed the edge of the laptop as she peered at the data.

"This dataset here, *NestMigration_MEX_2017*. It's tied to a multiyear climate change impact study. If we lose that, we lose five years of trends."

Olivia nodded, making a note. "Good. That's exactly what I needed. What else have you got?"

Her tone wasn't clipped or condescending, and held none of the mocking playfulness of earlier. Appreciative, perhaps, but mostly it possessed a brisk professionalism that Nyla fully identified with. It was more comforting than a warm hug at the moment.

She pointed to another folder. "That one, *Loggerhead_Bloodwork.csv*. Don't let that go, either. It's a match to necropsy records we digitized last year." She continued to identify data sets and files, while Olivia noted them and

Yasmin tapped away at her keyboard. Dionne had floated to the other side of them to quietly observe their work.

Olivia looked up when Nyla paused and met her gaze, holding it with an intensity that sent ripples of tension through Nyla's body. "Thanks," she said simply, but the smile that tugged at her lips changed the air between them, settling the defensiveness Nyla had carried since that morning.

She cleared her throat and moved to indicate another data set when Olivia's attention was snatched back to the screen. Without warning, Olivia's face hardened, her voice changing, becoming as sharp and clear as glass. "Wait—something in the quarantined files just woke up."

Her fingers flew across her keyboard. "Dareen, cut it off. Yasmin, double-check that it didn't touch the research server."

Jack, who had wandered back in with a stack of external hard drives, stopped in mid-step, his eyes growing large. "What's going on?"

Ignoring him, Yasmin was already typing. "No crossover. It was flagged just in time."

Nyla watched as Olivia exhaled, relief plain on her face. "Un-freaking-believable." Her eyes flicked up at Dionne, who had come to stand closer to her. "What the hell tripped that payload? Al? Feliz?"

"Manual activation?" Dionne suggested, scanning the activity log on a second screen.

"That's not even remotely funny," Yasmin responded, while all eyes were now pinned to Olivia. She was the de facto leader of this circus and everyone, including Yasmin, and even Nyla herself, was waiting for her to draw her conclusions. Meanwhile, Nyla's brain kept spinning with this new fact—Olivia had somehow thwarted a reactivation of the malware or some secondary execution, and she'd done so efficiently and decisively.

Un-freaking-believable, indeed.

The conversation taking place around her came rushing back into her awareness and one detail blasted away her sudden, adrenal response to Olivia's exercise in expertise.

"Wait. Manual? Are you suggesting that someone triggered an attack?" Nyla asked.

"Signal's bouncing through several VPNs, and there are no personal signatures. Code looks like a paid bogey, so it's hard to tell," Olivia answered almost distractedly as she typed away.

"English, please, though Spanish would be so much better," Anuar spoke up and it registered in Nyla's overheated brain that he had come into the room at a certain point and picked up on the conversation. He gave Nyla a quick wink when he caught her eye before settling in next to Dionne, who was taking in everything with that eagle-eyed sharpness Nyla had come to know so well. Nyla's attention had been so fixed on Olivia and the data to recover that she'd missed his entrance altogether. Now the room felt almost claustrophobic with so many people inside.

Yasmin stopped typing and looked up from her screen. "It means the attack left a kind of booby trap hidden in the backup files. The moment we touched them, it tried to trigger. Normally it's automatic, but Dionne's point is that this one might have been set off by a person."

"That would change the whole game," Dionne said.

"Like a land mine, set to detonate when the slightest pressure is applied." She looked up, catching Nyla's gaze instantly. "It's possible someone set it off on purpose, but for now we'll treat it as a delayed trap and keep moving."

Nyla nodded, bitterness curdling her stomach, and all of

a sudden she was back in Miami, sitting in front of a university panel, trying to convince a group of officials and professors that the data their golden boy had used to build his dissertation was in fact hers, and that he had passed it off as his without any consideration for the work she'd put into collecting it. Much like the projects Olivia was asking her to identify, the data she'd collected had been a decade in the making, in addition to all the white papers she'd put together in the buildup to her dissertation. The horror, the violation, the absolute sense of betrayal came roaring back in the form of a pounding heart, and her quickly shortening breath.

"I'm going to need a moment," Nyla said as she stepped quickly out of the conference room. She rushed past Jack, who had been hovering behind her, down the hall to the break room, with its pristine chrome fixtures and open blinds that let the sun seep in. It was nothing like the conference room she'd left, where everything was shut against natural light to help counteract the glare of the computer screens.

Her chest heaved from the memory of that time of her life, the stress of the last few days finally settling into her skin and weighing down her bones until she had to grip the counter for purchase.

Like a land mine, set to detonate at the slightest pressure.

Did she really suspect a targeted attack by a malevolent actor? But who? Why would anyone go out of their way to target a turtle rescue center, of all places?

Nyla shook herself, searching for the shield she used to bury her emotions and get things done. She pulled open the cupboards, searching for one of the generic mugs that she'd stocked in the two break rooms of the center alongside an abundant selection of tea, coffee and packaged snacks. She believed in a comfortable, collegial work environment, and food was a shortcut for creating that kind of environment.

She set about preparing a cup of herbal orange blossom tea, quite certain that she didn't need any more caffeine with the way she was feeling. Midway through her preparations, she stopped to rest her head against the cabinet and closed her eyes. For just a moment, she let herself imagine that the breach was over, all systems were back online, her data secure and her turtles recuperating in safety.

And then there was Olivia.

The K-Cup maker gave a loud sputter as it released its first burst of water, pulling Nyla out of the confusing miasma of her thoughts. The door of the break room squeaked open—she'd been meaning to oil the hinges. Awareness of the person behind her crept up her spine and she imagined it was Dionne, coming to soothe her. She swirled honey into her tea.

"It's too damned early for all this," she said. "No one should have an existential crisis before four in the afternoon."

"Oh, I entirely agree," came the sharp voice that was at once strange and too familiar. Nyla jerked to her full height, hot tea splashing onto the counter.

"*Aye, caramba*," she muttered.

"You sound like my cousin Val." Her steps moved closer and paper towels appeared out of the corner of Nyla's eye. "By the time she gets to the end of her shift in my uncle's restaurant, she's wearing the lunch menu."

Olivia glanced up at her and Nyla was shocked to find her standing so close to her she could see a thin line of foundation at her jawline. Funny enough, the color was perfectly blended on the other side of her perfectly shaped chin. She resisted the urge to reach out with her thumb and smudge the line away.

"Would you like a cup of coffee?" she asked, nervously wiping up the spill and tossing the wet towels into the recycle bin. They were made without dyes and fully biodegradable, something she'd made sure of for almost all the materials that went into the center. "I was thinking of relocating one of the K-Cup makers into the conference room so you can have coffee and tea whenever you like." She should have done it already. Her mother would have so much to say about this lapse in her manners.

Olivia chuckled. "Then we'd never get out of our chairs. It's an occupational hazard. It's better if we're forced to walk the long, endless mile to get our coffee."

Nyla tried to bite back the smile, but her body needed it and she let it bloom on her face. "You have a way with words."

"Sometimes." Olivia leaned against the counter now, watching Nyla pull out the supplies for Olivia's coffee. "I can make my own, you know."

Nyla shrugged, trying and failing to only focus on the coffee, allowing her gaze to flicker to where Olivia leaned so near to her against the counter. "I don't mind."

Olivia said nothing, and the weight of her stare was a tactile pressure against her skin. The silence was evident and persistent, but Nyla almost didn't mind it.

Finally, Olivia spoke again. "I know this is all very difficult. This is your kingdom, your people, your data. And here we are, a bunch of strangers with our rough tools trying to perform brain surgery."

It was uncanny how well she nailed exactly what was plaguing her. "Brain surgery?" Nyla laughed and this time, she didn't bother to hold it back.

"Okay, okay, more like spear fishing with a blunt stick. I don't know." They both laughed but Olivia pushed on. "What I'm trying to say is, we're going to fix this. And I won't let anything happen to your data or your center. I promise." Nyla was almost convinced she was serious. "CyberHunters vows to protect the way of the turtle to the very last string of code."

Nyla chuckled before turning away to replace the K-Cup holder with the coffee Olivia seemed to enjoy so much that morning. "Aren't you the CEO of your company?"

Olivia's brown eyes twinkled with a mischievous glint and she suddenly looked young and so pretty, the ache of it caught Nyla off guard. "The operative word being *my* company. I can be any way I want to be. Who is going to tell me differently?"

The water beginning to boil filled the background of the room. Nyla was grateful for the jarring sound. "What's your point?"

She continued, sweeping out a hand to take in the center. "This is your kingdom. You are entitled to protect it and suffer over it in any way you see fit. No one can tell you differently." Olivia paused and when Nyla glanced over, she saw something honest and real on Olivia's face that she couldn't tear her eyes away from.

"Just remember that we're on your side. I promise that."

Nyla paused on that.

In the end, Olivia was here for the center. And Nyla needed to start acting like she was a part of a team, and not just someone a bad situation had happened to. That was far too passive, and she had never been a passive person. Her data might be tied up, but she still had options. Olivia was showing her that.

"Thank you," she said at length. "Think I needed to hear that."

Olivia's smirk was wicked and irreverent. "I'll do almost anything for coffee. Even offer free therapy. It's my fatal weakness."

"Lucky for me." Nyla fixed the coffee the way Olivia liked before handing it to her. Olivia took the tumbler, but Nyla didn't let it go right away. She held Olivia's gaze, flecks of brown that appeared fractured under the cold light of the break room. Nyla sank into it, soft brown and textured like velvet in shadow, while her heartbeat kicked up its speed. The moment lingered, stretching taut between them until Nyla was sure it would snap.

Finally, she let the coffee go, its warmth still lingering on her fingertips.

Olivia inhaled loudly before clutching the tumbler Nyla had given her. "I…" She swallowed hard, her neck bobbing from the action. "Thanks again for the coffee. It'll be a real game changer."

"There's a great place just up the road," Nyla blurted out, for no good reason. "A little Puerto Rican shop. They make the best café con leche." Nyla rested her hand on the counter. "In case your team gets bored of the brew here."

Olivia grinned, as if she could read the inner workings of Nyla's mind and found them humorous. "That's good to know. Thank you."

With that, she gave her a quick wave before stepping out of the room and down the corridor.

Once she was gone, Nyla wilted against the counter. The conversation felt like it had lasted three hours. She placed a hand over her stomach to steady herself, as if she was recovering from a sudden jolt of electricity. What the hell had that been about?

Dionne's and Anuar's voices came from down the hall. Nyla straightened, chagrined that her tea had gotten cold. She popped it quickly into the microwave. By the time her friend and her in-house veterinarian were in the room, she had outwardly recovered, though inside, her stomach still trembled as if tickled by the wings of a thousand butterflies.

Chapter Six

Olivia

The next twenty-four hours were a grueling haze of emails, system checks and decryption code testing that blurred one hour into the next, leaving Olivia and her team hollow-eyed and running on nothing but caffeine and willpower.

As the day wound down, the glow from Olivia's laptop screen cast nebulous silver-blue shadows across the darkened conference room, making her feel like she was submerged in a tank of cold light. Dionne and Anuar had long since left. It was getting well into the evening, and Olivia had half a mind to just dismiss her team for the day. A glance over at her people showed her they were on their way to full exhaustion—Al was wilting from the insomnia he always experienced the first time he was forced to sleep in a bed that was not his, Feliz had only stood up twice to use the bathroom despite the way Olivia fussed at her to move around from her chair at least once an hour. Yasmin had her head down and was working away as if she hadn't been up half the night already, fueled by determination and grit. It was her system that had been attacked, after all, and Olivia couldn't help admire the girl's stamina.

And Nyla? She hadn't seen her. To be fair, after identifying the high-priority files that needed to be retrieved at all costs, there wasn't much need for her to be in the room while they worked.

That didn't mean Olivia wasn't sorry that she wasn't around. It was fun to fluster her, and her mind was as quick as a whip.

Olivia leaned in, fingers flying across the keyboard, another line of code unfurling like a stubborn riddle that didn't want to be solved, all while she counted down the minutes until she was scheduled to provide Nyla with the last update of the day before heading back to the bungalow for dinner and rest.

It wasn't just fascination with the pretty professor that drove Olivia's impatience to see her. She radiated misery and frustration with her situation. Nyla's reaction to Dionne's insinuation that any of this could have been intentional and targeted had been a double punch to Olivia's gut, though she had taken care not to dwell too long on it. It only made sense that Nyla would suffer that possibility even more acutely. This center mattered to her in the same way CyberHunters mattered to Olivia, with its mini army of oddball mischief-makers whose energies had been harnessed toward doing some good in the world. Because she saw liberating systems from techno-criminals as its own kind of justice. Except in Olivia's case, she expected to be paid a premium for her work. She didn't believe in giving her talents away for free. A girl had to make a living, after all.

Somehow, she had the feeling that as long as Nyla had enough to live on, she would do her work for free. That was a different kind of passion, one that deserved to be protected at all costs. And Olivia was the kind to get protective to the extreme when sufficiently motivated.

Olivia hadn't played up Dionne's observation about a manual triggering of the virus when she'd first proposed it.

There simply was no evidence except for timing, and that had most likely been a coincidence. Olivia chose to be realistic and not dwell on it until she had more to go on. The recovery script was clean so far. Backup files were slowly being restored without any further incident. She hadn't found any other pathways that would trigger the kind of cascade they'd seen earlier. She'd caught it in time, but that didn't mean there weren't any more of those packages ready to explode.

The idea of encountering something new got her heart pounding, because it was the kind of problem that held her attention. Working around contaminated systems, reverse-engineering codes and rebuilding networks was one kind of challenge. Hunting for a virus whose bits were buried in the architecture, designed to trigger the moment they tried to restore the backup files, was another.

Damn, but she couldn't help but admire the well-crafted piece of code.

"Olivia?"

Olivia looked up to see Dareen standing in the doorway. Her tired brain dropped automatically into Spanish. "*¿Que pasó?*"

"*Nada,* only that it's getting late and it's my turn to cook tonight. Think we could cut out of here?"

Olivia stretched, feeling the soft tug of material under her arm despite the tailoring. She'd go for business casual tomorrow, though she'd much rather be dressed like Yasmin, in a hoodie, T-shirt and sweatpants.

"Why don't you head back to the resort. I have a couple of things to finish up here and I still have to debrief Nyla on our work this afternoon."

Dareen stifled a yawn. "Want us to wait?"

Olivia had switched her attention back to her screen. "No,

I'll catch an Uber." She made a shooing gesture, knowing they'd wait hours if she asked them to. "Now go. Save me something to eat. You know what I like." They'd been working with each other long enough to know about allergies and preferences. "Just be sure to take the card."

Dareen pulled her phone out of her pocket. "Company card, ready to go."

Olivia gave her a quick wink before returning to her screen, leaving a short annotation on the code she'd been working on before switching to her project management program to document their work and time. She heard the shuffling of her team as they left, the sky darkening through the wide window behind their space. Olivia really liked the conference room setup. The glass partition separating the two rooms had been opened after their last meeting, doubling the area. Olivia didn't have to relocate her computer and towers to be close to her team.

She wondered if Nyla's hand had been in the design of the center and immediately concluded that yes, she must have been. There were too many touches that spoke to a loving heart in the design and execution of this space.

She noted how the stern, serious woman she'd met on the beach had suddenly become vulnerable in this very room. Olivia wanted this all to work out, not only for CyberHunters, but for Nyla. She wanted to find the culprit and wipe that vulnerability away. Did she have a bit of a savior complex? No doubt, because Olivia couldn't stand to see something that wasn't right play out in front of her without acting.

Olivia gathered her laptop and left the conference room. Her schedule indicated that Nyla would most likely be in the Nest, the equivalent of a turtle hospital. She could have called down, but Olivia wanted to puzzle out the layout of the center. She studied a map she'd been given, but found her way around easily because of the clearly posted signs near the ramps that served as an alternative to the elevators, taking her down each floor. Exhibits and demonstration spaces appeared and disappeared, while signs set at strategic intersections throughout the different spaces led her farther. Beyond the floor-to-ceiling windows, the beach unfurled in waves of sand that sent shivers up and down her spine. The setting sun set the sea on fire with pastels bleeding yellow, pink and purple until midnight blue crept in at the edges.

The public exhibit area was unexpectedly quiet, and though it was now after hours, Olivia imagined this same silence reigned during the day now that the malware had shut the center down, leaving it empty. The unfairness of it burned Olivia inside. She could only imagine how it made Nyla feel.

She knew she'd arrived when she looked up at a set of large, double metal doors beneath a sign that said The Nest imprinted with the giant sea turtle logo that was visible everywhere in the center.

Olivia pushed the doors but found them sealed. Stepping back, she suddenly regretted not calling ahead before taking the long walk down. A glance around her confirmed that there was a camera and a keypad, though she had no idea what the code would be. She decided to press the button, a buzzer sounding inside.

A series of clicking sounds came through the camera device, followed with a heavily accented young man's voice. "How can I help you?"

"I'm here to speak to Dr. Dávila," Olivia answered.

"Of course, Ms. Navarro. Come in." A buzzing sound, followed by the unclicking of the doors, indicated that Olivia could go inside. There, she found the Dr. Anuar Jimenez, the veterinarian she'd met the day before. He was a handsome young man about her height, no more than thirty, with large, wide-set brown eyes and light brown hair that cascaded in waves around his head, like Michelangelo's David come to life.

"Please call me Olivia," she said as she stepped inside, offering him her hand.

He smiled, his eyes crinkling sweetly at the edges. "Anuar, then. A pleasure to see you again. Follow me, I'll take you to Dr. D—I mean, Nyla."

Olivia smiled before taking in the room before her. She was quickly taken aback at the sheer size of the space. A name like the Nest implied a small, cozy place where baby animals were hatched and raised. This was the size of a small hangar, with hydraulic pipes running along the top and down columns that ended in blue structures resembling above-ground pools. There were about eight large ones and several smaller ones running the length of the aisle where she stood. Touch screen panels were affixed to the columns next to each pool, no doubt for monitoring the water and animals inside. Monitors whose screens were now black, their information gnarled by the virus.

Olivia would change that soon enough.

A soft voice floated across the space. Olivia followed the sound. As she approached, she recognized the gentle cadence of her words, not quite baby talk, but still a sharp contrast to the voice that Olivia had heard that night on the beach. Nyla was perched on a platform next to a large en-closure, twisting a valve that hung over the edge of the pool. She leaned over the edge, murmuring sweet nothings as her hand trailed through the water, her carefully twisted braids hanging over one shoulder. It was another snapshot of Nyla that slotted into place in Olivia's mind.

She couldn't tear her eyes away if she tried.

"Nyla?" Anuar's voice cut through the scene, shattering the moment. Olivia repressed a physical urge to pull him back and stop him from interrupting her.

Nyla turned away from the turtle she'd been sweet-talking in the pool, her eyes growing wide at the sight of Olivia.

"I didn't know turtle whisperer was one of your many skill sets," Olivia said by way of greeting.

Anuar gave a short laugh but quickly smothered it when Nyla straightened up from where she'd been kneeling, dusting her pants off. Even in her casual, beige capris, she looked tall and elegant, a queen overseeing her water kingdom. Her vulnerability of the day before swallowed up by the figure she presented now—competent, compassionate and fully in her element.

She handed a clipboard to Anuar. "I manually adjusted the pH levels in Tank B. All other tanks are offline and can regulate as normal. We just won't get any data."

"Sounds good. I'll add it to the daily rotation. I'll check on the last two tanks." He gave Olivia a grin that lit up his face. "I think Turtle Whisperer is kind of catchy. What do you think, Nyla?"

"Why is everyone trying to rebrand my center?" she asked instead of answering.

"You have to admit, it does have a nice ring to it," Olivia added.

Anuar tucked Nyla's chart under his arm, his olive-green polo with the center's logo a smooth compliment to his olive-tinted skin. "We should consider it for our upcoming beach cleanup event."

Olivia offered Anuar a fist to bump, which he returned enthusiastically. He looked like the kind of guy you could have fun with. "You see, Professor? I think my catchphrases have legs. Don't sleep on them."

Nyla threw both Anuar and Olivia a look. "I'll think about it. Think you can get that data into our spreadsheet before you leave tonight?" she said, smoothly redirecting Anuar's enthusiasm.

"*Si, Professora!*" he said cheerfully. He gave Olivia a cross between a wave and a salute. "Good night, Olivia Navarro."

The full name was not an improvement. "Good night, Anuar Jimenez."

He chuckled again. "Dr. Anuar Jimenez, Ms. Olivia Navarro." He waggled his eyes at Nyla before walking away with a skip in his step.

When he was out of hearing, Olivia murmured, "He's a character, that one."

"He is," Nyla said, climbing down the ladder and stepping over to where Olivia stood. "Never a dull moment."

Nyla's smile lit up her face and Olivia's head started to get a little swimmy. Oh no, she did not need to see Nyla like that. "So, what happens when the pH is off?"

Nyla indicated for Olivia to follow her. "Unfortunately, a whole host of complications. Acidic water can erode keratin, making turtles vulnerable to bacteria and fungi. Alkaline water can cause caustic shell irritation and lesions, while corneal exposure could lead to damage resulting in blindness, and you can imagine how difficult it would be for a blind turtle to survive in the wild. Not to mention, immune suppression, ammonia toxicity and general stress behaviors."

Olivia let out a low whistle. "I'd show stress behaviors too, if my entire organism was falling apart. The way of the turtle sounds rough."

Nyla snorted and it was the cutest thing Olivia had ever heard. "It's not. It's humans that make everything difficult."

"That's true for any animal species, including humans themselves."

Nyla gave a slight shake of her head, but her expression was almost indulgent. "I can't disagree with you there." They stopped in front of an office that seemed to have been added as an afterthought, built with modular walls, a window that looked out on the length of the Nest and a door Nyla now held open.

"Ready?" she asked.

Olivia gave her a smirk that always drove her cousin crazy but didn't seem to faze Nyla one bit.

"I'm always ready."

Chapter Seven

Olivia

Olivia stepped inside. It was a large office, impeccably organized, with a sturdy, metal-and-fiberglass desk and two chairs dominating the space, a similar worktable on the other side of the room with a stool under its high counter. A microscope sat on top, while shelves packed with binders, textbooks and what looked like field guides lined most of the walls. Where shelves didn't cover the walls, a whiteboard hung with coastal maps of every kind took up the remainder of the space. In another far corner sat a pair of filing cabinets, no doubt locked shut. The desk was piled high with file folders that were neatly labeled and organized. CDs, no doubt burned with legacy data, sat on a neat tower, while flash drives in a tray and three external drives were lined up neatly on a shelf.

"And I thought my office was packed," Olivia said, taking it all in. "Looks like your entire life is backed up in these four walls. Do you actually need me?"

Nyla took a seat on the other side of her desk.

"Yes," Nyla said, indicating the chair across from her. "I need you."

Olivia pinched her lip. Those words had an effect on her she wasn't interested in parsing out at the moment.

"I sent an email to Dionne and cc'd you with the same information I'm giving you now. I'll debrief you daily until the project is complete. However, as your area of expertise is not programming, I'll summarize my findings and you can ask me any questions you have."

Nyla nodded. "I appreciate the consideration."

Olivia flipped open her computer and turned it on so they could both see the screen. "I'd need the same support if you were talking turtle to me."

Nyla huffed out another short laugh. "You and your words."

Olivia spread her hands. "We've worked through a big chunk of the backup files and should have a better timeline soon for getting everything running again."

She listed it out simply. "Right now, we're focused on the essentials—finance, HR and the systems that keep the Nest running. Once those are stable, we'll circle back to the less urgent ones."

Nyla leaned back with a groan. "God, I forgot credit cards and HR records might be caught up in this, too."

Olivia nodded. "The university has strong protections in place. That data should be unreadable to whoever broke in, but we'll still make sure it's recovered."

A roll of thunder pulled their attention to the large window beyond Nyla's office. The darkness was total except for the outline of clouds and rain that sent needles of water against the pane of glass. A loud thunderclap made Olivia jump in her seat.

"What the—?" she muttered as lightning flashed, briefly lighting up the beach like it was midday. Her heart was rabbiting a mile a minute.

"I'm not going to be able to check my nests tonight," Nyla said, sliding a clipboard toward her from a tray that held several of them. "Weather app said it's going to last a little while. We've had so much erosion already." Nyla walked around her desk. Olivia got up to follow her toward the giant window.

"Erosion means less sand, right?" Olivia asked as Nyla turned down a switch, dimming the fluorescent lights above. She stood near the window, leaning against the long ledge that ran the length of the glass pane.

"Yes," Nyla answered. "The sand withdraws from the beach with the storm surge, but it usually recovers."

"That's too bad," Olivia practically growled.

She reached over and raised the dimmer, though not to the brightness it had been before. Nyla wrinkled her nose, and yet again, Olivia was only two gestures away from experiencing cuteness aggression. "You're seriously offended by sand on the beach? I thought that was a joke."

Olivia scoffed. "Oh please, the beach would be the perfect place if there wasn't any sand."

Nyla scrutinized her for longer than Olivia would have liked. Finally, she said, "If it bothers you so much, couldn't you stay up in your penthouse suite in the city or wherever your headquarters are and send your employees out to do the traveling? Perks of being the boss."

Olivia shook her head. "That could never be me. I'm not cut out for the corporate life. I'm not even sure how hacking into businesses for fun turned into this." She lived on the top floor of her brownstone apartment building, but that was as close as Olivia had ever come to a penthouse suite. "I'm a programmer, through and through. I'm at home right in front of my screen. I'd rather be in the middle of the job, not managing it from above."

Nyla stared at her intently, and Olivia almost had to turn away from the intensity of it. A sound came from the enclosure, startling them both. Nyla pushed off from the ledge and walked around the tank from earlier. She climbed up to the metal ledge and Olivia quickly followed. "I'm not much for the business end of things, either. Unfortunately, I've had to learn to be. I'd much rather be down here, doing my research all day. The well-being of my center demands that, in addition to being a research scientist, I should also be an educator, administrator, human resources manager, business manager and whatever else the center needs to keep it running."

"You should hire a business manager." Olivia peeked past her to try to see the turtle. It drifted through the water with slow, deliberate strokes, its shell catching light each time lightning flashed. Olivia had expected it to look smooth, like something polished by waves, but up close it was rougher, ridged like old stone. The color reminded her of rusted metal, dark and reddish. Across the shell ran a pair of jagged scars, pale against the darker plates. Olivia pointed at them.

"What happened to her?"

Nyla frowned, kneeling down to trail a hand through the water. "Ugly reminders of some boat's propeller. It's the leading cause of trauma in this part of Florida. These injuries often cause deep shell fractures, internal damage and even death."

The turtle swam placidly, carrying those injuries without fuss. She glided forward as if nothing could weigh her down. Watching the enormous creature, Olivia felt a faint twist in her chest, a familiar rage against the world, and awe at the creature's stubborn grace.

Nyla lifted her eyes from the turtle, her gaze snagging on Olivia's. They were a deep, crystalline hazel color that glittered in the dim lighting.

"This is what I try to do. Heal the injuries of the world on these creatures one turtle at a time."

Olivia turned her attention to the turtle as her front flippers moved lazily through the water. She wondered what the turtle might be thinking, swimming in circles, trying to find anything that might remind her of home and coming up short. Olivia could identify with the feeling from her experience with her mother, who had tried to live in the mainland after her divorce and couldn't. She'd gone back to Puerto Rico, leaving a teenage Olivia to live with her aunt and cousins.

Another thunderclap nearly sent Olivia headfirst into the water.

"This must be what a hurricane is like," Olivia nearly shouted at the shock of thunder.

Nyla shook her head. "This is nothing compared to a hurricane."

"I heard you guys recovered from a hurricane. What happened?"

"What didn't happen?" Nyla leaned back on her haunches, hugging herself. She didn't seem to care that she was dripping saltwater all over her outfit. Olivia sat next to her, legs crisscrossed. Her outfit was probably going to hell, too. "We were high enough not to get completely flooded, but we weren't immune to damage."

Olivia leaned her chin on her hand, watching Nyla speak. She was animated, using her hands and her body to speak. Olivia was captivated by her every move.

"The Nest's design was done intentionally to make sea turtle transport as easy as possible, but it put us at risk. Everything you see here is waterproof." Olivia swept her hand out to the hangar, with its large saltwater pools arranged in neat rows behind them. "The turtles we treat are wild animals that are being cared for with the eventual goal of releasing them back into their home environments. So the center was designed with that purpose in mind, but it makes hurricanes very inconvenient."

"I'm sorry about the damage. That was probably discouraging."

"Extremely," Nyla laughed, but there was an edge of sarcasm to it. "This center has been my sole focus for the last decade. Seeing it damaged like that—it was like a friend being injured. The community really united to make sure Soledad Bay got back on its feet."

"Reminds me of my hometown, East Ward. Everyone knows each other, and sometimes that can be a little claustrophobic, but when there's a crisis, we stand up for each other." Nyla's smile was wistful as she spoke, and it sent a warm sensation like a hug over her skin. "I had a feeling you might have had a hand in the design here."

Nyla's eyes grew wide. "Did you? How?"

Olivia shrugged. "From what I know about you so far, you're conscientious, logical and meticulous with details. The center just makes sense."

If Olivia didn't know better, she might have seen a blush creep across Nyla's soft-brown cheeks. There were few things Olivia understood more than a woman who hustled. Nyla was by far one of the most intelligent, prepared women she'd ever met, and her work was incredibly meaningful. Olivia, who wasn't typically intimidated by anyone, found herself a little in awe of her.

"You know, I haven't seen the Nest. Not in its entirety," Olivia said, glancing at the enormous space.

"Got a little time right now?" Nyla asked.

Olivia hadn't expected her to accept right away. It made her feel a little electric that their conversation was not quite at an end yet. "Been working nonstop all day. I could use a change of pace."

"This way," Nyla said, getting to her feet. Her voice was low, but sure. "We'll start in the lab."

Chapter Eight

Nyla

Nyla didn't wait to see if Olivia followed, but of course she did. Curious and observant, Olivia was already scanning the environment like it was a new system to map. Nyla didn't know a lot about Olivia, but she couldn't help but imagine her mind as an engine that was always running at full throttle. Nyla had seen the look on her face before, the one she wore when she was deep into a problem. She recognized that look on herself and in others who were caught up in their own passions. Except this wasn't code. It was Nyla's legacy, built brick by brick, revived after Hurricane Adaliz had tried to rip it all away.

"That corner," Nyla said, nodding toward a small alcove filled with glass tanks and microscopes, "is a new genetics station to replace the one that was destroyed. We almost lost all our sea turtle DNA data when the storm hit. Water came in through the ceiling and collapsed that whole wall. Luckily, we sealed the Nest so the damage was contained to this area."

Olivia's brow furrowed. "Did you have cloud-based backups of your DNA data?"

Of course she would ask the most logical thing in her mind. Nyla walked over to a hanging photograph, a group shot, five people knee-deep in mud, holding a turtle between them. Nyla was in the center, covered in grime, grinning like a fool. It had been a while since she'd smiled that way.

"Yes. Thanks to a grant I wrote, we were able to buy the right subscriptions. To think I almost said no to that. Sometimes, when you're focused on the actual work on the ground, the technical aspects fall by the wayside. Do you remember Jack?"

Olivia nodded. "Yes. I met him the first day. Very helpful. He's always shadowing Yasmin."

Nyla smiled at that description, because she wasn't wrong. Jack was charming, intelligent and had a special passion for computer science that he put to good use in both his research and helping Yasmin troubleshoot network issues. "He and Yasmin advocated for getting better servers and subscriptions. Thank God he did. When the storm hit, the power grid was down for over a week, but our information was safe because he'd had the forethought to push for those cloud backups. They're so important, especially the geotagging data. We're supposed to be releasing Yuno and Kayuga in a few weeks. We tag and track them after release, collect migration data for our studies."

Olivia tilted her head. "And the hack messes with that, doesn't it?"

Nyla's jaw tightened. "Yes, because without the systems back online, we can't access the geotagging software or log the baseline data. If I miss the release window, I lose a year of research. More importantly—" her voice dipped, almost speaking to herself "—the turtles lose vitality in captivity when they should be in the ocean. They have to be released, no matter what. I can't hold them indefinitely just because I need their data."

For a moment, Olivia didn't answer. She just looked at the

station, then at Nyla, something unreadable flickering in her expression before she finally said, "We're racing the clock."

"Yes." Nyla felt her mood fall. "This hack will make all our efforts be for nothing."

Olivia came to stand close behind her—Nyla sensed this more than felt it, like a beam of sunlight falling across her back, heating up her skin. "It's not all for nothing. We're going to get your data back and we're going to fix it so that nothing like this ever happens again."

Nyla's laugh was short and bitter. "Not if whoever is responsible for this isn't held accountable," Nyla said, moving deeper into the lab. "They'll just keep going after other targets, putting people through the same thing we're going through now. It's not fair."

"No, it's not," Olivia said, placing a warm hand on her shoulder that felt like comfort and something more Nyla didn't want to dwell on. "But if I find even a shred of evidence about who or what did this, I'll make sure it gets to the authorities. I do this work precisely because I can't stand criminals."

Nyla nodded, but it was clearly not the response Olivia was looking for. She stepped in front of where Nyla was staring out over the sea that was visible from where they stood, forcing her to look at her. "I promised I would fix this. It's literally the reason I'm paid to be here."

Nyla lifted her eyes, and though Olivia wasn't as tall as she was, she always gave the feeling that she had to look up to really see her.

"It stopped raining. Let's go outside. Hope you don't mind a little wet sand in your shoes." She walked past Olivia, carefully switching off the lights except for dim emergency lamps, without waiting for a reaction.

Beyond the secure doors separating the Nest from the

outside, moonlight bathed the landscape. The air smelled of fresh rain, salt and damp sand. Nyla led Olivia down the shell-lined path toward the outdoor enclosures, shielded by a sturdy roof from the fierce sun.

"This whole wing had to be rebuilt," Nyla said. "Roof peeled right off during the second night of the storm. We found seagrass in the supply closet. Fish in the hallway. That was wild."

They entered another building, similar to the main section of the Nest, but here, it was a large, compartmentalized lab. The air here was thick with antiseptic. Olivia scanned the room. Nyla observed the way she took in the boards, tanks and lab tables, and a fume hood that looked like a throwback to Nyla's high school biology class.

"It wasn't just the water," Nyla added. "It was time. For weeks, we couldn't come back in. The humidity. The rot. Everything we didn't lose to the wind and water, we lost to mold."

She walked to the largest tank and leaned on the edge. "This one came in two weeks ago. Fishing line around her flipper. She'll lose it, but she's strong."

Olivia stepped closer. "You named her?"

"Michiru," Nyla said with a smile. "From *Sailor Moon*."

"Wow, that's a blast from my past." Olivia smiled in exchange, bright and sincere. It nearly blinded Nyla.

"I was a quirky girl in school," Nyla said. "I started with manga, then went from boy love to girl love and never turned back."

Olivia furrowed her brow. "You mean yaoi and yuri? That's a lot of queer reads."

"My parents thought so, too. Maybe that's why they weren't surprised when I came out." Nyla tensed, realizing too late that she may have admitted to more than just her reading preferences. "Is that a problem?"

Olivia stared even harder at her until all the tension drained from her expression, leaving behind a wistfulness. "*Strawberry Panic* was my lesbian awakening, which is also a good way of describing my mother's reaction to my coming out." Olivia laughed. "All I remember was the look of shock on my mother's face, followed by constant prayer and at least two visits to the local priest to try to bless the lesbian out of me."

Nyla's eyes went wide. "You're joking."

Olivia looked out over the water, her expression unreadable. "Wish I was. Looking back, it's actually funny, but in the moment…" She let her words trail off before she added, "So no, I don't have a problem."

Nyla stopped in her tracks, seized by both horror and recognition. "I'm so sorry about your mom."

Olivia smiled. "She's a character. Where do you think I get it from?"

Despite her confession, Nyla couldn't help but smile. "Well, *Strawberry Panic* helped me figure myself out too, though it was campy as hell." They stepped out of the hangar and into the moonlit evening. "Do you remember *Aoi Hana*?"

Olivia smiled widely "A little too sweet for me." The smile on her face was smug and a little bit wicked.

"I see you, *fresca*," Nyla laughed. "You were going after the smutty scanlations, weren't you?"

Olivia shrugged. "If it didn't make me sweat, I wanted no part of it."

Nyla's laughter raced up and down the empty beach. She felt like a building shaking free of its scaffolding, everything that held it in place crumbling down to its very foundations. Olivia was like her, and now Nyla couldn't unsee the dangerous possibilities that presented. She cast a quick glance back at Olivia, who was giving her a look that was long and lingering and not altogether appropriate for the moment. She led them toward the vegetable garden, a riot of green and blooming colors held together by the geometry of irrigation tubing.

"I run a high school conservation club called the Turtle Warriors—"

"Of course you do," Olivia interjected but Nyla ignored her, continuing with her tour as if they hadn't just come out to each other in the nerdiest way. Olivia huffed out a laugh behind her but Nyla rolled with it. "We planted this on the same day we got power back. Some of those kids had lost everything. This gave them purpose as their families tried to rebuild. Something to water and nurture. Something that gave life. We use some of the vegetation to feed the turtles that are recuperating, but most of it is sent home with the kids."

This was the kind of initiative that Nyla lived for, and the center was fully onboard to support this. This was why resolving this hack was so important. How could anyone, even a hacker, harm a place that was trying to do so much good?

Nyla had never felt a more powerful urge to beat someone she had never met.

They stopped at the conservation dunes, windblown and stretching toward the dark waters of the gulf.

Nyla knelt, fingers brushing the roots of newly planted dune grass. "We almost lost the Nest entirely, it was so badly damaged. FEMA said it wasn't worth rebuilding. The insurance company fought us every step of the way. But the community wouldn't give it up."

She stood, met Olivia's eyes. "This isn't just science.

These turtles have been nesting here since they evolved into being. They thrived before we set up shop here, and everything we do hurts them. We are part of their community, but we don't act like it. We have a responsibility to protect them from the harm we cause. We couldn't let the Nest stay shuttered. The community came together the way we came together for everything that mattered in Soledad Bay after the hurricane. And now some hacker is going to take it all away?" She stepped close to Olivia, so close, it nearly forced her back. "I won't let them."

Olivia held her gaze, wearing defiance like a suit of armor for all the world to see. But Nyla was defiant in her own way. If Olivia was a tsunami who could wipe the beach clean in the blink of an eye, Nyla was the tide that rose and fell with the changing of the moon—constant, inexorable and unrelenting.

Olivia's gaze dropped down to her lips and Nyla had never wanted to kiss someone harder than at this moment. And the fact that it was within the realm of possibility made Nyla go queasy and weak inside.

Nyla stood on the dune, burning from the heat of the sun inside her. Olivia was so close, it made her reckless with need and want.

"It just occurred to me," Olivia said quietly.

"What?" Nyla whispered, the sea breeze making her barely audible.

Olivia snorted. "You are an amazing person."

Nyla felt her face go slack. "Really?"

"Yeah. You are. This is all amazing." Olivia closed her eyes, swaying as if she were suddenly dizzy. Nyla instinctively reached forward and caught her hand. The feeling of her palm softened by office work contrasted with Nyla's sand-and-salt-roughened one. She suddenly wanted them all over her body and recoiled immediately from that want.

"*¿Estás bien?*" Nyla asked, not missing the irony of her asking about Olivia's well-being when she herself was on the verge of spinning apart.

Olivia opened her eyes, looked at where their hands were joined. She didn't pull away immediately, allowing their hands to remain linked. Her gaze made its way to Nyla's, and a powerful wave of inexorability welled up inside, spilling over out of the boundary of her skin, and into the air around them. Olivia thought she was amazing, and while Nyla wasn't one to care much about the way people saw her, somehow, after only three days, Olivia's opinion mattered.

Three days?

Nyla gently pulled her hand away, the magic of their connection lingering in the warm evening air, not quite dissipating.

Olivia, face unreadable, dropped her hand to her side. "I should get back to my team. They're waiting for me at the hotel. Thank you for showing this to me."

Nyla gave a small smile at this. "*Gracias* for the personal debrief. It was…thorough."

"*Fue un placer.*" Olivia's *My pleasure* answered Nyla in a low, sensuous tone that she had never used before. It was the first time Olivia had spoken to her in Spanish, and the sound of it in her mouth made Nyla want to lick every syllable off her tongue.

Three days.

Nyla shut down that line of thinking. Olivia had to go.

"Wait," Nyla said, her addled brain snapping into place.

Olivia, who had begun to turn away, stopped in her tracks. "Go ahead."

"Your team is already at the resort. How are you getting home?"

The thought seemed to occur to Olivia for the first time. "Uber?"

Nyla shook her head. "Don't take Ubers at night. I'll drive you."

Olivia lifted her hair away from her neck, the wind whipping it against her cheek. "Are you sure? I don't want to put you out."

"Nonsense. My best friend Indya owns the place where you're staying, and I don't live far from there."

She moved down the dune toward the Nest before Olivia could answer, kicking up sand behind her as she walked. To Olivia's credit, she simply followed without fuss, which Nyla could already guess was not like her.

Nyla threw a glance behind her, attempting to cool the mood that lay thick between them. "I'll meet you at my car. You know where I'm parked."

"Sure. Just follow the turtle-mobile," Olivia quipped, heading inside, as well. The Nest's lights were bright, which surprised Nyla, as she had left them dimmed to help the turtles sleep. She made a note to herself to check the timers. She quickly locked up the facility, activated the alarms and left the center proper to find Olivia already leaning against her Jeep. She was texting away and hadn't noticed Nyla, allowing her to enjoy the sight of her—shorter than Nyla, her legs still made up 80 percent of her body. Her waist was tiny, her hips soft and round, and her breasts were the perfect size to hold—

Nyla blinked away her thoughts. She never looked at people she worked with like that. She sensed her attraction, how drawn she was to Olivia, especially now that she knew that it could be reciprocated, but it was absurd. They barely knew each other.

You could just get to know her a treacherous part of her whispered.

She took out and pressed her key fob, the beeping echoing across the dark lot. Olivia jumped, startled by the noise. Nyla bit back a smile. *"Perdón."*

Olivia scowled at her. "You did that on purpose." She picked up her messenger bag, which she had set against the windshield.

"I might have," Nyla answered, unable to hold back her smile.

Three days.

But the Nyla of today felt very different from the Nyla of three days ago.

The drive started out quietly, Olivia sitting up straight in the passenger seat, watching the occasional traffic light come and go as they drove in from the edge of the national park, where the center was located, to Soledad Bay's downtown. Nyla kept both hands firm on the wheel, the hum of the Jeep Olivia had christened the turtle-mobile filling the silence. Their moment on the beach lingered here in the cab, as well.

It was Olivia who cracked it first.

"So…only child?" she asked, glancing up from the glow of her screen.

Nyla gave a short laugh. "In what universe? I'm the oldest of six, plus three stepsiblings. Add all the first and second cousins and their kids, and it's basically a small nation. Sunday dinner looks like a block party."

Olivia whistled low. "How did you survive? With your reserved ways?"

Nyla flicked the signal indicator to turn at the next light. "I'm an introvert, but I'm not antisocial. I just have to hide in the bathroom a lot."

"Tried-and-true strategy." Olivia shifted in her seat. "I grew up as the lone kid of a single mom. She left me with her sister's family when she went back to Puerto Rico for school. Val, Rafi and Nati—they're my cousins, but honestly? They feel more like my siblings."

Nyla shot her a sideways look. "So you got all the sibling chaos without the actual parental supervision. That explains a lot."

Olivia pressed a hand to her chest. "Are you calling me undisciplined? I'm offended."

"Not undisciplined," Nyla corrected, fighting a smile. "You were probably the kind of kid who knew how to hack into your uncle's accounts to watch shows you weren't allowed to watch."

"That is a very specific accusation," Olivia said in mock offense. "And totally accurate."

Nyla chuckled, shaking her head. "Meanwhile, I was the bookish one hiding from my extroverted relatives. At the time, my mother was a science teacher at Soledad Bay High before she became principal. She knew every one of my teachers before I even walked into their classrooms. No such thing as mischief when your mother is at the same school."

"Brutal," Olivia said. "I bet you got voluntold for every club and fundraiser."

"I still do," Nyla admitted. "That's how the Turtle Warriors got started. A club to keep students busy, but somehow it's become a part of my life's work."

Pulling into the parking lot of Alba's Beachside Resort, Nyla maneuvered into a space and set the car in Park. She glanced over to catch Olivia leaning her head against the seat, eyes shining as she stared at Nyla. "That's the difference between us. You grew up in a crowd, trying to carve out space. I grew up alone, trying to prove I deserved space at all, especially in my mother's life."

The blunt honesty in her tone made Nyla's chest tighten. She opened her mouth, but Olivia's phone buzzed, sliding off her lap and onto the console between them. They both reached for it at the same time. Nyla's hand brushed against Olivia's, and she quickly became confounded by the soft, warm, sweetness of her skin. For one suspended second, Nyla forgot about the center, her family and the lot they were now parked in—everything except the way Olivia's fingers seemed to reach for hers.

Their faces tilted almost instinctively toward each other. Olivia's lips were so close, Nyla could just see the remnants of lip gloss in the soft creases of their pillowy fullness. Mere inches separated them, their breaths mingling in the dark interior.

Just as Nyla had resigned herself to surrender, to pressing her lips to Olivia's, the phone buzzed again. This time, the sound rent the air like the lightning of earlier. Nyla snapped back, pulling her hand away as if burned.

"Got it," she muttered, shoving the phone into Olivia's palm without looking at her. Olivia glanced down at her phone for the source of the interruption.

"It's my team. They have dinner waiting for me. I should go." Olivia unbuckled her seat belt slowly, eyes fixed on Nyla with something unreadable. "Thanks for the ride," she said softly, fingers tightening around her phone like it was keeping her from floating away.

"Of course," Nyla answered, her throat tight. She didn't trust herself to say more.

Olivia gave her a small, wry smile before slipping out

of the car. Nyla watched her walk up the path, shoulders squared against the night air, before disappearing into the glow of the lobby.

She'd had every intention of going in to see her friend Indya, or say hi to Jade, the front-end manager at the resort. Indya and her best friend Rayne were fixtures in her life since she was just a girl running amok on the beach, and she'd been traveling in the same queer social circles as Jade since they were both in high school.

However, as she watched a tremor course through her hands, which still itched to hold Olivia, she thought better of it.

Nyla exhaled, gripping the wheel like it could keep her steady. Mere days ago, Olivia hadn't existed in her sphere. She didn't even know of a company called CyberHunters. And now, Nyla was too undone to think about anything— or anyone else.

Chapter Nine

Olivia made her way across the boardwalk, the sand wet and matted under her sandals. Funny, she hadn't thought of the sand even once when she was out on the dunes with Nyla. It was as if her body, primed to perceive every kind of discomfort related to that horrible substance, had made the executive decision to ignore it completely when in the company of Nyla.

She thrummed with a restless, half-wild energy she hadn't felt in years. Not since Aleysha, and maybe not even then. Everything around her felt heightened by a factor of a thousand—the warm ocean air smelled too sweet, the salt too sharp and tangy. She clenched and unclenched her fists, palms and fingers still burning where they'd touched Nyla, a simple squeeze, professional and restrained, but her skin remembered it like a brand.

She had wanted to kiss her. God, she had wanted it more than a drowning person wants to breathe. And she didn't care what kind of composure Nyla had projected; for a moment, she wanted it, too. And the thought that any of this was possible drove Olivia to distraction.

She is just like me. It put all the weird interactions into perspective. Nyla was just like Olivia and now she couldn't unthink all the scenarios that truth invited.

There had been a heartbeat where the whole world had gone still, and Olivia could have sworn that if she had leaned forward, if she had closed those brief, final inches between them, Nyla would have met her halfway.

Instead, Olivia's phone had buzzed and, like a movie cliché, reality cut into the moment, forcing them apart. Forcing them back to the limits of the real world.

It was probably for the best. Work and pleasure rarely mixed well. But at that moment, Olivia hadn't been thinking about their work situation. They were just two women sitting in a Jeep, risking a professional complication while unable to resist each other.

Olivia squared her shoulders and forced her body into a controlled rhythm as she approached the entrance of the bungalow. Her heart hammered against her ribs like it wanted to break free, but she reined it in with several deep breaths.

The last time she had let herself believe in someone, it had cost her more than just her pride. Olivia's jaw tightened at the memory of Aleysha, with her good times and total rejection. She had wanted so much out of that relationship, thought she'd never stop loving her.

And yet Olivia had been so easy to leave behind.

She thought she needed the words, needed to hear Aleysha say: *I was never going to stay. It was never going to be you.*

But the only closure she needed was the life she was building without her.

Olivia reached for her hotel card and swiped, listening to the latch unlock before she stepped inside. She leaned briefly against the doorframe, shoring herself up. She had to pull herself back together before meeting her team. Their voices floated down the corridor along with the smell of spices that reminded her she hadn't eaten. She stepped toward the sounds and smells, drawn more by the need to put something in her stomach than by a desire for company. She really wanted to be alone with her thoughts of Nyla.

Feliz glanced up from the kitchen island and straightened when she saw her.

"Hey, boss!" Feliz grinned. "We went to this amazing Colombian restaurant downtown and brought you back a box."

Olivia perked up, her stomach answering with a quiet rumble. "What's on the menu, little one?" she said, her voice steady again.

"You're okay with me not cooking tonight?" Dareen asked. "I was too tired and ended up taking a nap when I got in."

Olivia shrugged as she pulled the paper bag reserved for her, the containers inside still warm enough to eat. "You can have my turn tomorrow."

Dareen pursed her lips. "Are you trading with me or just exercising your executive privilege?"

"I would never." Olivia feigned outrage. "Can't have cooked people cooking food. That's like cannibalism or something."

Al, who was sitting on the other side of the counter, tapping on his phone, raised an eyebrow at her. After working with him for three years, Olivia still couldn't fathom why he was typing so much. "You realize that nothing we've said here is even remotely related to cannibalism. Just throwing that out there."

"It felt cannibalistic," Olivia retorted. "Or maybe it's incestuous."

"Stop while you're still ahead," Al said. Dareen and Feliz laughed as they moved around the kitchen, taking out wineglasses and a bottle of wine, which they uncorked. Feliz poured the glasses and Al stopped typing long enough to distribute them.

"Now, wine is something I can get behind," Dareen said.

Feliz raised her glass. "Cheers to another successful day."

There were murmurs of assent before everyone downed their wine. Al and Feliz refilled their glasses, while Olivia dug into her meal of *pescado frito*, fried fish served with sides of coconut rice, fried plantains and salad. She liberated an avocado from its wrapping of wax paper and gave a sound of delight.

"My favorite. Thank you," Olivia said around a mouthful of plantains.

Dareen beamed. "We're going to start a new series before going to bed. Want to join us?"

The intensity of the day, together with the weight of *wanting*, had settled into Olivia's bones. She wasn't in the mood to be alone. She knew if she was, she'd end up thinking about Nyla, and she needed to cool down, or the first thing she would do tomorrow upon arriving at the center was something unprofessional, like finish the kiss they'd started. Not the worst possible outcome, but not the wisest, either.

"Yeah, I'll watch with you." She picked up her container and moved to the living room, determined to continue her meal and hope the Korean historical zombie drama would take her mind off the kiss she was certain she would have shared with Nyla if her technology hadn't stepped in to head off a possible disaster in the making.

Olivia lay awake in her aquamarine bedroom long after the others had gone to sleep. The room was steeped in the soft hush of the waves and the low hum of the ceiling fan. After only a few nights, the sounds of the bungalow were still strange and alien. The sheets felt wrong against her skin, too smooth, too clean, as if they'd been laid out for someone else. It would take another day or so for her to become immune to the ambient noises of this place.

Her laptop blinked from across the room, the green light pulsing like a reminder of everything still left to do. She turned her back to it, reaching instead for her phone. Nyla's name sat in her contacts, neat and unassuming, as if it didn't carry the weight of what had almost happened in the Jeep tonight.

Her thumb hovered before slowly typing out *Still awake?* The words sat on the screen for three seconds before she erased them, one sharp tap at a time.

What would she even say if Nyla answered? *Sorry we almost kissed? Sorry I wanted to? Sorry I still want to?*

The glow of the phone burned her eyes until she clicked it dark and dropped it onto the pillow beside her. She stared at the ceiling fan, the slow tick of its blades as loud as her own pulse.

Aleysha's face flickered in her mind, the silence that had stretched out in those last days sharp and final. Nyla wasn't Aleysha, could never and should never be. And yet her chest tightened anyway, and for an unbearable moment, she couldn't tell for whom she ached. All she knew was that the sensation was too close and far too familiar.

She pressed the heel of her palm to her eyes until sparks danced behind them. *Sleep,* she ordered herself. *Think about the breach, about the job. Not her.*

But when sleep finally claimed her, it wasn't network maps or corrupted code that followed her. The usual compulsive thinking about breakups and reunions kept their distance.

It was Nyla's hand in hers, warm and steady, with the unbearable sweetness of *almost* that carried her into sleep.

Early the next morning, the clop of Yasmin's Keds echoed down the hallway long before she appeared in the doorway of the conference room. Olivia looked up from her laptop, freshly brewed coffee heating her tumbler. She'd barely slept, too wired from her never-ending list of things to do, but mostly her sleep paid the consequences for the time she spent with Nyla.

Now Yasmin stood in front of her with a frown on her face, clutching a manila folder and her laptop to her chest.

"Houston, we have a problem," Yasmin said without preamble. She shut the door behind her and set her things down.

Olivia straightened. "Hit me with it."

Since the breach, Yasmin had been combing through recovery logs and time-stamped irregularities—leftovers from the hurricane-era data loss that still haunted the Nest. Nothing catastrophic, just a system that showed scars from its reconstruction.

"We're clean," Yasmin said finally, rubbing the bridge of her nose. "But there are signs that we aren't the only ones accessing logs."

"Meaning?" Olivia asked.

"Meaning someone in-house is taking an unusual interest in our cleanup. I can't prove it yet, but I can feel it."

Olivia trusted Yasmin's intuition. This was her system, and so far, her instincts had yet to be wrong.

Yasmin's voice had barely settled into the silence when the door creaked open.

"Morning," Jack said, strolling in with his easy grin, a travel mug in hand and a large pastry box in the other. A ladened plastic bag was hooked around two of his fingers.

His eyes quickly scanned the room, pausing on the printouts spread out over the table, then the open laptops, and arched a brow. "Wow, you two are up early. Everything okay?"

Olivia's pulse jolted. She flicked her gaze at Yasmin, who didn't hesitate, sweeping the papers inside the folder in one clean motion.

"I'd say the same for you," Yasmin retorted. "You're here awfully early on a Saturday."

"I'm behind on my data collection, what with the hack and all. I have no choice but to come out on the weekend and try to keep up." He glanced at Olivia. "Dr. Jimenez is here, as well."

His explanation made sense. "System audit," Olivia interjected, circling back to his original question. She didn't have to dumb things down for Jack. He had a good grasp of the fundamentals of her work. "Routine checks. You know the drill."

Jack set the box down and lifted the lid, the waft of vanilla and sugar spreading through the room. "Dedication is good, but don't work on an empty stomach," he said, sliding the box in Yasmin's direction. "Best bakery in town."

Yasmin's eyes grew wide while Olivia closed hers to take in the aroma of doughnuts, croissants, jelly and cream-filled pastries and slices of moist pound cake wrapped in wax paper. "This smells like heaven."

"La Isla? Their stuff is amazing," Yasmin exclaimed, digging a couple of napkins out of the bag and handing one to Olivia. Jack declined when she offered one to him, as well.

"No thanks, I had one this morning on the way in to work. They're too hard to resist when they're fresh."

"Tell me about it." Yasmin smiled. She didn't often smile at anyone that Olivia had seen, and yet with Jack, she was easy.

Jack raised his coffee tumbler as if in a toast. "Hope the tech team enjoys them."

"I'm sure they will," Olivia answered. Soon, he shut the door behind him. Olivia exchanged a look with Yasmin.

"We'll need to keep an eye on system access," Olivia said once the door closed behind Jack. "Could just be noise from too many cooks in the pot."

Yasmin nodded. "Everyone's poking through the archives trying to help. It's a miracle anything still syncs right now."

"Talking about too many cooks," Olivia said, unable to resist teasing Yasmin, "feels like you are a fan favorite of one of our cooks."

Yasmin didn't react to Olivia's words, but her eyes betrayed her, flicking instinctively to the door Jack had closed.

"Hmm-hmm," Olivia said in response, finishing off her treat with one bite. "That's what I thought."

"He's just a co-worker who's trying to be more." Yasmin still giving nothing away except for the dust of pink spreading across the top of her cheeks. It only served to emphasize her normally pale freckles.

"And how successful has he been? You know, about being more?"

"Shush," Yasmin said, pulling a cackle of delight from Olivia. "I have no comment."

"Okay, okay, I get the hint." Humor still tugged at Olvia's voice. "Let's run a fresh audit this week, just to be safe."

"Already scheduled," Yasmin replied, reaching for her pastry. "And for what it's worth, these things are amazing. Whatever else is broken, at least La Isla is still functioning."

"I know. It's good that your co-worker knows what you like."

"Whatever," Yasmin said, but there was no bite to her

response as she gathered up her folder and her pastry and left the conference room.

Olivia leaned back in her chair, chewing thoughtfully on a cream puff. She thought of Nyla and wondered which pastry she would enjoy. But she wasn't at the center this morning. She tried not to dwell too much on the disappointment that came from this fact.

Chapter Ten

Nyla

Nyla stumbled out of bed on Sunday morning nearly two days after her near kiss with Olivia, more out of habit than anything else. She wasn't much for sleeping in except when she was sick. Most of the time, she was grateful for what her best friends, Indya and Rayne, would call her super-human ability to wake up before the sun. It was the best time of her day. She normally found the routine soothing, whether it was a weekday doing her rounds or documenting her findings, or the weekend rhythms of journaling and re-flection. Now that she was forced to do everything on pen and paper, she was rediscovering that there was something about writing things by hand that quieted her anxieties and reminded her that the world could still be captured in steady lines and neat numbers.

And she needed the calm now more than ever, because her mind wouldn't stop replaying those moments alone with Olivia.

Her Jeep still carried the ghost of it—the dark hush of ocean outside her cab juxtaposed with the near touch of Olivia's skin against hers. The silence between them had thickened and become electric, raising the soft hairs at the back of Nyla's neck, clear as the tide turning. For one dangerous breath, she had been certain that if Olivia had only leaned in a little farther, she would have met her halfway and fused their lips together.

The thought rattled her more than she wanted to admit. Of all the people to be drawn to, why Olivia? The outsider. Her savior. The woman who had already upended her thoughts and left her scrambling for solid ground.

Nyla shuffled to her kitchen, brewed her first coffee of the day, then floated to her home office in a daze, sinking as if boneless down into the soft, pale cream–colored chair at the desk. She looked out at the sky bleeding sunrise pinks into midnight blues. She had bought a Florida stilt house back when houses were still affordable, painted it a soft green with pale yellow accents, like the colors of her grandmother's house in Santo Domingo, planted several mango, papaya and banana trees, and called it home. If the center was the core of who she was professionally, her home was the essence of Nyla, stripped of all the trappings of education and career.

She tightened her grip on the pen, her handwriting neat and deliberate, as though ink on paper could steady what her mind could not. But the source of her restlessness was still there. She had wanted that kiss. And no matter how many times she told herself it was a mistake, or reminded herself that relationships at work should be a big no-no, she couldn't stop wondering what it would mean if she gave in and asked for more.

She wrote in painstaking detail the events of that night, hoping that by transferring the memory of Olivia's proximity onto paper, she could purge it from her mind and let it live, unrequited, on the pages of her leather journal.

Just as she was putting the finishing touches on her writing session, her cell phone rang, cutting through her spiraling thoughts. Rayne's name flashed across the screen, pulling her back into the daylight.

"*Professora!*" Rayne shouted. Nyla had to pull the phone away from her ear to keep from suffering hearing loss.

"*Mala*, why are you shouting? It's too damned early for that."

"I'm not shouting. That's my baseline volume. Tell me that hacking business isn't dragging you into work on this fine Sunday morning."

She should. How could she relax when her center had been infected with a vicious virus that was making everyone miserable.

"Welllll…" Nyla said, drawing out the word. "I have a rare free morning. What have you got in mind?"

The sound of her best friend's joy pushed away the melancholy. The stress of the hack, together with her endless thinking about Olivia, needed an outlet, and her friends knew how to provide the perfect relief.

Rayne's voice came across the phone in decibels of high-pitched excitement. "What do I have in mind? How about you, me and Indya having brunch and throwing back mimosas on the beach?"

Nyla leaned her head back against the chair, smiling up at her wooden ceiling. "Why do I feel like everything on that list is optional except for the mimosas?"

"*Ay, por favor*, you know you love a good buzz." She dropped her voice, the tone as close to serious as Rayne was ever going to get. The shift was so rare, it put Nyla on alert. "We want to get together because we're worried about you. We had to find out about the hack from the newspaper and your mother. Why didn't you tell us what was happening?"

Nyla glanced out the kitchen window, watching two small seabirds race across the balcony railing of her house,

Rayne's words landing sharper than she'd expected. She gripped the phone a little tighter, searching for an answer that didn't make her feel like she was unraveling.

Why didn't I?

It wasn't that she didn't trust them. Indya and Rayne had been her lifelines since elementary school. Their friendship was woven in colorful threads of love and heartbreak through every major stage of her life. But this felt different. Heavier. Like if she spoke it aloud, the whole fragile thing would shatter.

She'd felt the exact same way when Ethan had nearly stolen her dissertation. Like the whole thing had been her own personal failure, even if she was the victim in both instances.

She pressed her thumb against the desktop, grounding herself. The truth was harsher than she wanted to admit: This fight, this fear, was something only the people experiencing it along with her could really understand. Yasmin, Olivia and her team, who worked so hard to salvage systems they barely controlled. Only they could truly understand what it meant to try to unravel the mess that this virus had inflicted.

Somehow, in the middle of the chaos, it was Olivia's voice she was learning to trust the most. The woman who understood what it felt like to have no choice but to be vigilant, to hold the line when everything was slipping through your fingers.

Nyla closed her eyes briefly, wanting to find the right words, something true that didn't sound like an excuse.

"I... I didn't know how to talk about it," she said finally, her voice quieter than she intended.

"Well, *hermana*," Rayne said with equal solemnity, until Nyla could almost hear the grin break through her words, "you are going to talk about it today, so you better prepare yourself, because your therapists are in the house."

An unexpected chuckle broke out of her, making her feel normal for the first time in a week. She had truly fallen into tunnel vision with this hack, and Rayne's words were like a lifeline, lifting her out of quicksand. She'd hooked her with mimosas, but what her friends were offering was so much more than that, and she'd never loved them more for it.

"You're not normal," Nyla said between chuckles.

Rayne scoffed. "Normal is overrated. Usual time, usual place?"

"You're the one inviting," Nyla retorted. "You tell me where to go."

"That's my feisty girl! Waterfront dining and afternoon drinking, it is! Meet you at the diner at eleven o'clock on the dot."

"As if I'm the one who gets to places late."

Rayne's laughter chimed crystalline over the phone line. "I might not be *on* time, but I'm always there at the *right* time."

"Bye, *Mala*," Nyla practically singsonged, ending the call on another peal of Rayne's laughter.

And that's how Nyla found herself in front of the local gift shop's window display later that morning, scanning the towers stuffed with ocean-themed trinkets such as ceramic octopus wind chimes, sea turtle lamps and a Save the Turtles necklace that looked similar to one the research center stocked in its gift shop.

Except the center's gift shop terminals were down. Everything at the center was down, and there was absolutely nothing she could do about it.

Nyla pivoted on her heel before she got into her head again and faced the street instead, with its slanted parking spaces and old-fashioned meters that had been replaced throughout the downtown area after the hurricane except for this strip of Ocean Avenue. Residents and business owners had been adamant that, while modernizations and improvements were more than welcome in the rebuilding of the downtown area, they wanted to retain the familiar touches that contributed to the quaint, small-town vibe of Soledad Bay.

Nyla was about to move on when she heard her name being called from the direction she'd walked from. In the distance, she saw Rayne waving to catch her attention.

"*Hola, Mala,*" Nyla said when Rayne caught up to her. Nyla opened her arms, knowing her best friend would fling herself into them, whether she was ready to receive her or not. She was wearing a sheer white linen dress with a bright yellow, thinly knitted bolero sweater that emphasized her long, swan-like neck, the color making her light brown skin gleam in the sun. Her curls were perfectly styled, the aroma of coconut and argan oil winding around her before the sea breeze swept it away.

Nyla laughed when Rayne's hug nearly sent both of them tumbling to the ground. "Ny-Ny," she cooed, "I'm so glad to see you. How are you, Mama?"

"*Ahí, luchando.* Just hanging in there."

They linked arms and chatted as they walked in the direction of Alba's Beachside Resort, the business Indya owned with her parents. As they walked past the shops, Rayne waved at the owner of La Isla, who made the most incredible pastries in town, and Nyla followed suit. Rayne knew everyone, and not only because she was beautiful and fashionable and larger than life. A former film and creative writing student, she'd turned her talents for creating catchy, addictive short videos into a small business as an influencer who specialized in beach-town living. Everyone in town tapped her to create social media campaigns that promoted their newly revitalized businesses. She was more than happy to put her enormous follower count to good use.

They reached the pool area of Alba's Beachside Resort just in time to see Indya laying a kiss on a tall, handsome man's lips. Nyla couldn't help her indulgent smile at Indya and her fiancé Santiago's affection. At that moment, he looked up and waved at them, which they returned with a wave of their own, Rayne's practically lifting her off her feet.

"I'm sorry I didn't come out to meet you. We had a tour group check in and it's been pure chaos trying to get all the rooms ready when half your staff is down with the flu." Indya clutched her wallet, waving one last time to Santiago, who smiled at her as if she'd hung the moon. Their love affair had come out of the blue, like lightning striking the middle of the ocean, but it worked, and Nyla had never seen two happier people.

As soon as they made it to the boardwalk, Rayne cast a quick glance behind them. "I see commitment has made Santiago a snackier-snack than ever."

Nyla wrinkled her face and Indya stared at her in shock. "Really, Rayne?"

"I'm paying you a compliment, *amiga*. Clearly, whatever it is you're doing has had a transformative effect on that man. *Parece un hombre nuevo*. A man with a new lease on life. He was so serious all the time when he first came to Soledad Bay."

"He had serious problems, *Mala*," Nyla answered. "Of course he looked serious. Now his daughter is with him, and he's getting married to one of the finest women in this town." Indya beamed, accepting the compliment, which was new for her, as well. Indya projected confidence, but she was plagued with insecurities. "I'd be smiling all the time too, if I was him."

Rayne put her hands together in an exaggerated prayer. "I'm just asking, when will it be my turn, Lord?"

"You are the silliest person in the world, you know that?" Indya said, flinging an arm around Rayne's shoulder. She was taller than the petite firebrand, though still a few inches shorter than Nyla, with golden, wavy hair the color of honey. She was the most put together of the three of them, with her sleeveless, pale yellow silk blouse, beige pencil skirt and matching pale-yellow sandals.

Indya turned to thread her fingers through Nyla's. "And you, *Mami*? How are you holding up?"

Nyla sighed, shaking her head. Indya released Rayne and took Nyla's face in her hands. "*Aye, bendito.* You can break it down for us while we eat."

Nyla huffed out a small laugh, realizing how much she needed to do exactly that.

They walked down to their usual dining spot with their arms linked, a seafood diner at the edge of the historic downtown area that only sold the fresh catch of that day. The owner went down to the docks and bought whatever the fishermen brought in. Nyla wondered if Olivia liked seafood. Would she go for a restaurant like this one?

Why was Nyla even thinking of that?

"I hate to be repetitive, but I'm really sorry to hear about the center. I know how much it means to you," Rayne said.

Indya shook her head. "I can't even imagine it. Is the entire center shut down? There's nothing you can do?"

Nyla shook her head. "Unfortunately not. While the university has a contractor working on restoring my data, my biggest priority is to make sure my research assistants continue to be paid. Thankfully, those grants have already been approved and the funds disbursed. I'm still able to continue paying my regular employees out of our emergency funds, but the center needs to get up and running again. We can only fund a closure for so long."

"It's good that you think of your workers first," Indya said. A server arrived at their table and paused, smiling brightly at them. Nyla instantly recognized the young woman who was a former member of the Turtle Warriors.

Nyla stood. "Sofia, it's so good to see you."

They hugged for a moment before Nyla took her seat.

"I can't believe I get to be your server today. I'll take good care of you. Sorry to hear about the center. That's just wrong."

Nyla nodded. "It's been rough, but we have good people working on solving the problem."

Sofia dug a notepad out of her pocket. "My friends and I practically grew up at the center. I'm studying ecology because of it. I hope they fix things so you can reopen soon."

The girl's words warmed Nyla's heart. "I love that. Thank you."

Sofia beamed before taking their order. When she left, Nyla leaned back, taking a long drink of water. "It's not just my employees. I need to keep the lights on and electricity going for my turtles. I can release most of the other turtles, but Kayuga isn't strong enough to be out in the open water yet."

"I'm sure things will sort themselves out soon," Rayne said.

"That's insane. Why would hackers even bother with a research center in a little town like ours?" Indya asked.

"We're nowhere near trying to figure out who the hackers are, or if they'll bother to claim the crime. The way it was explained to me, these entities create viruses and look for easy targets, like schools and local institutions—"

"And research centers—" Indya interrupted.

"Exactly. They usually come through as a link in an email. Unfortunately, one of our people clicked on it and inadvertently downloaded it onto the servers. The systems were locked down by the virus. The only way to unlock the system is to use a code only the hackers know, and to get that code, we must pay them a stupid amount of money."

"If you want your data back, you have to pay for it? That's horrible. How do you know if, once you pay, they still can't lock you back again? What's to stop them from extorting you for more money whenever they feel like it?" Indya asked.

Nyla picked up her toast, then dropped it again. "That's why you don't pay. The state hired someone independent to handle it. Apparently, the center isn't the only place in the state that they've hit, and CyberHunters are working on the problem, trying to reverse-engineer the key."

"That's a good thing, right?" Indya said.

"Yes," Nyla said, picking up her glass of mimosa. "Of course it is."

"You don't seem to be enthusiastic about these Cyber-Hunters," Indya pressed.

"Oh, they're great. Really. Nothing bad to say about them." Nyla had a flash of Olivia waltzing by her as she worked in their conference room superimposed with her walking away from her on the beach, all brashness and bravado, claiming she'd be done in a matter of weeks. Then her face appeared as it had in her Jeep, the pupils of her dark eyes blown wide, her lips half parted, as if waiting for Nyla to close the space between them.

"Are you sure? They're supposed to be helping you. If you have any reservations, you should communicate them to someone important," Indya pressed. That was Indya's way of thinking—she was always a little suspicious of people, especially in a professional context. She ran her family's hotel and, before that, had spent years living in Sarasota, closed off to anything that wasn't work or taking care of her daughter. Her fiancé had gone a long way toward getting her to open up to other aspects of life, but she was a businesswoman and an employer. Nyla wasn't surprised that her mind would quickly jump to a human resource solution.

"I have no reservations. Not really. I mean, the owner is…something else. Can you believe that in our first meeting, she said she'd be done with the code decryption in half the time it usually took, which is wild, because I did the research. Her timelines are insane." She shook her head at Olivia's audacity. She should have found it more annoying, but something about Olivia's bluster charmed her, and brought a smile to her face.

Indya and Rayne spoke at the same time.

"She sounds cocky," Indya said.

"She sounds confident," said Rayne.

"She's both." Nyla shrugged, chuckling to herself. She wasn't as comfortable expressing her feelings as she was talking about facts related to her work. "She's brilliant, that's clear. She's earnest and works with integrity. She has a lot of leadership qualities, and when it's time to be serious, she's almost intimidating." Nyla toyed with her glass as she brought her thoughts together. "I wasn't sure I could trust her at first. She can be brash to the point of off-putting, and sarcastic to the point of exasperation, but it's also part of what makes her funny. I wouldn't want to change any of that about her."

Nyla had been staring off into the waves, her thoughts pouring out of her like water out of a seashell. When she refocused her attention, her friends were staring at her. Indya's eyes were wide, and Rayne was covering a giggle behind her hand.

"What?" Nyla said, irritation creeping into her voice.

Rayne took a long sip of her mimosa while Indya continued to stare.

Nyla lost patience. "Why are you two looking at me like that?"

"Nothing," Rayne said, blotting the edges of her lips with a linen napkin. "So what is this CEO's name?"

"Olivia," Nyla said warily. "Olivia Navarro."

"Hmm," Indya said. "You have a lot to say about this Olivia Navarro."

"Of course I do," Nyla said, sensing a shift in the mood. Indya exchanged a glance with Rayne and it was starting to annoy Nyla. "My center can only stay closed so long before we become insolvent. I know, insurance," she said, heading off Indya's reply. "But you know how long that can take to come through. In the meantime, turtles will be hatching soon, and I have to release my turtles before the season is over. This hack couldn't have happened at a worse time and I have no choice but to depend on someone else to solve the problem, because it's outside of my field of expertise."

Indya opened her mouth to say something but seemed to think better of it. Instead, she put a hand on Nyla's and gave her a gentle squeeze. "Sometimes we catastrophize because we're terrified of what could happen. I have a feeling you and the center will come out of the other side of this."

"Yeah, it's not like this town is going to let the center go under." Rayne smiled. "You might consider a fundraiser to bridge the gap in funds. I'm sure that the town would come out for that."

Indya perked up. "Yes! Let me think." She pulled out a

notebook from her Celine bag and put it on the table. The food hadn't arrived yet, so she had space to maneuver. "Alba's Beachside Resort could host a Lights Out Gala." Her hands flew as she tried to paint a visual of the scene. "One night on the beach, dinner by candlelight, no artificial lights at all. We'd turn the blackout into the whole point of the event and show people how important darkness is for hatchlings. We can raise money by selling tickets for a fixed menu and a silent auction afterward. We'll make it an experience."

Rayne clapped her hands. "And I'll claim the daytime! We can host an Arts on the Sea event featuring a sandcastle contest on Saturday morning, live music and local art booths on both days, and then a community beach cleanup to close it out on Sunday afternoon. Families, tourists, influencers, the whole shebang. It'll get us buzz online *and* bodies on the sand."

"The center's employees and students have been getting a little stir-crazy because they can't get their research done. They can help with the organization, and it will boost everyone's mood," Nyla said.

"And you know local restaurants would love to get in on the action," Indya said, already jotting notes into her agenda. This was the space she thrived in—making plans, organizing people and getting things done.

Rayne was on her phone, punching in notes. "It will make the whole town come to life with a full weekend of saving turtles, Soledad-Bay style. Now first things first—we need to get the word out."

"My mother has connections with City Hall," Nyla offered, feeling more alive and excited than she had since this whole hacking started. "She can get the permits expedited."

"And my restaurant…" Indya began, then grinned at both of them. "Well, it's my restaurant and I can do what I want."

Rayne high-fived her. "That's my girl boss."

Indya set her pen down. "Oh, I am a woman boss."

"Especially of that man of yours," Nyla interjected.

Indya, Rayne and Nyla each exchanged looks with one other for several beats before simultaneously bursting into raucous laughter. They drew the attention of other diners but they didn't care. People knew them by now, and it was to be expected that they would act up at some point wherever they went.

Nyla laughed so hard, she had tears in her eyes. Somehow tears of joy turned to tears of gratitude, and as the laughter died down for Indya and Rayne, her laughter gave way to tears that streamed unchecked down her face. "I'm so grateful to you both. What would I do without you?"

"Oh, baby," Indya said, getting up from her chair to give Nyla a hug. "We're your sisters. We'll do anything for you."

"That's right," Rayne said, clutching her hand, leaving a kiss on her knuckles. "You know we'd never leave you alone. You'd be lost without us."

Nyla released a wet laugh followed by a sob. But it was just what she needed—an outlet for her stress and a plan.

Indya snorted while Nyla sniffled. "*Sin vergüenza,*" they said in unison, while Rayne laughed and laughed at being called shameless.

Their food finally arrived, and they spent the remainder of the meal drawing up plans and to-do lists that they could accomplish within an extremely short timeline. There was so much laughter that it was a wonder they got anything done.

After the trio finished their meal and drafted their plans, they walked companionably down the boardwalk for a couple of miles before doubling back to Alba's Beachside Resort. Nyla only half listened to Indya and Rayne's conversation, now that they had moved on to other topics.

She found her thoughts turning again to Olivia. She didn't know Olivia well, but she sometimes reminded her of Indya, yet possessed some of Rayne's chaotic, irreverent energy. Olivia even reminded Nyla of her own mother in the stubborn persistence she'd revealed when she was hard at work on a problem.

But contrary to many people Nyla knew, Olivia wasn't ashamed to change her opinion or admit she was wrong. She had a certain intellectual humility in the way she accepted new information and apologized when that new information proved her wrong. If she had been a little more obstinate or a little more chaotic, Nyla might have been endlessly annoyed by her. But she had just the right balance of characteristics and behaviors Nyla found familiar and even comforting. It was no wonder, then, that she had wanted to kiss her. She was proving with every layer of her character that she revealed to be someone that Nyla was finding harder and harder to resist.

The day ended the way the best days always did—with laughter that was almost a little too loud for the quiet evening sidewalks of Soledad Bay. They'd had dessert at a favorite ice cream shop, visited a craft market that was taking place in the plaza and then walked with arms linked along the shoreline, their shoes tucked safely in their bags. Nyla's heart felt lighter than it had all week, her chest unknotted by the familiarity of their easy affection.

The dim, soft yellow resort lights twinkled ahead, haloed by the misty sea air. Rayne checked her phone and groaned about an early call time for a brand deal in the morning. Indya peeled off toward the staff entrance of her resort with a mock salute and kisses blown wildly in the wind. And just like that, Nyla was alone again, walking the path back toward the town center where she'd parked, the evening whispering around her.

That's when she saw her.

Olivia, emerging from the shadowed curve of the board-walk, head bowed as if weighed down by more than just work.

Nyla's steps faltered. For a moment, the world compressed around her. She hadn't expected to see her tonight. And she definitely hadn't expected the violent lurch that her heart gave at the sight.

"Hey," she called, pitching her words casually, trying in every way to banish the lingering memory of nearly kissing Olivia.

Olivia startled slightly, then lifted her head. For a breathless second, something flickered in her eyes. Recognition, maybe, or even relief. But it was gone too fast, replaced by a weary, shuttered look Nyla didn't know how to read. Nyla's attention flew to her computer bag slung heavily across one shoulder.

"Hey," Olivia said. Her voice was hoarse, frayed at the edges.

Olivia looked exhausted, the kind of exhaustion that seemed etched into her bones. There were smudges beneath her eyes that even the soft light couldn't hide.

"Are you just getting back from work on a Sunday?" Nyla asked, searching her face.

"Yeah. Long day." Olivia shifted her bag higher on her shoulder, the motion almost defensive. "Did you have a good day?"

"I did," Nyla said, a little too quickly, a little too brightly. "Went out with some friends."

"Good. You needed it."

"Looks like you do, too."

Olivia gave a soft snort that lacked real energy, more like an exhale than a laugh. Nyla hesitated, hoping Olivia would give a clue that she wanted her to linger. It came in the form of Olivia taking her bag off and setting it on the ground against the wooden railing of the boardwalk. "We made some progress with the virus key." Olivia leaned against the wood. "I swear I am going to throw the biggest party once I break that code."

"Funny. So will I," Nyla added, leaning on the railing, as well.

Olivia snorted and her laugh went a long way toward making her look less drained. But the exhaustion was still visible in the corners of her eyes, and the slight downturn of her lips.

"Have you eaten?" Nyla asked gently.

Olivia dropped her eyes, then seemed to look up at her from underneath the lashes, a gesture that was achingly sweet and more vulnerable than anything she'd shown Nyla until now.

"Not really. But it's so late."

"Nope," Nyla answered, filled with an assertive courage she could only attribute to the afternoon she'd spent with her friends. They had filled her well and she felt like a superwoman. "There's a taco truck up the beach that's still open for another couple hours on Sunday." She indicated with a jut of her chin toward the resort. "Drop off your bag. I'll take you there."

The smile Olivia gave her was wry, so much closer to the Olivia she'd come to know during these few short days.

"Well, alright, bossy lady. Come on. I'll show you my luxury digs." She hoisted the bag over her shoulder and led the way to the bungalow. Nyla couldn't believe her own audacity. She had to consider channeling her friends' energy more often, especially if it meant that it gave her the courage to spend more time with Olivia.

Chapter Eleven

Olivia

Olivia unlocked the bungalow and shouldered the door open with a practiced nudge, stepping aside to allow Nyla to pass through.

"So this is our temporary home away from home," Olivia said, uncharacteristically nervous as she gave a tour of the bungalow that no one asked for. "Kitchen is on the right. Up ahead is the living room with an entire entertainment system. There's even a turntable, which is kind of wild." Olivia glanced back at Nyla, who wore a small, indulgent smile. She switched on lights in the living room after making sure the blinds were closed.

"See, I'm a quick study," Olivia said.

"Yes, you are," Nyla answered, approval in every syllable. This buoyed Olivia. She took a quick survey of the common area, the blast of cool air from the air conditioner smelling faintly of the citrus cleaner housekeeping used to clean the place while Olivia and her team were gone all day. The couch was neat, with a folded throw blanket on the armrest while a tangle of charging cables seemed to engulf the surface of the coffee table. The silence of the bungalow had the temporary quality of an empty space that would soon fill up again.

"It's impressive, isn't it? I remember when Indya remodeled the units after the hurricane." Nyla's expression was full of fondness. Olivia liked when Nyla didn't hide her smiles.

"Figures you'd know. You're best friends with the owner of this place."

"What can I say? I've got connections."

Olivia stood in front of her, the silence carrying the electric charge of crackling static. Making herself immune to Nyla's magnetic hazel eyes, she turned toward the kitchen.

"Can I offer you a drink?" Olivia said.

"No, I'm good. Mind if I step outside on the porch while you get ready?" Nyla asked, moving toward the heavy curtains. She switched off a lamp closest to the sliding glass doors.

"Uh, no. I'll be ready in about fifteen minutes."

"Okay." Nyla's eyes twinkled even in the dim light as she slid the doors open. "Don't rush. I can amuse myself."

Olivia was sure she could. She was made for the sand and sea that she now stepped toward. The sound of the door sealing shut behind Nyla shook Olivia into action, and suddenly she was racing to her room. Her phone buzzed the second she crossed the threshold to her bedroom.

Group chat: Hey, boss. We're at the Craft Coven in the plaza on the beach, downtown Soledad Bay. Quick walk from the resort. Meet us when you get home.

Dareen had sent a wide shot of the boardwalk, all canvas tents and twinkling lights. Feliz replied with eight heart-eye emojis and a close-up of crocheted sea creatures, the octopus winning by a landslide in Olivia's opinion. Al had added a photo of a hand-carved wave sculpture, captioned: If I buy this, will it count as a carry-on? And Yasmin, who had become as much a part of the team as everyone Olivia had brought with her, had already located the paleta cart and posted a strawberry-lime popsicle, the caption simply: evidence-based joy.

Jack and Anuar were mixed into the background pictures the team posted. Seemed like the whole gang was there and having a blast.

Olivia typed one-handed while toeing off her shoes. Showering and running out to grab something to eat. Save me a churro or I'll spam your email.

Dareen responded with a skull emoji.

She made a beeline for the bathroom, turning the water on as hot as the temperature would allow to help her relax. She was wound up tighter than the lid on an old jar of pickles.

Fast showers were a professional specialty: two minutes to shampoo, one to rinse, another ninety seconds to scrub off the day. Steam fogged the mirror by the time she stepped out and wrapped up in a towel, the tightness between her shoulder blades easing for the first time since Yasmin had shared the pattern of failed backups, the ones she wasn't telling Nyla about.

She pushed the uneasy feeling away and concentrated on getting dressed. She put on a soft black tank top, crisp linen overshirt she could roll to the elbows and dark linen pants that looked loose and cool. She paused, eyeing the makeup bag and going for the minimum. A touch of concealer, a sweep of brow gel, mascara. She hesitated and then added a slim line of eyeliner—just bold enough to look like she'd made an effort. She applied lip gloss with the faintest tint. She didn't overthink the why.

Phone, wallet, keycard. She opened the door and stopped, the hush of the shore clearer now that the day had shifted toward evening. The bungalow sat a short sandy walk off the main boardwalk, perched on low stilts. The porch creaked in that charming way old wood did. Beyond the steps, the sand rose in gentle mounds punctuated by beach grass and the occasional stake-and-twine marker that signaled a protected nest.

Nyla was out there, where the first slope of the dune met the path. She moved slowly, deliberately, eyes scanning the sand with the concentration Olivia had come to recognize when Nyla worked: quiet, serious and fully present.

Olivia let the screen door whisper shut behind her and took the steps down, dusting sand from the rail before she realized how automatic the gesture had become. "You casing the joint?" she said softly.

Nyla glanced over her shoulder, a small smile flickering on her face. "Something like that."

"What are you looking for?" Olivia closed the distance, the sand sucking slightly at the soles of her sandals. She removed them and let her toes feel the cool rasp of it against her skin. Her discomfort was not as acute as the first day she'd arrived. She decided that she and sand were on speaking terms now.

"Tracks. Scrapes. Sinkholes. Anything indicating that a turtle might have been here looking for a place to nest." Nyla crouched, brushing the surface lightly with the back of her fingers. "I don't expect one right up against an occupied bungalow, but sometimes they'll surprise you."

Olivia followed her gaze. "Isn't it too close to lights? Noise?"

"Usually," Nyla said, standing. The wind lifted a curl at her temple and she smoothed it absently. "Turtles prefer darker, quieter stretches of sand. They're skittish when they nest. But every season, a stubborn mama comes along and does what she wants. If she decides this is the spot, then it's the spot."

Olivia's mouth tugged up. "I respect a woman with a vision."

"Exactly." Nyla tipped her head toward a low, fenced square farther down. "Those stakes mark an active nest. It's a bit close, but the resort's been cooperative about it."

"They better be. The owner's your bestie, after all."

Nyla's face split into a grin. "You like that, don't you?"

Olivia shrugged, swinging her sandals. "Reminds me of East Ward, and my family, how we're all connected to each other. Community is important."

"It is."

Olivia bit her lip as she watched Nyla check a cluster of seagrasses. "Do you do this everywhere you go?" Olivia asked. "Scan for turtle evidence the way I scan for unsecured routers?"

Nyla shrugged, sheepish and proud at the same time. "Occupational hazard. My brain's always half on night patrol."

Olivia pretended to be purely neutral about how charming that was and failed. "Well, if we find a turtle under my porch, I'm moving out."

"We'd move you out," Nyla said, too matter-of-fact to be teasing. "And reroute foot traffic. And slap tarps over any light spill. And post signs. And then I'd spend the remainder of the season checking her nest twice a week until they hatch, so please don't manifest that into existence unless you like being moved around."

"Duly noted." Olivia looked out toward the line where the boardwalk cut parallel to the beach. The evening crowd had thinned a bit, but there was still movement on the boardwalk: couples in flip-flops, families herding sunburned kids to bed, a few runners taking advantage of the cool evening. The breeze carried the buttery-sweet smell of frying batter and something fruity-bright. Olivia's stomach made a polite, hopeful sound. "You said tacos?"

"I did." Nyla straightened up from where she'd been searching behind a small dune. "Ready?"

"Always." Olivia fell in beside her as they stepped onto the path, where walking didn't feel like sinking in quicksand. The boardwalk was slatted underfoot, weather-silvered and warm. String lights blinked above them as the moon continued to rise, making the whole stretch look like a postcard.

They didn't rush conversation. It was a new rhythm tonight, perhaps because they were both tired. No forced chatter, no obligation to fill silence. Olivia liked that she could be quiet around Nyla. She'd point out a patch of sea oats that was rebounding after last winter's storms, or gesture toward a tern banking low over the water and name it without turning into a know-it-all. Olivia chimed in where she wanted to, asked about hatch windows and how many nests were active this season, because she was picking up these concepts as she worked. It was practical talk with the kind of subtext that didn't need decoding: *I like seeing what you see and I like knowing what you know.*

By the time they reached a row of food trucks, the boardwalk had pooled into a small plaza with benches and a guitarist working through a set of old beach staples like Jimmy Buffett and the Gipsy Kings. The taco stand sat under a hand-painted sign whose edges had been salt-sanded over the years: El Faro Taquería. A string of *papel picado* fluttered overhead, colors snapping like flags, and a chalkboard listed the day's specials in slanted script: *carnitas, pescado al ajillo, rajas con queso, elote, agua fresca—sabór de piña o de limón.*

Olivia followed Nyla up to the counter, where an older

couple moved with the smooth choreography of people who'd been doing this together forever. He flipped tortillas on the plancha with a quick flick of the wrist; she dressed plates with a steady hand, sprinkling onion and cilantro like confetti. At the register, a tip jar read *Para la universidad* in marker, surrounded by doodled caps and diplomas. Olivia could appreciate a good hustle.

"Evening, *Profe*," the woman called when she spotted them. "You bring me turtles?"

"No turtles, just hunger," Nyla said, smiling. "Señora Garcia, this is Olivia."

Señora Garcia, who was now helping her husband fill a plate with toasted tortillas, smiled while her husband lifted his chin in greeting. *"Buenas noches. ¿Cómo les puedo servir?"*

Olivia leaned an elbow on the counter, soothed by the hiss of the plancha and the citrus-salt air. "I've been told you ruin people for other tacos."

"We don't ruin anyone," Señora Garcia said in mock offense. "We set the standard."

"Dangerous." Olivia glanced at the chalkboard. *"Dos pescados, una raja* and… I'm open to being bossed around for the fourth."

"Carnitas," Nyla and Señora Garcia said in unison. They laughed, the kind of easy overlap that told Olivia this was a regular stop on Nyla's nightly excursions.

"Carnitas it is," Olivia said. *"Por favor."*

"And two *aguitas*," Nyla added. *"Una de piña y una de limón."*

"Coming up." Señora Garcia slid a glance at Olivia, her eyes kind. "Is she your computer person, *Profe*?"

Olivia blushed as Nyla answered. *"Sí, señora."* She wondered when they might have had a chance to talk about her.

"Our son is studying computer science," she said, tipping her head toward the jar. "He threatens to replace my cash box with a QR code."

"If he does," Señor Garcia said over the sizzle, "then the tourists maybe will tip less and he won't have money for college."

"He should make sure you have both," Olivia suggested. "It's always good to have options." She felt Nyla's amused look and tried not to glow under it.

"I heard the center is still closed. When will it open again?" the older gentleman asked.

"We're working on the center's systems," Olivia answered, keeping it light.

"*Bueno*," Señora Garcia said, her voice softening. "Turtles are the symbol of this town. We need that place to open again."

"It will," Olivia said with simple sincerity. She held Nyla's gaze as she continued. "I promise." Nyla's lips quirked but she said nothing more.

They didn't press for further details, and Olivia liked them for that. The plate arrived lined with parchment: tortillas barely blistered, the fish crispy-edged and lemony, *rajas* glossy with roasted peppers and *carnitas* with those soft, perfect browned ends that meant whoever made them knew what they were doing. Lime wedges perched on each side like quotation marks.

"Here you go," Señor Garcia said, pushing two plates forward. *"Bienvenida a nuestro pueblito."*

"I feel very welcomed. Thank you," Olivia said with sincere gratitude. She would have to bring her team back here.

Olivia reached for her wallet, but Señora Garcia waved a hand. "The first visit with *Profe's* friends is always free."

Olivia made to protest but Señora Garcia raised a finger. "You are not allowed to argue with your elders."

"But—" Olivia began.

"Don't argue," Nyla murmured, sliding the plate toward Olivia. "Just accept it. You'll never talk them out of it."

Olivia did what she was told, thanking the Garcias profusely, but didn't leave without digging into her pocket for a handful of bills and dumping them in the tip jar. The older woman tsked, but she had no choice but to let it slide.

"*Gracias*," Olivia repeated as she and Nyla took their plates and drinks to one of the standing tables. The first bite was an immediate explosion of rich flavors. She closed her eyes and nearly did a little dance but remembered that she was in public. "Okay," she called out to the Garcias, who waited for her verdict with a smile. "I am now officially ruined for any other tacos. I'm moving in with you."

Señora Garcia preened. "You see?" she reminded them. "Standards."

Olivia lifted the *aguita*, cool and not too sweet, and offered it as a toast to Nyla. "You were right."

"I'm going to need that in writing," Nyla said, tapping her cup against Olivia's. "I want to reread that statement over and over again."

"Ha-ha," Olivia said, savoring the tacos in combination with the delicious, flavored water. She could eat these tacos until she was ready to burst. She glanced over at Nyla, who was watching her eat.

"You really do enjoy tacos," Nyla said, popping a piece of tortilla into her mouth.

"They are unreal. Is there something in the water that ensures every meal is amazing?"

"The effect of a perfect beach," Nyla said with obvious pride.

"Whatever it is, you need to market it somehow. People would flock here, knowing the food is delicious and the people are beautiful."

Nyla waved a hand as if brushing the comment away. "You exaggerate."

"I speak from experience." Olivia leaned her cheek on her hand. "Though they'll have to manage their expectations, because I'm biased. I happen to be in the company of the prettiest woman in this town."

Nyla sucked her teeth, but the pleasure from the compliment lit her face up. *"Coqueta."*

Olivia downed her drink. "What can I say? I have game."

Nyla launched a balled-up paper towel at Olivia, which she caught flawlessly.

Olivia glanced toward the plaza. A banner for the craft festival bobbed above the walkway like a flag calling them onward. The group chat pinged again: a photo of Yasmin with a crocheted turtle hat balanced on her head and a caption from Feliz: Peer-reviewed drip. Olivia snorted, then held up her phone for Nyla to see. "I think the kids are waiting for us."

"Finish your tacos," Nyla said, half stern, half fond. "Food first, then crafts."

Olivia took another bite, chewed and let the knot under her ribs loosen one more notch. She hadn't realized how much she'd needed something simple: food made by people who liked you, a walk that didn't have an end point, company that didn't require anything more than her eating until her stomach was full. She tapped the plate with her thumb, a quiet rhythm she didn't notice she'd adopted until Nyla's eyes dropped to it and back up, reading her in that precise, gentle way she always did.

"Impatient to get your own crocheted hat?"

"It's the must-have accessory of the season." Olivia stood, collecting her tray and tossing the garbage in the correct recycle bin.

"Ready?" Nyla asked.

Olivia wiped her hands, nodded and fell into step beside her, the two of them angling back toward the hum of the festival, the taste of lime, salt and flirtation still bright on her tongue.

The craft festival was more packed than Olivia had expected. The sounds of conversation and music were layered and sometimes competing with each other: a kid hammering nails into a make-your-own birdhouse, a troupe of dancers stomping out a *folklórico* routine on a temporary stage, the occasional squeal from someone discovering their friend behind a booth. The boardwalk had been transformed into a riot of color and sound, stalls spilling over with textiles, ceramics, beadwork, driftwood sculptures, tie-dyed shirts, hand-tooled leather and jewelry strung with shells and polished glass.

Olivia tugged at the hem of her black tank, as if that might anchor her in the chaos. She was good with noise when it came from servers and machines; human chatter was another matter. But Nyla moved through the festival like she belonged, greeting stall owners by name, stopping to admire a child's drawing and slipping money into tip jars. People called out to her—"Doctor!" "Nyla!" *"Profe!"*—and Olivia registered how the whole town seemed to know her, like she was a local landmark in her own right.

She caught herself staring at Nyla time and again—at her composure, her sweetness, the respect with which she addressed everyone. She could watch her and nothing else, and that alarmed Olivia. It had barely been a week, yet she felt like she'd known Nyla for ages.

She forced her attention away. Across the plaza, Dareen was waving both arms in the air to catch her attention, her silver bangles catching the light. Feliz stood beside her, balancing a paper plate loaded with arepas, while Jack gestured animatedly toward something carved out of driftwood. Anuar and Al seemed to occupy their own universe, oblivious to everything around them. Yasmin trailed a step behind them, hoodie tied around her waist, her expression set in that calm look Olivia recognized from hours of recovery work.

"Crew sighting, ten o'clock," Olivia murmured, tipping her chin.

Nyla followed her glance, smiled, and steered them through the crowd. Al and Anuar were in mid-debate when they arrived.

"—no, no, the tensile strength wouldn't hold," Al was insisting. "You can't make a hammock out of driftwood."

"You absolutely can if you bind the joints properly," Anuar argued, a gleam of challenge in his eye.

"Yeah, and then you fall on your ass in the first five minutes," Feliz added around a mouthful of arepa, utterly unconcerned about decorum.

"I still don't get why we're making hammocks out of driftwood. Sounds uncomfortable," Yasmin murmured, though her tone was distracted, her eyes flicking to a stall loaded with crystals of every kind.

Jack jumped in, his voice smooth. "What about reinforcing with epoxy? It could work if—"

"Not everything is a lab experiment, Jack," Anuar groaned, throwing his hands up. "Sometimes a chair is just a chair."

"Better than old, moldy wood," Jack mumbled petulantly.

Olivia cut through before the debate could spiral further. "Anyone else dying for a sugar overload from festival food?" She tilted her head toward the side street where a painted sign in pastel swirls announced Helados del Sol. "Because I vote for ice cream."

"Yes!" Dareen cheered instantly. "Best idea you've had all week, boss."

"I'm in," Feliz said, polishing off her plate. "I saw someone walking by with a scoop the size of my head."

"Count me in," Al added. "Need to cool down after fighting for science."

"You were fighting for nonsense," Dareen shot back, but her grin betrayed her words.

"Pure nonsense," Anuar said in agreement, but he was more charmed than exasperated and Al did something he rarely did—he laughed out loud.

"*Helados*, please," Anuar said. "They have the best coconut flavor."

Al's eyes grew bright. "I love coconut."

"Another thing we have in common, *sí*?" Anuar said, shoulder bumping Al.

Nyla laughed, her curls catching the breeze. "Looks like you have your answer, Olivia."

Olivia quirked a smile, enjoying the sight of her blended team bickering and smiling instead of staring hollow-eyed at screens. She flicked a glance toward Nyla. "Ice cream is always the right answer."

They set off as a pack, weaving through the crowd. Anuar and Al continued their debate at full volume, their banter drawing side-glances from festivalgoers who couldn't help but grin. Feliz snapped pictures of booths as they passed, narrating each shot for her social media backlog. Yasmin walked ahead, gesturing to Jack, who hovered at her shoulder like a satellite caught in her orbit.

Olivia found herself next to Nyla, their shoulders almost brushing as they moved. She walked with that effortless authority she carried everywhere. Her hand brushed absently against Nyla's thigh when they got too close, a warm, electric sensation she was far too fond of. She tried to focus on the stalls, the music, the colorful crowd ahead of her, but it was Nyla's presence that captured her attention.

When they reached Helados del Sol, the line was already snaking out the door, but the cheerful chaos inside made the wait feel short. The shop smelled of sugar and fruit, large bamboo fans humming overhead. A mural of sea turtles painted in bright acrylics covered the wall, their shells patterned like stained glass in the same style as the giant turtle on the side of the center. Olivia felt her lips tug upward. She would never look at turtles the same way again.

The group spilled inside, everyone pointing at different tubs: pale coconut, mango gold, deep chocolate, strawberry marbled with cream. The chatter rose until Nyla leaned toward Olivia, voice pitched low. "This is Soledad Bay distilled—turtles, sunshine and everyone talking over each other."

Olivia smirked. "Sounds like the kind of chaos that would drive an introverted scientist out of her mind."

"It does sometimes," Nyla admitted. "But it's also the kind I could never live without."

Olivia understood. East Ward had a kind of chaos that spoke to her and felt as familiar as her name.

By the time they each had cones or cups in hand, the festival air had turned quieter, families heading out to leave the young and adventurous to carry the festivities to the end. Some stalls had packed up, but the music was still vibrant.

In Olivia's town, they would have to be done by midnight, and she imagined it would be the same here. The group wove through the changing crowd of the plaza, laughter trailing behind them like a banner. Anuar and Al were now comparing scoop sizes like competitive athletes. Jack and Yasmin held their heads close together as they talked. Dareen threatened to steal bites from anyone not guarding their dessert. Feliz documented everything with merciless efficiency through her camera—Olivia would have to ask to see the pictures, because Feliz's photos were always so good.

Nyla used her plastic spoon to steal a scoop of Olivia's pistachio ice cream. She laughed and returned the gesture, approving of Nyla's fruit flavors. Nyla nudged her elbow lightly. "I think two couples are forming already," she said under her breath, nodding toward Al and Anuar's banter, then toward Yasmin and Jack's lopsided orbit.

Olivia followed her gaze, smirk tugging at her lips. "At least two," she agreed. She licked a stripe of melting cream from her spoon, then added with mock casualness, "Or maybe there are three."

She stole another spoonful of Nyla's ice cream, waggling her eyebrows as the mango melted on her tongue. The words hovered in the air like the dragonflies that were everywhere during the day. Nyla's eyebrows rose, not in shock, but in that sly way that told Olivia she was amused by the insinuation. She bumped her shoulder, light and warm, and said, "You're funny, Olivia Navarro."

"Oh ho, watch out. She used my full name." Olivia tried not to grin too widely, though she felt like she could breathe for the first time all day. The hack was a mystery to unravel, and there were still some secrets Olivia was forced to hold close to her chest. But for a fleeting moment, she let herself believe in what the night had promised and delivered:

laughter, company, easy closeness and the possibility of something more curling at the edges.

The festival slowly wound down. Stall owners packed up in a well-practiced rhythm, the laughter fading into tired but satisfied chatter. The group split naturally in two when they reached the low wooden arch that marked the edge of the resort property: Olivia's team veered toward the cluster of bungalows, while Nyla's staff peeled off toward the parking lot. If Al and Anuar hung back to talk longer, Olivia said nothing. Who was she to criticize when she was convinced that she was developing a crush on Anuar's boss?

There were hugs, shoulder claps and good-nights exchanged in a chorus of voices. Dareen promised to text pictures of her "driftwood hammock prototype, done properly" once she finished it. Feliz insisted they all come with her the next weekend to explore a locally famous artisan market "two towns over" to buy homemade jewelry and crystals for her sacred stone collection. Anuar gave Al one of the woven bracelets he'd bought, dangling it from his fingers like a casual gift that left Al staring at it far longer than necessary. Yasmin rolled her eyes at Jack's overeager offer to walk her to her car, but she didn't refuse.

One by one, the group thinned until only Olivia and Nyla were left standing near the sand. The night air had cooled down, the salt tang sharpening as the tide crept up to shore. The golden and amber lights of the boardwalk spilled only so far, leaving long stretches of beach in shadow by design. The hum of generators from the bungalows was muted by the steady hush of the waves.

Olivia slipped off her shoes without thinking, toes curling instinctively into the cool, wet sand. She had always hated the grit, the way it clung to her feet and worked its way into her clothes. But tonight, she found it almost pleasant. The sand was just another texture, another grounding point to a world she floated above every time she was with Nyla.

Nyla noticed immediately. She tilted her head, her bundle of braids curling over her shoulder as she studied Olivia's bare feet. "You," she said softly, her tone halfway between amusement and wonder, "are standing in sand. Voluntarily."

Olivia let out a low chuckle, flexing her toes. "I'm adapting, like your turtles." She glanced up at Nyla, her hazel gaze boring straight through Olivia's soul. "At least I'm not jumping away from imaginary snakes anymore."

The laugh that burst out of Nyla was brighter than any festival light, pinning Olivia's eyes to her perfectly shaped face. "I will never let you live that down," she teased, her voice warm with memory.

"I figured. That's why I got ahead of it," Olivia admitted, and she didn't mind. Not when Nyla's laugh smoothed the edges of everything jagged in her chest.

They walked slowly, side by side, the soft give of wet sand pulling at their steps. Olivia was exhausted, but she was also wound up. Nyla's presence did that to her. Neither spoke for a while. Nyla looked tired, as well. Her shoulders drooped, and her voice, when she did comment on the moon's reflection, was softened by fatigue. Yet she remained cheerful, her words touched with affection, her smile lingering, even when her eyes looked ready to close.

Their hands brushed once, then again. The second time, Olivia didn't pull away. Instead, she turned her palm deliberately, her fingers sliding against Nyla's until they twined together. The contact sent a quiet jolt through her, like static snapped something deeper into place.

Nyla turned her gaze forward, lips parted, letting the gesture speak for her. Olivia squeezed gently, reassured when Nyla squeezed back.

A few steps later, Olivia stopped, still holding Nyla's hand. She lifted it to her lips and pressed a kiss against her knuckles. The gesture was old-fashioned and impulsive, but it pulled a sigh from Nyla that sounded like it had been waiting in her chest for years to escape.

Olivia let her kiss linger a second longer before lowering their hands. "Sorry," she murmured, though she didn't feel or sound sorry at all.

"Don't be," Nyla whispered, her voice husky.

The tide surged closer, foamy edges licking at their feet. Olivia tilted her head toward her. The moon hung low over the water, silvering the line of Nyla's cheek, catching in the strands of her braids. The buildings behind them were shrouded in shadow, the world pared down to moonlight and surf around the woman standing inches away.

Olivia leaned in first. To her relief and pleasure, Nyla met her halfway.

The kiss was unhurried, tentative at first, just a brush of warm lips, both a test and a promise. Then Nyla pulled her closer, her free hand finding Olivia's shoulder, and the promise deepened into something undeniable. The taste of ice cream still lingered on her lips, the scent of ocean, sunblock and Nyla's warm skin filling Olivia's senses until there was no room for anything else.

When they broke apart, they pressed their foreheads together. Neither moved to fill the silence, content to breathe each other in, to let the waves mark time for them.

Finally, Nyla whispered, "You make it hard to remember that I'm supposed to be smart about this."

Olivia smiled, brushing her thumb across Nyla's knuckles again. "Maybe smart is overrated."

Nyla's answering smile was tired but radiant. She gave Olivia's hand one last squeeze before letting go. Olivia was disappointed. She wanted more time, even if exhaustion was making her head feel swimmy.

Nyla read her expression and smiled in understanding, "Do you know how long it takes hatchlings to crawl out of their nest once they hatch?"

Olivia shook her head. "A couple of hours?"

"Try days," Nyla corrected. "Days of digging, of crawling over each other. Of waiting for the night to fall before they race across the sand and into the water."

"Persistent little guys."

Nyla nodded. "Persistent and patient. It's always served me well in my life."

Olivia nodded, understanding. "I'm not that good at waiting. I'm made for that last sprint toward the water."

"I see that, *impulsiva*." She smiled when she said this. "And sometimes, I slow myself down with too much thinking. There's value in both, but you have to know when to be which way. I struggle with that."

Olivia raised a hand, cupping Nyla's cheek. "Nice to know I'm not the only one."

Nyla put a hand over Olivia's, holding it in place as she nuzzled into the palm. "Good night, Olivia."

"Goodnight, *Profe*," Olivia echoed, her quavering voice reflecting the storm in her chest.

She watched Nyla walk up the boardwalk path, her figure swallowed by shadows and the glow of the resort lights beyond. Then Olivia turned toward the bungalow, slipping her shoes back on, her anxieties of the day all but washed away in the tide.

Inside the bungalow, her team had already settled in for the night. Olivia's pulse still thrummed from the kiss, but even in the warmth of it, stray doubts tugged at her. She'd been here before, swept up, reckless, convinced she could sprint toward something without looking back. It wasn't quite the same, though. It felt different with Nyla, steadier somehow, yet a thin seam of unease threaded through the sweetness. There were things she hadn't said, truths and revelations about herself she had learned to hold close until she could untangle them. For now, she pushed the thought down, letting herself cling to the memory of Nyla's hands and lips pressed against hers.

The taste of Nyla's kiss pulled her back into the clouds, sharp and sweet as the salt air and ice cream.

Chapter Twelve

The bell above the bakery door chimed as Nyla slipped inside, the warm air fragrant with butter, sugar and competing savory spices. She hummed under her breath, a tune she couldn't quite place, as she scanned the glass case lined with guava turnovers, pastelitos de carne and glossy Danishes. Monday mornings called for reinforcements, and a box of pastries for her staff felt like the right start to the week. She'd completed her morning routine, all turtle nest temperatures measured and documented, and her mind was clear enough to finally dive into planning the Arts on the Sea weekend with the Lights Out Gala at its heart. She'd been messaging Indya and Rayne and she felt like she had a real handle on the vision for this fundraiser, and she'd already reached out to her mother, who would handle her permits.

Even with the taco truck detour and the festival's bright chaos, the idea had been simmering quietly in the back of her thoughts. Now she and her friends would shape it into something real, something the whole town could rally behind. She placed her order, watching Lara Fuentes, the middle-aged daughter of the bakery owner, tuck each pastry into a pink cardboard box, and caught herself smiling for no reason at all. Well, not for *no* reason. Olivia's laughter had followed her into her dreams, and the memory of their walk, of the kiss on her knuckles and the sweeter kiss on her lips, soft as the incoming tide, stirred heat beneath her skin.

"And that little smile?" Lara teased, placing gold foil stickers on the edges of the box to seal it shut before packing up the sugar packets and stirrers for the box of café con leche that Nyla had ordered. *"Hay sonrisas que confiesan lo que los labios callan."*

Nyla grinned at the saying—*There are smiles that confess what lips keep quiet.*

"It's a beautiful Monday morning, isn't it?" Nyla evaded.

Lara chuckled. "That's okay. A woman needs her secrets, doesn't she?"

Nyla handed Lara the exact change and left a few dollars in the tip jar. Her crush on Olivia was her secret and she wanted to cherish that intimate knowledge until she understood what, if anything, it would turn into. "She certainly does. *Cuidate, linda.*"

"Igual." Lara waved her off. Nyla strode down the sidewalk toward her Jeep, balancing the boxes of pastries and coffee while mentally ticking through a list of calls to make for additional permits, volunteers and silent auction donations. It was the perfect way to distract herself from Olivia, images of whom constantly invaded her thoughts—her laugh, her sarcastic comments, her office-soft hands and plump lips.

Nyla needed to do anything but dwell on Olivia's smart mouth.

The Lights Out Gala and Arts on the Sea weekend had gone from half-baked brainstorms with Indya and Rayne to something she could almost taste. For once, the future felt like more than triage.

But even as she planned menus and auction tables in her

head, her thoughts drifted. To the taco truck, to the festival lights, to Olivia's hand closing around hers and the taste of salt and ice cream when their lips finally met. She shook her head, amused and exasperated at herself in equal measure. She had turtles to save, a fundraiser to plan, a community to keep afloat—and still, Olivia had a way of slipping into every thought, like sunlight spilling through cracks in the shutters. If she could just keep her mind on the task at hand and not on that wicked, wonderful woman.

She made the short drive, parked and walked into the center, carrying her boxes of treats as she made her way to the conference room that CyberHunters had claimed as ground zero for their work. Yasmin was already in place, half-zipped hoodie pulled down over her head, her posture terrible as she hunched over her screen. Nyla tsked. "Sit properly or you're going to strain your back."

Yasmin looked up and instantly did what she was told.

"Where's Olivia?" she asked, setting the box of treats down.

Yasmin stood from her chair, walked over to the glass partition that separated the conference room from the adjacent workroom where the rest of Olivia's team was working and rapped on it. Olivia's head popped out from the side. Nyla nearly jumped, but Olivia only smiled and waved before she was on the move, opening and stepping through the door that separated the spaces.

"I figured you all might need a break," Nyla said by way of greeting.

Olivia's eyes grew wide as she broke the seals and opened the box. "Is this the bakery where Jack bought those cream pastries? La Isla?" She inhaled the aroma that wafted up the box.

"The bakery downtown, yes," Nyla answered. "They

make these guava-and-cheese turnovers that will make your soul want to leave your body."

Olivia nodded in approval. "This reminds me of the bakery my friend Javi runs with his brother in East Ward. There is nothing like that Caribbean touch."

"I couldn't agree more," Nyla said as Olivia waved the team over.

Dareen entered the room, followed by Feliz and Al. "This is better than room service."

Nyla met Olivia's eyes, just briefly. "And *café con leche* for everyone, obviously. That's not something my little coffee maker can do."

Al, Feliz and Dareen had already descended on the box with a gratitude that bordered on reverence.

"Are these sweet *arepas*?" Feliz whispered like she'd found treasure at the bottom of the sea. "There's gooey cheese in this one. I can live on these forever."

"I made sure to keep them hot," Nyla said. She indicated the outdoors. "You know, this is the best time of the day. The air is still fresh, and the waves are gentle." Her eyes slid to where Olivia still stood, before she turned to look at her team again. "There's a picnic area outside if you need a break."

"That sounds divine," Dareen said, while Al poured out coffee for everyone. "Hey, text Anuar and Jack." She winked at Al. "You know you want to."

"Already did," he said in that even way he had. "That okay, boss?"

"Of course," Olivia said, sliding her eyes to Nyla and quickly away again. "The more the merrier."

The group, joined by Jack and Anuar, claimed their prizes among the *arepas, empanadas,* guava turnovers, classic croissants, freshly made jelly doughnuts, *quesitos* and assorted butter cookies. They filed out with plates piled high, chattering happily.

Olivia stepped around the table to stand near Nyla. She was wearing a floral jumper that managed to look feminine and practical at the same time. "That's so much food. Thank you. Seriously."

Nyla shrugged, but she couldn't hide the hint of softness in her expression. "You're doing good work. I figured it was time I acknowledged it. Plus—" she dropped her voice low "—I wanted to steal a little bit of the CEO's time for myself."

Olivia's olive-gold skin flushed an undertone of pretty pink. "You don't need food as an excuse to do that."

They made their way out to the picnic area, settling down on one of the tables. Olivia made a show of dusting sand off the bench, though they were clean.

"I thought you ended your beef with sand," Nyla teased.

"It's more like a cease-fire." When Olivia smiled at Nyla, she forgot for a moment how to breathe. She quietly counted backward from five before picking up a *bacalaito*. The taste of cod fish and savory seasonings flooded her mouth, momentarily breaking the spell Olivia's presence had spun around her.

They ate in companionable silence, the sound of birds rustling and chirping forming the symphonic background with the soft rush of the sea.

Olivia picked up an *alcapurria*, admiring it, while Nyla's attention kept getting tangled up in Olivia.

They sat beneath the shade of a large oak hung with thick Spanish moss. The morning sun was soft and mild as it filtered between the branches, the breezy sea air whisper soft and mild against her skin.

"So," Olivia said, sounding casual, "why turtles?"

Nyla paused mid-bite, a crumb of the salted fritter clinging to her thumb. "I grew up here," she said. "I've always loved the sea. But it wasn't until I was seven years old that I knew I wanted to work with sea turtles."

Olivia smiled, waiting. Nyla remembered her own words at the festival, telling Olivia that if she was patient, she would reveal herself. And she had listened, because she waited with a patience that belied her nature.

Nyla continued. "My *tío* had invited my family to his beach house to have dinner and play on the beach afterward. It got late and we decided to take a walk along the boardwalk for ice cream."

Nyla could see the lanky little girl she'd once been, a bit tall for her age, maybe a little shy until she got to know a person. She wore a pink-and-white sundress, and little white flip-flops, streaks of dry sand clinging to her legs.

"I ran off when my family wasn't looking and headed down the sand dunes. I had never felt so free." She smiled, and even now, with Olivia's eyes on her, and the sea just beyond, Nyla watched that little girl racing away from her adults without a care for rules or danger.

"Then I saw her. A leatherback, though I had no idea at the time what kind of turtle I was looking at. And she was *huge*." Nyla laughed at the memory of that night. "She had crawled between these two dunes that looked like mountains to someone as small as me. She was digging away, slow and powerful and, to me, unstoppable. She had these ridges on her back like carved stone, and horrible pale scars, cutting across her shell. I thought she looked like an ancient sea warrior."

Nyla's voice quieted, reverent now.

"I couldn't move. My family was calling from the boardwalk, but I didn't hear them. My father carried me away when he finally found me. I wasn't crying, or scared. I scared the hell out of everyone else, though. I just… I kept wondering over and over, what happened to her? Did she finish digging? Will she ever come back?" Nyla shook her head.

"I cried myself to sleep when I found out what those scars meant," Nyla admitted. "Healed injuries from boat strikes, propellers and industrial fishing nets. I remember telling my mom, who was a high school teacher at the time, that I was going to fix it."

"Fix what?" Olivia asked softly. Her full attention was on Nyla, like there was nothing else in the world but her.

"Fix *her*," Nyla said. "Fix that turtle and any other creature that crawled out of the sea, injured by the things we do."

There was a pause. Nyla couldn't breathe, couldn't look away. She was watching her own story unfold as if in real time.

"You did," Olivia said, voice low, sure. "You kept that promise."

"I try. Lord knows, every time I go out and find another one of God's creatures hurt because of our carelessness, I try. And when I'm successful—" Nyla shook her head, the sun shining like a halo on them both "—there's no better feeling."

Without warning, Olivia reached across the narrow table and brushed her thumb gently at the corner of Nyla's mouth, where the crumb of *bacalaito* clung stubbornly to her skin.

"There," she said softly. "You had a little…"

Nyla's breath caught and it shocked them back into reality. Olivia pulled her hand back, mortification written across her face. Nyla glanced around, but Dareen was distributing the remaining snacks to the team at a table near the shore. She had clearly returned for seconds, fussing over the younger team members like a mother hen.

Olivia spoke, her voice weak and unsteady. "Sorry. I—"

"Don't be." Nyla didn't look away. She picked up a napkin and blotted her lips. "You're good at that."

Olivia's brows furrowed at her words. "At what?"

Crushing the napkin, she pushed it into the pocket of her pants and picked up a turnover. "Seeing people."

Olivia dropped her head in obvious embarrassment. "Only the ones worth seeing."

Nyla smiled at that and Olivia answered with one of her own. She was smiling a lot lately, and Nyla was captivated. Somewhere a gull cried overhead. But Nyla heard only her heart beating loud, wild and thunderously full.

She took a bite of the pastry, but the taste, so perfect before, barely registered now. Her senses were full of Olivia—the cadence of her voice, the earnest fire in her eyes, the way the shadows cast by the sun through the branches painted her cheekbones in shades of pale copper and gold.

At the table behind them, Feliz let out a laugh, probably at one of Dareen's terrible puns. The clatter of plasticware and the rustle of paper plates reminded Nyla that they weren't completely alone, even if it felt like the rest of the world had been temporarily put on mute.

Nyla reached for one of the cafés con leche, no doubt cooled from sitting without being touched. Olivia picked up the other one. "There's something I want to show you," Nyla said casually, but there was a brightness behind her words that didn't feel casual at all.

Olivia raised a brow. "Yeah?"

"There's a rehabilitation enclosure offshore. We fit each turtle with trackers when we treat them. It's the last stop before they are released to the sea," Nyla said. "We have a juvenile green turtle out there right now recovering from buoyancy syndrome. Boat injury, poor thing. She's a tough one, though. Her name is Aniki. We have a window of opportunity that's closing before we're forced to release them without uplinking their data to our systems. But you know all this."

"I do." Olivia paused, then said, "Wait, Aniki? The one who punches gods? From *Record of Ragnarok*?" She laughed, and Nyla felt herself slowly coming down from the high of the last half hour. "That's amazing."

"The kids named her. They have a funny sense of humor."

"Not unlike their professor," Olivia teased.

Nyla dipped her head in acknowledgment before continuing. "The enclosure isn't directly accessible by land," she went on. "Too shallow to dock a boat, and there's no walkway yet. We usually just kayak out."

She sipped her coffee, then met Olivia's eyes again. "I thought, if you're up early tomorrow, we could go. Before you and your team start up work again. It's quiet out there in the morning. Peaceful. It's a nice way to start the day."

There was a certain kind of awe in Olivia's expression. Perhaps she understood what this meant for Nyla, how sacred her turtles were to her. "Yeah. Yeah, I'd like that a lot."

"I was hoping you might." Nyla's smile was subtle, but she hoped unmistakable. All her smiles today felt like a secret version of herself that she was sharing only with Olivia.

The gulls circled lazily overhead. The sea rolled in and rolled back out again.

"I've seen powerful networks crash, and business leaders lose their minds," Olivia said, her voice as dreamy as the air around them. "I'm rarely confronted by the divine in my day-to-day, but in your work, I can see the hand of something beautiful and intentional." She turned her face away, as if she'd said too much.

Nyla, moved by the unexpected beauty of her words,

reached across and took her hand, this time not caring who might see them. "I feel like I commune with the divine every day I spend with those turtles. That's why their well-being means everything to me."

Olivia squeezed her hand back. "So, sunrise, then?"

"Sunrise," Nyla confirmed, and stood slowly, collecting their empty plates and cups. "Wear a swimsuit. And don't be late."

"As if I were capable of being late," Olivia quipped.

As they walked toward the table where their team sat chatting away, Nyla felt a return of the weight of that earlier moment settle over her like salt air, something ancient and healing that clung to her hair and skin. A moment she wanted to sit in together with Olivia, like those turtles who felt healing hands on them and were made whole by loving, gentle attention.

Nyla prepared her hair, rinsing her braids until they were heavy with fresh water, the drops streaming in thick rivulets down her back. She gently squeezed as much water as she could out of them before massaging reef-safe conditioner into each braid, a process she could do with her eyes closed. She tried to chase away her nervousness by listening to the newest Bad Bunny album as she got dressed, the music streaming in through the wireless speaker system she'd installed when she first bought her house on the canal. The salsa, plena and reggaetón beats threaded through the room, surrounding her, smoothing out the tumultuous swells of her mood while snaking through the very center of her, spreading its rhythm through her nerve endings.

Nyla suppressed a shiver as she twisted the braids around her head, and pinned them in place before pulling the multicolored swim cap down over them and an expertly twisted shawl over that. She paused, trying to ease her mood away from intense anticipation. Dressing for anything that might require her to get her hair wet had never been more than a checklist of things to strap on, like a knight putting on each piece of armor in methodical order. It was a necessary ritual she'd been performing ever since she had done her first deep-sea dive as a teenager, when she had learned that spending as much time as she could in the water was a key to her well-being, away from the endless noise of interacting with people. But to find that escape, she had learned to care for her hair and protect it from the very environment she loved so much.

But all her habits and procedures failed her before Olivia's impending presence, the arrival of which she felt in the air the way she could smell rain before the skies opened up. She'd be here, on her kayak, in her ocean, in her space, and it made Nyla's breath grow shallow and weak, the last thing she needed when she was about to take the kayak out. She had to reach deep to be as calm and completely unbothered as Olivia, who seemed to be undeterred by anything.

She dressed, putting on a T-shirt with a giant sea turtle encircled by the words *Sea Turtle Research and Education Center* in bold lettering on the back, and a pair of jean shorts. She lavished sunscreen on every exposed inch of skin, applying a high SPF to her face. She nearly put it away, then remembered that Olivia was a city slicker and possibly unprepared for the sun. She tucked the portable tube in her backpack, together with water and turtle treats. She completed the last step in her routine, dabbing a drop of Florida water on each pulse point for good luck the way her grandmother taught her.

She drove through the sleeping streets to Beachfront Drive, winding through the familiar national park road that took her directly to the front parking lot of the center. She pulled in to find Anuar's truck already in place. Once she parked the Jeep and gathered her things, she walked through a side door that led directly to the Nest. She wasn't surprised to see Anuar, in a tank top and swim shorts, standing waist-deep in a saltwater pool. He was no doubt examining Kayuga for buoyancy, even as the turtle ambled at a respectable distance from him.

Anuar glanced up from his waterproof notebook, the first shaft of morning lighting up his hair and turning the water crystalline.

"*Hola, Madrugadora*," he teased, eyes crinkling with a smile as he rested his forearms on the pool's edge. "It's a rare morning when I beat you here."

Nyla climbed the ladder to the platform above the tank, peering in at Kayuga, who floated lazily in the water, her broad shell dappled with light and shadows. "Couldn't sleep, so I'm heading out to the enclosure this morning," she hedged.

"Hmm." Anuar's gaze sharpened, kicking into doctor mode. "Couldn't sleep? Or maybe you couldn't stop thinking?"

She wouldn't bother denying it, but she wasn't ready to elaborate, either. Instead, she trailed a finger over the water's edge, watching tiny ripples fan out. "How's Kayuga?"

Anuar's gaze lingered on her, but eventually he allowed the conversation to be deflected. "Better today." He slid a hand along the turtle's shell, palpating gently. "The antibiotics are kicking in. She's a fighter."

Nyla nodded, her throat tight. "Good. I need her to heal."

Anuar let that sit for a beat, then hoisted himself out of the pool with practiced ease, dripping water everywhere as he grabbed a towel. "This hack is weighing heavily on you."

She leaned back on her heels, then sighed. "It weighs on all of us."

Anuar lowered his head. "I'm so sorry."

"No," she said. "You're not allowed to do that. You're not allowed to take on this responsibility. Governments and institutions all over the world get hacked all the time." Nyla wanted to kick the railing around the tank. "All it takes is a well-put-together email and one click. It could have been any of us. It's not an individual failure. It's a systemic problem and no one has a solution." She reached out to put a hand on his shoulder. "You wouldn't let Yasmin feel guilty about this, so why should you?"

Anuar wiped his nose and Nyla realized he'd been close to tears. "I know, I just—"

"*Nada,*" she said with finality. "Don't carry this. Take that energy and put it toward our babies. This—" she pointed at Kayuga floating without a care in the world "—this is what matters."

He patted the hand that still rested on his shoulder. "*Gracias.*"

She nodded before she flicked her gaze toward the docks, where the sea shimmered in the growing light. "I'm meeting Olivia in—" she checked her watch "—fifteen minutes. We're going to the enclosure."

Anuar paused, one brow arching as he towel-dried his hair. "Really? You don't usually take outsiders there."

"It's important that she sees everything that we do with her own eyes." Nyla's lips pressed into a line. "It's her job to fix what's broken. I figured...at least I can show her what's at stake."

Anuar gave her a long, knowing look. "And this has nothing to do with the way you've been acting every time you two are in the same room?"

Nyla shot him a death glare, but her ears warmed beneath the edge of her swim cap. "Don't start all that. This isn't one of those reality TV shows you like so much."

He grinned, utterly unrepentant, while slinging the towel around his neck. "Hey, I'm just saying. She's…intense. But my instincts tell me that she's good, Nyla. I think you can trust her."

"That's the problem." Nyla stood, brushing grit off her shorts. "I don't want to put my trust and everything that matters to me into the hands of one person."

Anuar chuckled, crossing his arms. "Everyone needs a knight in shining armor."

She rolled her eyes, but a reluctant smile tugged at the corner of her mouth. "Look, I need you to keep an eye on things here while I'm out. Just in case."

"Always do." He sobered, getting to his feet. "But try not to internalize this so much. This center, these turtles, they're yours. No one's taking them from you."

Nyla crossed her arms, holding herself tight. "I know, but seeing it closed like this, without visitors or tour groups— it's starting to wear on me, you know? I think the fundraiser could go a long way to at least make sure everyone is okay for however long it takes to get this fixed."

"I loved the idea when you shared it after the debrief yesterday." Anuar bumped her shoulder. "But wait, I thought you didn't like people."

Nyla smiled. "There are a *few* people I like."

"Like a certain cybersecurity expert whose initials start with Olivia Navarro?"

Nyla bumped him back. "*No seas tonto.* I meant you, my family and friends, and my students."

"I'm not being foolish!" Anuar retorted, flicking a few

drops of water on her bare legs. "I see the vision. I had a feeling she was queer when I first saw her."

"Did you? I didn't see it right away."

"Because your mind was on other things. But it was clear as day in the way she looked at you from the first moment, *amiga*. My gaydar is clearly better than yours."

"Like the way it worked on Al?" she teased.

Anuar's smile was smug and unashamed. "Need I say more?"

"Well, aren't you my clever Anu," Nyla said, using his nickname. "Wish you had clued me in sooner."

"It's barely been two weeks." He jerked his chin toward the dock. "Go on. She'll be here any minute. Try not to let her float away into the gulf."

Nyla laughed, the sound breaking through her tension like sunlight through the mist. "Can't make any promises." Her phone buzzed with a message from Olivia indicating she'd just arrived and would meet her in the atrium of the center. Olivia had been granted full access to the property for the purposes of her work, but never treated it as her personal playground. Olivia had clear boundaries when it came to her job, and Nyla respected that about her.

Nyla looked up to see Anuar watching her with a wry smile.

"Not another word from you," Nyla tossed out before turning on her heel to find Olivia and take her out to the open sea.

Chapter Thirteen

Olivia

Olivia paced as she waited in the quiet atrium. The early light streaming through the high windows cast a soft geometric pattern on the floor. She held a paper bag in one hand and a tray with two coffees in the other, unable to quell her excitement. She tried focusing on the giant posters announcing events and coming exhibitions, and not on the fact that she was spending time yet again with Nyla in the space of a few days.

Olivia looked up when she heard the tapping of shoes on the floor, her stomach giving a familiar clench at the sight of Nyla. For a moment, they just regarded each other, the sleepy quiet of dawn stretching between them.

"You're early," Nyla said, adjusting the strap of her waterproof bag.

"I'm always early," Olivia replied. She wore a pair of denim overall shorts with a swimsuit underneath, and sport sandals that she made sure were waterproof. "It's a compulsion."

Nyla smiled faintly. "Good. I'm an early bird too, and I hate waiting."

Olivia handed her the paper bag. "I do recall that about you." She removed one coffee from the carrier and handed it to Nyla as well, keeping the other one for herself. "Picked this up from that bakery we all seem to love. I might have a verifiable addiction."

Nyla took the coffee and the bakery bag, touched by Olivia's consideration. "Thank you. Add it to your love of tacos." She glanced at the smaller snack bag in Olivia's hand. "What's that?"

Olivia held up the small foil bag with the telltale yellow goldfish, shaking it lightly. "Found these in your vending machine. Either this place is the very definition of old school or someone's got a retro snack obsession."

"Goldfish crackers aren't retro." Nyla laughed, shaking her head as she motioned for Olivia to follow. "And that would be Anuar's doing. He keeps this place stocked like it's a high school lunchroom, because so many of our visitors are school age."

They made their way through the center, the sound of their footsteps mingling with the distant wash of waves. "I respect the choice. Salty, crunchy and aquatic-themed—it fits."

They reached the rear doors, where a sliver of rising sun glinted off the kayaks stacked neatly by the dock. Nyla paused, pulling her keys from her pocket to unlock the gate, feeling Olivia's gaze slide over the water with quiet assessment.

"Looks peaceful out here," Olivia said after a moment. "This is so different from anything I'm used to."

"I imagine it is, city girl," Nyla agreed. She glanced over her shoulder, lips twitching from a barely repressed smile. "So much sand."

Olivia smirked, popping a Goldfish into her mouth. "Don't remind me."

As they stepped out onto the dock, a light breeze caught

at their clothes. Nyla sipped the coffee, humming in approval that it had been prepared exactly to her tastes. "Did you tell the owner that this was for me?"

"I might have." Olivia pinched her lip. "I know how you like it by now." Olivia had to turn away before Nyla clocked her embarrassment. She focused on the brighter glow of the sky as Nyla led them to a white gazebo.

They settled on a bench next to each other. When Nyla opened the bag, Olivia was hit with the vanilla-sweet aroma of the hunk of fluffy, sticky sweet bread tucked inside. It was like a slice of heaven. Nyla offered a piece to Olivia, which she accepted, before taking a bite of the rich, decadent treat. "Sometimes I just come out here by myself. It's hard to find the right people to share something like this with."

"And who are the right people for you?" Olivia asked, taking another sip of her coffee.

Nyla glanced away from the sea, an eyebrow raised in challenge. "My friends, family, some of my graduate students."

"Coworkers? Like Anuar? He's a lot of fun."

"Absolutely." She tugged at a rope, checking the knot, and gave Olivia a sideways glance. "You know, Anuar would be very gratified to know that you think well of him. He likes you."

"Does he, now?" Olivia flushed with pleasure at this fact. "I'm not for everyone. Only people with very good taste tend to like me."

"Oh, okay," Nyla said, her hazel gaze finding and holding Olivia's. "Then I must have very good taste."

Olivia couldn't resist the magnetic pull of her eyes. She leaned forward, the smell of vanilla and vegetation engulfing her in a cocoon that triggered all her appetites. She kissed Nyla's soft lips, licking the vanilla and sugar from them. When her lips fell open, Olivia slipped inside, tasting deeply from the sweetness that was only partly because of the sweet bread. Olivia thrilled at the return kiss, the way Nyla's hand slid up her arm, hooked behind her neck and pulled her in closer.

A soft moan escaped Olivia, low and involuntary. It evaporated into the air, followed by an answering one from Nyla. It drove Olivia to the edge of sanity, flooding her body with need.

When they pulled apart, Olivia whispered, "I knew you weren't as serious as you first appeared, Professor."

"Oh, I am," Nyla answered with a voice raspy with hunger and need. "But I'm also interesting and fun." She pulled back, inhaling deeply. "I'm literally rowing you out to the open ocean on a kayak to see a turtle rescue enclosure, just because I can."

"Let's see this turtle enclosure you're so proud of, then, ma'am." They stood, Nyla collecting their detritus and discarding everything in a recycle bin. She led Olivia farther down the dock, their banter easy and more relaxed than Olivia ever thought it could be after a kiss like the one they'd just shared.

As they approached the kayaks, Olivia slowly relaxed, her earlier arousal softened by Nyla's comfortable presence and the pull of the sea. Whatever the day brought, professional or otherwise, it had already started to feel like the tide was shifting within her. Regardless of who was responsible for this hack, Olivia would fix this situation and make things right for Nyla and the center. She refused to fail her.

Uplifted by this determination, buoyed by Nyla's presence and awash in the sun and ocean she was learning to love, Olivia followed Nyla with determination, helping her ease the kayak down from where it was perched in its holder.

They crouched down, and Nyla taught her how to double-check the life vests and paddles, Nyla's strong hands moving with practiced ease. She also taught Olivia to adjust the numerous straps and inspect everything with an eye to safety.

When it came to boarding, however, Olivia stood beside Nyla, arms crossed, eyeing the kayak with obvious skepticism.

"I'm going to go with the assumption that you don't do this very often," Nyla teased.

"Do I look like someone who spends her weekends kayaking?" Olivia's gaze flicked to the narrow boat, then back to Nyla. "The paddleboats in Central Park are the extent of my seafaring experience."

Nyla straightened up, grabbing a vest and tossing it her way. "Time to add a new skill to your résumé."

Olivia caught it, flipping it over in her hands like it might bite. It looked uncomfortable and unwieldy. She slid it on, muttering under her breath, "I can hack a federal database, but sure, let's make balancing in a floating piece of plastic my challenge of the day."

"Are you supposed to admit that out loud?"

Olivia froze. "Probably not."

Nyla laughed, especially when Olivia cursed while struggling to put on the life vest. She was sure most of her outfits were more complicated to wear than this contraption, so she wasn't sure why this was defeating her so soundly. Nyla stepped closer to help secure the straps, unable to resist teasing her.

"Landlubber," Nyla said, her fingers flying over her straps. Olivia stared at her, the wind tossing the loose hair of her bob so that it whipped against Nyla's cheek. Nyla glanced up and when they made eye contact, it was Olivia's fatal mistake. She could see nothing else but Nyla, and her closeness made her skin tingle, especially when Nyla's fingers brushed her shoulder beneath her T-shirt. Olivia's pulse answered by skipping a beat with a loud thud that ricocheted through her chest.

"Thank God for the local YMCA swim club," Olivia murmured, making an anemic attempt at a joke.

"Relax," Nyla said slowly, adjusting the fit around Olivia's waist. "I won't let you drown. We'll take it slow and easy."

Olivia swallowed hard as she imagined all the things that they could do slow and easy. She turned away before she did something foolish, like lick the line of Nyla's throat to capture the fading tension of her muscles.

"I'm holding you to that," Olivia answered, her voice thick and loaded with all the things that moved through her body, making her feel heavy and liquid.

"Okay," Nyla said shakily, slipping her own vest on and adjusting it much more quickly than Olivia's. She stepped into the kayak with the grace of someone who'd done it a thousand times and steadied it with her body and a firm hand on the deck. "Your turn, hacker girl. Sit down *gently*. You want your weight low and centered."

Olivia crouched down awkwardly, one hand gripping the side of the kayak, the other still clutching her bag of Goldfish. "Low and centered, got it."

She tried to step in, wobbled immediately and froze mid-move. "Nope. Nope. This is a mistake."

"Here." Nyla stepped out of the kayak, landing in the water. She steadied the kayak with one hand, offering the other to Olivia. "I got you. Slow and easy."

Olivia growled but accepted Nyla's hand, sliding into the front seat with exaggerated caution. For a moment, she sat ramrod straight, shoulders tense as the kayak rocked lightly beneath her. She glanced behind her with wide-eyed fear.

"This is unnatural," she muttered, gripping the sides with white-knuckled determination. "Human beings are not meant to do this."

"There is evidence of human seafaring as early as eight hundred thousand years ago. Some scientists even believe Neanderthals were traveling waterways with rudimentary rafts before the evolution of modern humans."

"Thanks for the TED Talk," Olivia groused, her grip numbing her fingers.

Nyla's chuckle came from behind Olivia as she pushed them gently away from the dock. "You're doing fine. Now relax. I'll do all the work."

With a quick, practiced motion, Nyla settled in behind her, the kayak gliding forward smoothly as she dipped her paddle into the water.

They headed away from the beachhead and took a parallel path along the clusters of mangrove trees that sprouted from the water until they cleared the brackish water and moved toward the sandbar, beyond which lay the enclosure.

"Ooo-kay," Olivia breathed, adjusting her posture, still gripping the sides a little too tightly. "This is…doable."

"You're overthinking it," Nyla said, guiding them out toward open water. "Loosen up your shoulders or you're going to snap your spinal column."

Olivia turned so only her profile was visible. "Ha-ha. Easy for you to say. You're basically an amphibian."

"Oooh, now you're talking my language," Nyla retorted. The rhythmic splash of her paddle was the only sound for several otherwise calm minutes. The water stretched wide and empty around them, the sun casting a shimmer like molten gold across the water's surface.

The morning was calm and still, the water stretching smooth and glassy between them and the sky, except for the disruption of the oar sinking in and rising from the water. Olivia's hands slid off the sides and rested on her lap. There was a kind of peace that was new to Olivia, healing the wound of endless chatter and noise in their day-to-day. Instead, the waters of Soledad Bay were doing all the talking.

Nyla's voice came from behind her, low and reverent.

"Most people don't look twice at this bay," she said quietly. "It's not a giant one, like Apalachicola Bay, nor does it possess the majesty of the coral reef islands of south Florida. People look at this beach and see something average, a strip of sand dirtied by plants and roots, and an ocean that becomes interesting only when we approach the sandbar. But it's old and rich, full of life, where nothing and everything changes at once. Land shifts and species adapt. It's fragile, but it also persists, and every version of it is a manifestation of the universe's benevolence on earth." Nyla paused. "And it's my home, as much as it's the home of every creature that climbs on this beach."

She dipped her paddle again, her movements precise. Something welled up in Olivia's chest as Nyla continued. "I never get used to how beautiful it is, and I'll never abandon it," she said, and this time Olivia couldn't help herself. She glanced back, just once, and met Nyla's eyes. There was more emotion in them than she'd ever seen since Olivia arrived at the center. She had no idea what tides moved through Nyla, but they were deep and true, and worth protecting at every cost.

Olivia trailed her hand in the water, enjoying the pace of Nyla's paddling. She couldn't imagine how much work it was to paddle this far out, and promised herself she would offer to paddle back. Nyla's hypnotic description of the bay lingered in the air like the smell of the vegetation as they entered the water. It threaded through Olivia's thoughts like a melody on repeat.

She had let Nyla carry her on this journey, let her words lull her with their magic, and through her eyes, she saw the bay—quiet, and peaceful, but also thrumming with a vibrant life force beneath the stillness. Beds of seagrass shifted lazily below the water, while the beige line of sand running along the shore felt like a part of something far bigger than them, something that still echoed the cadence of Nyla's voice even though she was no longer speaking.

Ahead, the sandbar came into focus, narrow and low, a pale ribbon against the deeper blue. The enclosure bobbed nearby, its simple frame tugging at the moorings with every change of current.

Nyla's voice broke the quiet. "We'll pull up there. The water's shallower and it will be easier to get in and out of the kayak from the sandbar."

The kayak banked onto the sand. Nyla gracefully leaped out and pulled the prow the rest of the way onto the sandbar. Olivia's eyes dropped to Nyla's back, admiring the steady strength of her shoulders as she moved. There was purpose and clarity in everything she did. That precision, together with her seriousness, her frankly terrifying intelligence and her beauty, made it increasingly difficult for Olivia to keep from feeling strongly about her.

Olivia turned back to the open water, swallowing hard. *This is her home.* Not just where she lived, but where she *belonged.* Every word, every glance told Olivia that.

A new thought pressed up unexpectedly from her. *Would she ever leave? Could she?*

It was ridiculous, of course. They barely knew each other. Olivia had no right to wonder, no reason to care. But still, the question echoed through her with ringing clarity. She thought about Aleysha, and how she had preferred breaking up with Olivia rather than allowing her to move to Florida to help her care for her mother. The rejection had hurt so deeply, she still felt the edges of the cut even now, after all this time.

But Nyla? Nyla was as solid as the oak trees that lined the path leading to the center. From what she could gather, Nyla didn't have an inconstant bone in her body. That solidity, strong and solid as steel, settled something in Olivia, a quivering, tender thing that she hadn't even been aware of how until it came up against Nyla's fierce intractability.

She's rooted here, Olivia thought, watching Nyla guide them in. *And me? I'm just passing through.*

The realization settled, heavy and bittersweet, like the tang of salt on her lips.

When the kayak was stable enough, Olivia stood. Nyla offered her a hand, which she took. The strong, rough texture felt like silk in her palm. Nyla gave her a small smile as she stepped onto the sand. When she was on terra firma again, she took a long look around her. The beach they'd departed from seemed so far away, and Olivia was again astounded by Nyla's strength in ferrying them this far.

Olivia dug the tip of her sandal into the sand. "You know, despite the sand, which I still abhor—" Nyla paused in the work of tying down the kayak to listen to her "—this isn't half bad."

"Do I sense a newfound passion for the way of the turtle?" Nyla teased, amusement sparkling in her voice.

Olivia frowned thoughtfully. "Yeah, that too, I guess. I just mean that you could probably escape being around people whenever you needed to by coming out here. The idea holds a certain appeal for someone like me."

"It's the perfect way to recover from social overload," she agreed. "Which, sadly, I experience frequently."

Olivia studied her. "You do it because you're an introvert. I do it because I can't stand the human species. We are not the same."

That made Nyla laugh so loud, the sound exploded across the open water. "You really have no brain-mouth filter, do you?"

Olivia shrugged. "Diplomacy is also overrated."

Nyla thought back to Olivia's words. "We're not the same," Nyla mused, still chuckling to herself, "but not so different, either."

Just ahead, the floating enclosure bobbed gently, a circular ring moored in place, its netting shimmering beneath the surface like a secret veil, with a tarp that shaded the enclosure from above.

"You built that?" Olivia asked.

Nyla approached from behind, her arms snaking around Olivia's waist. Nyla rested her chin on Olivia's shoulder and the boldness of it made Olivia's knees weak. It was weird, with the bulk of their life vests between them, but Nyla's arms were warm and strong. "I bought it with a grant from the Ocean Heart Foundation. They sponsor our rehab work, especially when they involve injuries from propeller strikes and boat collisions. This enclosure is modular, so we can pack it up in the event of a storm or expand it if we need to."

Olivia tried to focus on her words, ignoring the press of Nyla's chin on her shoulder. "Modular like…what, marine IKEA?"

Nyla chuckled. Olivia felt the sound settle over her, warmer than the sunlight slowly easing over the water.

"Pretty much. Only each piece costs a fortune, and if the current shifted the wrong way, the entire thing would become warped. We had to raise money to install an anchoring system after the last storm and we still have to take it apart before every major storm."

Olivia's mind went into the logistics of building a modular structure with the movement of so many ocean currents. "How do you do something like that in the water?"

"The anchors had to be done by a certified installation expert, which is why we needed additional grant money. But the enclosure itself wasn't too difficult to assemble because we did it on the sandbar."

Olivia was about to ask another question when Nyla stepped away and began to unbutton her shorts.

Nyla was starting to *undress*, and while it made sense, Olivia grew a bit lightheaded at the thought of whatever her clothes were hiding underneath.

First her life vest, the straps dangling as she flung it into the kayak. Then she removed her T-shirt, which she tugged up and over her head, revealing the wide sweep of her strong shoulders and the inviting dip of her cleavage, damp with sweat.

Olivia's brain short-circuited.

"Uh…what are…are you…?" Her voice came out higher and rougher than she had intended. She stumbled back, pulse suddenly hammering in her veins.

Nyla didn't answer. She shimmied out of her shorts next, kicking them aside like they were nothing, and stood there in just her hot-pink swimsuit that picked up the pink coloring in the headscarf. Sunlight glinted off her dewy brown skin, making her radiant. The muscles in her thighs bunched with power, the high cut of the surf suit revealing the enticing skin that flowed from her hips into her legs.

Oh God, this woman was breathtaking.

Olivia cleared her throat, her eyes *refusing* to look away

even though her brain was screaming *look away*! "Are we…
is this…a thing that's happening right now or what?"

Nyla finally turned, one brow arched in that maddeningly
clinical way she had of assessing a thing with the precision
of a scalpel. "What are you talking about?"

Olivia gestured vaguely, her hand flapping uselessly toward all the bare skin. "*This*. You. Taking off your clothes."

Nyla blinked, then finally laughed, low and throaty. "Oh
my God, Olivia. I'm not stripping down for a skinny-dip.
I'm preparing to swim the last few yards out to the enclosure. I'm not about to drag my jeans through salt water."

Olivia's mouth opened. Closed. Opened again. "Right.
Of course. Obviously."

Her voice had gone higher than a prepubescent boy's,
and she could *feel* the heat rising in her face in burning in-
crements, but there was no stopping it now. Nyla was still
smiling, all sharp-eyed and smug as she tucked her clothes
safely into the kayak and pulled out two sets of goggles.

She carefully unwound the scarf around her head, revealing a snug swim cap. She folded the material and added it to
her pile. Then she flipped her goggles down over her head.
"You coming?" Nyla asked, smirking. "Or are you just going
to sit there and stare at me all morning?"

"Staring's…a real option right about now," Olivia blurted
out, making Nyla's laugh ring out again, bright and teasing
as she waded into the water.

And when Nyla dived cleanly beneath the surface, Olivia
sat there gripping the straps of her jumper, her heart hammering out a staccato rhythm, while she muttered under her
breath, "Jesus Christ. I'm in trouble."

Once Olivia recovered from the life-altering sight of Nyla
in a swimsuit, she stripped down, yanked on the dive goggles and waded into the water before gliding behind Nyla.

The gulf was warm and gentle, perfect for a swim, though there were currents beneath that tugged at Olivia's legs. Nyla was already at the enclosure and had climbed onto its makeshift platform. It wasn't as broad or as sturdy as the one in the center. She watched Olivia swim toward her with far less grace than Nyla had possessed.

Olivia managed to get herself up next to Nyla. She pushed the dive goggles back onto her head and rubbed the salt water from her face. Nyla was biting her lip when Olivia glared at her. "What?"

Nyla could barely repress her laughter. "You swim like you grew up in the city."

"I did grow up in a city!" Olivia retorted, shaking the water out of her hair, making sure Nyla was in the blast radius.

"Hey!" Nyla screamed, droplets spraying her face. She paused to wipe them away when a small flipper broke the surface, followed by a carapace dappled with healed scarring.

"There she is," Nyla said softly. "Aniki. I think I told you. She washed up with a boat strike injury. She's still recovering from buoyancy syndrome." At Olivia's confused expression, Nyla clarified, "She floats at the wrong angle, and can't quite dive properly yet. This enclosure lets her swim without getting lost or stuck at the surface."

Olivia watched as the turtle moved through the water, tilting slightly but with determination. "She's trying so hard."

"They all do. It's their survival instinct. We just give them a safe space to get there." Nyla slid gently into the water, holding a small pouch. Knowing Nyla, it was probably biodegradable. "She'll gain her freedom—but only when she's strong enough to survive."

Olivia shifted to hang her legs in the water. She didn't

want to spook the poor turtle by entering the water suddenly. "That's kind of beautiful."

Nyla tilted her head up to look at Olivia, and it struck Olivia that she was usually the one looking up at Nyla, and not the other way around. "You'd be surprised how much you learn about people from watching animals."

Olivia's huff of laughter came low and short. "I can't tell if you're trying to impress me or if this is just you all the time."

"I don't try to impress anyone," Nyla said softly. "Not when it comes to this."

Their eyes locked again. Sunlight flickered warm and bright between them. Olivia felt a tug in her chest that had been growing since the night she'd stumbled on Nyla on the beach, with her weirdly outfitted wagon, her amber light and her disapproval. She could draw the thread that connected her desire now to that first yearning in her soul masquerading as admiration.

Olivia dropped her eyes to the sweet, soft bow of Nyla's lips, the shape of which lured her in. Nyla didn't move away, but watched the trajectory of Olivia's lips as they drifted down on her.

A sudden surge of water hit Olivia's face as Aniki surfaced with dramatic flair, her flippers slapping the water with a forceful *thwap*! Olivia pitched backward with a startled yelp, nearly losing her balance and ending up in the sea on the other side of the platform.

Nyla's laugh came bright and clear. "Okay, okay, message received."

Olivia, who was running out of things to dry herself with, blinked rapidly, while her heart hammered. "Did she just—did your turtle just cockblock me?"

"She's been known to have strong opinions," Nyla said,

opening the pack she'd brought and pulling out an assortment of vegetables. She approached an arrangement of PVC pipes and fed them through the holes so that it looked like a tiny, floating garden.

"Why not just feed her directly?" Olivia asked, glad for the distraction from their near kiss.

Nyla put the empty pouch inside the bag and zippered it shut. "She needs to be able to forage and feed herself. Since she can't dive for her own food yet, we need to make sure she can find food closer to the surface. Otherwise, she'll starve."

"We don't want that." The turtle approached and Olivia found herself annoyed at the interloper and how she'd insinuated herself between them. "I can't believe I have beef with a sideways-floating turtle."

"Be nice," Nyla gently scolded. Olivia smiled, sliding her wet hair behind her ear. It felt so domestic, she didn't want it to end.

Nyla swam over and stared at her for a moment before handing her a tube she pulled from her pack. "The sun starts to bite about this time. Get some of this on your face and shoulders. You can thank me later."

Olivia grasped her hand as she tried to withdraw it. "I'll thank you now. Before Miss Turtle Cockblocker over there finishes her snack."

Nyla shook her head but lifted her chin in easy abandon. As kisses went, it might not have been a romantic lead-in. But as Olivia lowered her head to where Nyla floated waist-deep and dripped like a mermaid, she placed a hand around her neck, just below her swim cap. It felt perfect. A rip current had taken up space in her chest where her heart lived, whipping it about with the force of a hurricane. It was better than coming up for air after being submerged under water.

When Nyla opened for her, she fell deeper into the kiss.

Her tongue wandered and tasted hers, a reminder of sea and air, as if Nyla had sprung up like Venus from the sea. Olivia kissed and kissed her with passion and promises and her own hidden wants—to be held, to be cherished, to be considered, to be desired.

Olivia knew something about desire. She wanted Nyla, pure and simple.

When they broke away, Nyla's eyes were large and glassy, even with the sun climbing higher and higher into the sky, making everything brighter and hotter. She recognized the want in Nyla's eyes, as well. It reduced Olivia's brain to a jumble of circuitry with no clear design.

"You taste—" But Olivia couldn't finish the sentence. She was staring at Nyla's lips and she wanted more.

"Good? Please tell me I taste good."

Olivia's eyes pinned to her lower lip, which she wanted to bite and kiss and soothe. "More than good. You're beautiful and amazing. You taste better than the sweet bread I brought you. And you're so smart, it's kind of scary and wonderful at the same time." Olivia traced a thumb over her cheekbone, her skin smooth and soft. "I'm gonna kiss you again, okay?"

Nyla, whose mouth had fallen open as if on command, nodded slowly and breathed, "Yes."

Olivia nodded in return and kissed her again. She was on her hands and knees, and this time, it was Nyla who pulled her in close. Olivia was flooded with a fierce need, worse than before. She kissed her long and deep, Nyla anchoring herself against Olivia with her strong swimmer arms. She was trapped, body and soul, and she wanted to stay that way until all their responsibilities melted away.

Another splash of water pulled them apart and Olivia

turned to see the turtle half submerged, one fin above the water, creating the chaos.

"Now what did I ever do to you?" Olivia demanded.

The turtle splashed again in response.

"It's okay, Aniki," Nyla cooed gently, careful not to touch it, letting her voice be her comfort. "She's a good one. You can trust her."

There was so much reverence in the interaction, in the way Nyla spoke and held herself, as if at every turn trying to reassure and care for the turtle without startling or terrifying it. Clearly, the turtle sensed Nyla's intentions, because she moved serenely around her, without fear.

Nyla held so much goodness in her heart that even wild animals perceived it, and Olivia felt that rush of protectiveness she usually reserved for her closest family. She wanted to protect that core that Nyla possessed from a world that would just as soon batter and hurt her.

Well, not on *her* freaking watch.

When Nyla looked away from Aniki to glance up at Olivia, she caught whatever was on her face, because she paused. "What is it?"

"Nothing," Olivia said quickly, running a hand up her own arms and pausing at her shoulders. "My shoulders are starting to burn."

"Get that cream on," Nyla fussed. "Otherwise you'll have regrets."

Olivia smiled, thinking, *I have no regrets*.

But what she said was, "I'm on it, *Profe*."

Chapter Fourteen

Nyla

Olivia insisted on rowing them back to land, and Nyla
let her, because Olivia said that she hadn't been useful for
much more than walking upright and being a passenger in a
kayak. Nyla hesitated—she didn't want Olivia's first kayaking experience to be characterized by effort and exhaustion.

"Are you sure about that? You'll be going against the
current."

Lifting her chin defiantly, Olivia retorted, "Don't under-
estimate me, *Profe*. I got this."

Nyla shook her head, unreasonably charmed by this
stubborn woman she'd just kissed, not once, not twice, but
three times. They hadn't been pecks on the cheek either, and
she could have kept kissing her all day. "I don't underesti-
mate you. But I think you are underestimating the sea." She
clasped her vest shut, after checking that Olivia had done up
hers properly. "I have my oar, just in case you need a hand."

"You just sit there and look pretty," Olivia said, settling
into the kayak, this time behind Nyla.

"Whatever you say, *traviesa*." She pulled the kayak off
the sand bank and expertly stepped in and settled into her
seat while Olivia used her oar to push completely off.

"This is where you find out what your dominant side

is. You'll have to compensate for that as you paddle," Nyla coached, glancing back and smiling at the fierce look of determination on Olivia's face. "You'll also notice that the current vectors pushing toward the beach and those running parallel create a diagonal path toward the shore. You'll have to compensate for that, too."

"Only vectors I know are viral vectors," Olivia complained but kept going, at first paddling zigzag and every which way, getting pushed off the straight path toward the shoreline altogether. However, Olivia was a quick learner and despite acting like she was infinitely annoyed with Nyla's instructions, she followed each one, refusing to allow Nyla to put her oars in the water. Finally, they reached the beach head a bit north of where they'd launched, but still within reach of the center.

Nyla jumped out to stabilize the kayak so that Olivia could step out, as well. Nyla was sure it wasn't her imagination that Olivia seemed to stumble out of the narrow red vessel.

"Not bad. You were only off by a little."

Olivia smiled sheepishly. She could take being teased mercilessly, but a genuine compliment undid her. "Told you I could do it."

"Yes, you did." She patted her cheek, impressed by her fearless kayak partner. "Come on. Let's drag this baby back home."

They each took a lead rope and pulled the kayak along the shallows where the current had already broken, leaving eddies of water in the deep wells of sand. It was still morning and the tide was low, so the water's movements didn't pull the kayak away from them. Olivia pulled quietly, casting a glance every now and again at Nyla that she caught. Each time she did, Olivia gave her a smirk that pulled a smile out of Nyla. It thrilled her because she hadn't felt this giddy in a long time, and it gave her an immense amount of pleasure to know that Olivia felt the same way.

When they arrived, Olivia helped Nyla rinse off the kayak and put it up on the rack. When they were done, there was a moment of awkwardness. They both needed to change out of their wet clothes and prepare to confront the rest of the day, but everything was so new and raw between them, Nyla was at a loss and Olivia was clearly as unsure as she was. Finally, Nyla shrugged, stepped forward and kissed Olivia, not as heated as the one they had shared at the enclosure. It was more of a desire for connection, a declaration of understanding and an attempt at normalizing the affection that Nyla wanted to give her.

When they pulled apart, Olivia kept a hold on her hands, staring at her fingertips as she spoke. "I don't know what this all means, but I'd like a chance to do this again." She looked up at Nyla, her wicked, clever dark eyes gone soft and vulnerable.

Nyla almost quipped that maybe they could invite Aniki, but the mood didn't feel right for that. Instead, she nodded and said, sincerely, "Tomorrow night? I'm meeting my mother tonight about a fundraising weekend I'm organizing, but we can visit the artist's quarter."

"I'd like that." Olivia squeezed both her hands before dropping them. "Preferably without that contrary turtle."

Nyla's laughter burst out of her. "Why was I just thinking about her, too?"

"The little stinker left a lasting impression on us."

"She's part of our history now." Nyla faltered, remembering that Olivia had a whole life somewhere else. But she was here now, and Nyla chose to focus on that.

"I have to go. I have a network to bring back online."

Olivia seemed to interpret Nyla's sudden shift in mood to be a reaction to the reminder of the hack, because she added, "I'm going to clean it up and I'm going to ransomware-proof your systems. I am committed to that, regardless of whether I get to kiss the director or not."

"I know you will." Nyla pulled herself together. She couldn't kiss someone and then behave so weirdly. That was not her way. "Can you believe I didn't think about the ransomware attack even once while we were out there?"

Olivia grinned at this. "The power I wield."

"God, woman." Nyla laughed. "Where is your humility?"

"I lost it after I kissed you. Now I'm going to be the most unbearable person in the world."

"*¡Vete!*" Nyla said, ordering Olivia to go. "Get to work already."

Olivia put up her hands in mock surrender. "I'm leaving, I'm leaving. Bye." She turned then paused. "I better see you later."

"*Presuntuosa,*" Nyla retorted, because Nyla knew she would go out of her way to see Olivia, no matter what Nyla was experiencing at this moment. She'd come to depend on their little interactions to bring a sparkle to her day. "Of course I'll see you. I practically live at the center."

With that, Olivia made her way up the path. When she had disappeared from view, Nyla crouched near the gear box, searching through the supplies for a tool that the enclosure would need the next time someone went out. The sun had done a good job of drying most of her clothes, though part of her bottoms were still soaked after putting them over her wet bathing suit. Thank God it was too early for anyone to be out on the beach. At least there would be no witnesses to her trying to gather her thoughts.

She wasn't usually thrown off-balance, especially in her

environment. Water had always been her element, her anchor. But Olivia's sharp mind, careful silences and sudden bursts of humor were unsettling in the best, most dangerous way.

She had leaned in for kisses. And Nyla hadn't stopped her.

But then Aniki had launched herself out of the water like she'd read the moment and appointed herself chaperone.

Nyla snorted as she took a seat on one of the many benches along this strip of beach. "Little traitor," she muttered under her breath, glancing out at the enclosure.

Aniki wasn't a traitor. She was a reminder that the ocean didn't care about timing or hormones. It had its own rhythm that everyone had to respect. Just like healing. Just like falling in love.

The timing for this feeling between her and Olivia was the worst. The center was Olivia's client, and they had a professional responsibility to behave…professionally. And Olivia wasn't here for the long haul. She lived in another corner of the country and had roots there that were as deep as Nyla's. Olivia would leave. And Nyla had never been one to have trysts. She didn't have time to waste on useless pursuits like that. She had a rhythm and she wasn't sure where Olivia fit into it.

But this tension between her and Olivia was real and relentless. And she'd opened the can of worms by not only letting her kiss her, but by kissing her back. More than once. For a long time.

So what was she going to do about it?

That question plagued her as she returned to the center and hopped into the employee showers, taking care to rinse out and moisturize her curls. She could never be too careful with her hair.

Nyla spotted Jack coming down the hallway from Yasmin's office just as she rounded the corner from the dressing room. His gait was relaxed, almost lazy, and he perked up when he saw her.

"Hey, Jack," she called out. She shifted the clipboard in her hands, tapping the schedule as she approached. "I was looking at Aniki's feeding schedule and I was wondering if you'd like to trade with me? I need coverage for tomorrow. You're free, aren't you?"

Jack's smile was lightning quick. "Say less, boss. I've got it."

Nyla made a note on the clipboard. "You're an actual lifesaver." She smiled at him. "Thank you for always stepping up."

Jack visibly preened at the praise. "Hey, we're a team, right? If you need anything at all, with the turtles or with this hacking nonsense, I'm prepared to do my part."

Nyla wanted to hug Jack, but didn't want to overstep his boundaries. Instead, she shook his hand. "You are the best."

"No," he said, giving her hand a final shake before dropping it. "I really think you are the best. You always have been." He beamed. "I'm lucky to work with someone like you."

"Stop," Nyla chuckled. "Now you're laying it on thick."

"Never," he answered. "You need to hear it. Now," he said, changing subjects so fast, it gave Nyla whiplash, "I'm off to help Yasmin go through some backup logs. Between you and me, I think we might be close to decrypting one of our major backup servers, which holds most of our research data."

Nyla felt her eyes grow wide. "Are you serious? Oh my God. Don't raise my hopes like that." If that was true, their turtle migration records would finally be accessible to her, and they'd be able to release the turtles without delays or losing a chance to track them in the wild. "That's wonderful! What does Olivia have to say about it?"

"She obviously has a hand in the work, with this being her project and all, but—" Jack shrugged, spreading his hands "—Yasmin and I are a pretty incredible team, too."

"I'll have to check in with Olivia and her team. Thank you for that update."

"No problem." Jack gave Nyla a million-watt smile. "Well, I'm off. I'll make sure Aniki is taken care of."

After she thanked him once more, Jack left with almost a skip in his step. Nyla was so grateful for him, and it was wonderful that Yasmin thought him up to the task of reviewing code. And if they were on the edge of a breakthrough with the backup servers, she should be over the moon, shouldn't she? That meant Olivia was slowly making progress to the end of her contract.

Nyla didn't really want to think too hard about what that meant.

She had a sudden, overwhelming urge to see Olivia again, but scolded herself. She'd just seen her, and they both had work to do. Planning for the upcoming community event would be a better use of her time. It would make her feel more in control and temporarily take her mind off Olivia and their upcoming date.

They met the next evening, just after sunset, when the sky was already painted in broad, moody strokes of lavender and coral. Nyla spotted Olivia waiting at the edge of the plaza, illuminated by the orange glow of the streetlights, and despite how cool and composed she wanted to be, her stomach flipped the way it always did when she was in Olivia's presence.

"Hope you're hungry," Nyla said as soon as Olivia reached her. Olivia wore her black wide-leg linen pants with a bright shawl around her waist and a white three-quarter-sleeve top. Around her neck lay a necklace with a single large opal hanging from the chain. She looked sleek, universally fashionable and, in Nyla's opinion, good enough to eat.

"I'm always hungry," Olivia replied, eyeing the orange-and-yellow-striped trapeze dress Nyla had chosen for the evening. It covered Nyla from top to bottom, but the dress gave her confidence because it hugged her curves in all the right places. From the way Olivia was looking at her, she thought the same.

"The downtown has such a different vibe tonight," Olivia observed. When they'd last been there, the plaza had been packed with stalls selling colorful wares and wonderful live music on a makeshift stage. Now it was full of people strolling across the giant compass in the middle, with distances to all the major cities of the world etched onto its bronze face. Jazz now played, the mood slower and more refined. During the day, water spouted from strategic holes in the ground, turning it into a free splash pad where children played for hours. It was a joyous little spot, and Nyla loved every corner of her quirky little town.

"Besides turtles, this town is known for the art district on the canal which you can reach by taking the side streets to the east. They're lined with shops, art booths, food trucks and pop-up workshops.

Olivia gave her that wicked, teasing smile that always drove Nyla out of her mind. "Say less. Lead the way, *Profe*."

Nyla couldn't stop smiling as they walked to the opposite end of the plaza and down one of the busier side streets. Nyla was enchanted by Olivia's presence in this otherwise very normal part of her life. Bright colors and golden lanterns illuminated the sidewalks, while laughter spilled out from the tiny tables crammed together like gossiping old friends. Soledad Bay's downtown restaurants and businesses were part of the rainbow directory, projecting the feeling of safety and tolerance that could not be said of every small town in North Florida.

They sampled their way through the food trucks. Cuban sandwiches sliced into thick, juicy wedges, fried plantains drizzled with savory, garlic-rich *mojo*, fresh mango chunks garnishing roasted meat—the culinary choices were endless. They bought a plate to share, piled high with shrimp, lobster legs and grilled scallops, bright yellow wedges of lemon lining the plate. They settled at a tall table with two uncapped bottles of El Presidente beers. Olivia took one bite of tender lobster and closed her eyes in bliss.

"This is what I'm talking about," Olivia said around a mouthful.

Nyla couldn't help laughing. "You can't say that you didn't anticipate how good the food would be here, not after the taco stand." She took a bite of her chimichanga dripping in rich mole sauce and felt the earth move under her feet, it was that good.

"Okay, you might have a point," Olivia retorted, picking up another lobster leg and pulling the meat out with a disposable lobster pick, moaning in a way that made Nyla's skin tingle. Olivia in the throes of surrender must be a sight to behold, and Nyla crossed her fingers and toes, hoping someday, she'd get to see it.

Nyla picked up the habanero pepper, pinched the tip and squeezed out the juices onto a jumbo shrimp. The biting aroma struck Nyla's nose. Olivia watched with a smirk before picking up her own pepper and did the same. Nyla lifted an eyebrow.

"You like it spicy?" she asked.

Olivia waved her hand, as if dismissing her question. "Girl, please, I *am* the spice. The spice bows down to me."

"*Tonta*," Nyla said around a laugh before giving in to the pleasure of the delicious meal. This was her joy besides the turtles, these tiny, familiar moments in the places that brought her comfort. They stitched through the fabric of her otherwise tame existence. But now Olivia was a part of it, weaving herself into Nyla's days until she blended in perfectly. Maybe too perfectly for someone who had only just arrived and might be leaving all too soon.

They lingered over their food, talking about the usual topics—work, the best coffee spots, the worst team meetings. All the while, Nyla felt a buzz grow beneath her skin, the pull of something deeper they didn't dare say out loud. When Olivia caught her gaze and held it just a second too long, Nyla's breath faltered. She looked away, finishing the last of the fried dough she'd picked up for dessert, as if the sugar and cinnamon could ground her.

They walked along, lazily taking in tents full of art, when Olivia pointed to a glass studio tucked in behind a booth selling shell jewelry.

"*The Sea Glass Collective—Make Your Own Keepsake*," Olivia read. "You ever tried it?"

"Once," Nyla answered, glancing through the open door. "They use recycled glass from beach cleanups. It's one of the local conservation projects. You can book a short workshop to learn how to blow glass."

"That sounds like your kind of thing," Olivia said. "And mine too, apparently. I've been told I look great in safety goggles."

Nyla chuckled. "Want to go in?"

Olivia nodded gleefully. "I'd love to."

Inside, the workshop smelled faintly of salt and sand. Bowls of crushed glass shimmered under the lights in sparkles of greens, blues and ambers. The instructor was beginning a demonstration and Olivia watched, eyes glued to the process as if memorizing every step for later practice, except for the hand Olivia slipped into Nyla's. She glanced down to where they were joined as if they'd been holding hands forever. Nyla couldn't focus on the selection of molds, or the mixing of colors when Olivia's skin was pressed so closely to hers.

Somehow, minutes or ages passed until a beautiful pendant with colors streaked through like a rainbow began to form under the heat of the torch and the expert manipulation of the instructor.

"All those broken pieces melting together so perfectly," Olivia said quietly. "I'd love to learn to do that."

"Maybe they have workshops for glassblowing in your hometown," Nyla suggested, though each word tasted like ash as she said them.

"Not the same," Olivia said, stepping away from the remaining demonstration. Their hands separated, falling listlessly to their sides. Olivia glanced up at Nyla, her chocolate-brown eyes dark and unreadable. She opened her mouth, shaped words that never came before she said, "Walk with me?"

Nyla nodded, a *yes* already lodged in her throat before she could think about how dangerous it would be to keep saying yes to this woman.

They wandered out of the shop toward the quieter end of the boardwalk, where the lights out ordinances were fully enforced, the noise of the plaza fading behind them. Night had settled like a soft, downy blanket made of the swish of the sea waves and balmy humidity. The moon had thinned to almost nothing and would slowly fill out soon and hang like a bright wedge in the sky. Nyla's heart beat too fast, each step another tiny betrayal of her common sense.

"So," Olivia said, bumping her shoulder lightly, "tell me something about you I don't know."

Nyla smirked, folding her arms like armor. "That's an incredibly broad request, ma'am."

"Okay," Olivia said, tapping her finger in mock concentration. "Family. Tell me about your family."

That made Nyla hesitate, because wasn't it always like this? Olivia asked questions like she wanted to dig down to the root of her. Nyla had spent years learning to hold her cards close to her chest, to be the stereotypically strong, unshakeable one. But with Olivia, she didn't want to be so guarded. She didn't want to hide behind layers of self-protection. With her, she wanted to drop the carapace and let her reach out and touch the tender flesh beneath.

"Big family," she said finally. "Loud. Close. Dad's side of the family are all Southern Black, born and raised on the Florida-Georgia border. My mother's people are from the Caribbean—mostly the Dominican Republic, but also Puerto Rico, and I even have some relatives from Guinea. I'm still meeting new relatives even today." Nyla chuckled and Olivia's smile followed suit. "Mami's been in the school system one way or another all my life, so I grew up with everyone knowing who I was. I used to hate that. I couldn't get away with anything."

Olivia's eyes went comically wide. "Nothing?"

"Nothing." Nyla chuckled. "If I spoke out of turn, boom, email Mami. Tardy to class? Email Mami. Try to sneak in shorts to change after the end of biology class because that teacher was stupidly obsessed with dress code to the point of giving me a nervous breakdown?"

"Email Mami," Olivia finished.

"You got it. And when she became the high school principal in my senior year, I was never more relieved to be graduating. She would punish me harder than anyone else because she didn't want any accusations of favoritism." Nyla kicked a stone off the boardwalk. "She would say, 'You're not just representing me as a student of this school, but you are also representing me as my daughter. So make your school and your family proud.'"

"That must have been hard." Olivia's soft voice lingered like a caress in the night.

"It was. But it was worth it. It gave me that extra motivation when my own reason for doing things wasn't enough to push me. I wouldn't change a thing."

Olivia nodded at this. "It was the exact opposite for me."

Nyla shot her a sidelong glance. "Really?"

Olivia's face softened, her tone dipping into something almost hesitant. "When I was young, it was just me and my mom. She worked her ass off. East Ward wasn't exactly the easiest place to grow up, but we made it work, with the help of my aunt and uncle. But then she decided to go back to Puerto Rico."

"Without you, right?"

Olivia nodded. "The minute I turned sixteen, she said she had put up with the mainland long enough, that if I wanted to stay, Tío Enrique could use another woman around the place, since his wife had passed away. As if I was ever going to be good at cooking or housekeeping." Olivia chuckled mirthlessly at that. "So she sent me to live with him and his three kids and she went back to Puerto Rico. Left me with them to finish high school."

God. Nyla's chest ached at the matter-of-fact way Olivia

said it, as if it were no big deal, as if something like that didn't leave a scar behind. "That's…a lot."

Olivia shrugged. "It was. But my cousins, they're more like siblings to me, you know? They don't leave me out of anything, even to this day. And my tío Enrique? He is the sweetest man you'll ever meet. It wasn't perfect, but it was ours. Navarros, man, we ride or die for each other."

The tightness in Nyla's chest left little room for oxygen, and it was all she could do to not pant with the weight of it all. "You lucked out. But that still had to sting a little."

"Well, yeah," Olivia said, expertly sweeping her hair back into the shortest ponytail Nyla had ever seen. "You'd think your mother would at least think you're worth sticking around for." Olivia took a deep breath and forced it roughly out of her lungs. "It is what it is. You know, my aunt who died was her sister, and they were close. I wouldn't be surprised if East Ward became unbearable to her after Titi Gabriela's death. Anyway, my uncle didn't do too badly."

"No, clearly he's a good man." Nyla felt the pressure in her chest ease a little at the thought that Olivia had been met with kindness and not cruelty after her mother left her. "And your dad?"

Olivia spread her hands. "A child support check in the mail each month. That's it."

Nyla swallowed hard, wanting to say something that mattered, something that showed she *understood*, but Olivia's gaze was on the ocean now, her thoughts far-off and unreachable.

"I guess that's why I built my life around East Ward," Olivia concluded. "It's where everything started for me. It's my home."

They walked in silence for a while, their steps falling into an easy rhythm. But inside Nyla's head, her thoughts were anything but easy. They ping-ponged and ricocheted off each other, never quite coming to rest. What was she doing? Letting herself feel things for someone who would be gone soon, back to a world she felt as closely tied to as Nyla felt to her own. There wasn't a city in the world that could replace Soledad Bay for her. Was East Ward Olivia's Soledad Bay?

Olivia's fingers brushed hers, just a soft request for contact, or comfort, Nyla didn't know and didn't care which. She didn't pull away. She fell into it, opened herself up to the question that warmed the tips of Olivia's fingers and answered her with a touch of her own.

They stopped as if by common accord on the boardwalk, two looming sand dunes in the distance pocketed with the deep grooves of a sea turtle excavating a home for her babies. The view of the sea beyond stretched out before them like a postcard: the plaza's glow long abandoned behind them, the ocean winking in ripples and undulations under the sliver of moonlight. Nyla looked down at their joined hands and took a fierce, visceral pleasure in seeing them joined together—Olivia's moonlit-kissed paler ones against the sun-worshipped brown of Nyla's skin. They were two beautiful women. Magnificent. And just a tiny bit unlucky.

"I would never leave here," Nyla said finally, her voice a little rougher than she meant it to be. "My family, my friends and my life's work are all located here. Who else can say that they have everything that defines them in one place?"

Olivia didn't hesitate. "I hear you. My company, my colleagues, my family and friends. My entire life is there." She passed Nyla to look out over the water, her face caught between light and shadow. "I get it. Even my wounds are tied up in East Ward. All my bruises and bumps have a name and a place connected to them."

Nyla looked down at Olivia, seeking out her eyes, which were hidden from her. Her heart was somewhere down between her feet. Nyla's connection to her home was her single most defining feature and, of course, the person she was beginning to care about more than anyone else was just as tied to theirs.

"Have you ever been to the Dominican Republic? Or visited their mountains? I've heard they're beautiful." Olivia asked, and Nyla accepted the topic change.

"I've been to the DR, which was amazing. I've also been to the mountains—" Nyla hesitated before continuing "—but they made me feel claustrophobic, like I was surrounded on all sides."

"And the ocean doesn't make you feel surrounded? It's literally everywhere," Olivia teased.

Nyla's lips twitched. "It doesn't feel the same. I could be Elastic Girl, stretch my arms out for miles and not reach the horizon, and I'd still be surrounded by water. And that's just the gulf. The Atlantic is even more amazing. It goes on forever." She looked at Olivia, at the way her eyes darkened just a fraction, and her breath caught. "But it doesn't make me feel crowded. I can't explain it."

"I'm teasing you about the sea, you know," Olivia said quietly. "I've spent my entire life on the shores of a river. My family comes from an island. So I get the difference, though I admit, I also enjoy mountains. And canyons. Snow and sun. I still think sand is a wicked invention, but everything is beautiful to me, maybe because I grew up surrounded by concrete and steel, and nature looks like a miracle."

Nyla smiled, but melancholy had settled in the gaps of their conversation. She hated the reminder that Olivia's time in Soledad Bay was temporary.

But now that she'd gotten to know Olivia and scratched

a little below the abrasive surface to discover a funny, intelligent and sensitive person, it pained her that she might no longer be a fixed presence in her life. Life could be so unfair.

Olivia caught Nyla's expression and lifted her hand to caress Nyla's face, as if she could wipe the mood away. Finally, she looked into Olivia's eyes. She couldn't know the doubts this conversation was seeding in Nyla's thoughts.

"Did you think I was going to fight you on your preference?" Olivia asked, softer now. "Your preferences are valid, even if people don't agree with them."

"I know, but thank you for reminding me," Nyla said, letting that explanation stand and not the other, deeper disappointment that was taking root in her heart.

Olivia's lips curled into one of those devilish smiles that undid Nyla so much. "I mean, I'll argue with you all day," she said, "but I'll never tell you that it's wrong to feel the way you do."

Nyla laughed, the sound catching a little at the end. "And how did I know you'd be argumentative, even about my preferences?"

Olivia shrugged, her eyes bright. "I am here to make you question all your assumptions."

"Lucky me. Maybe that's exactly what I need."

But was it? Nyla looked out at the water, feeling it again, that impossible chasm between desire and reality, where she currently resided. This couldn't last. And when Olivia left, Nyla knew she'd be the one left standing here, holding the ache of it like the bay held the waters that rushed in from the gulf.

Still… She turned back toward Olivia, who was smiling up at her, the fingers she'd used to caress her face tracing the lines of her cheekbones, the curve of her lips. She was a brilliant scientist, but when it came to matters of the heart, maybe she wasn't the smartest person in the world. That's why Nyla wanted to catch this smile and all her other ones and drink them down until she was full to bursting, even though it was destined to go nowhere.

As these thoughts tormented Nyla, Olivia lifted her head, offering her delicate lips, covered only in gloss, as if she knew the petal-pink tint would be enough to draw Nyla in. She licked into the fragrant sweetness of a mouth that hid so much behind the jokes and sarcasm. She was like a ripe fruit that was waiting for someone to pluck it, to lick and taste its nectar until their mouth was bathed in it. Nyla kissed Olivia, and Olivia, who didn't know what restraint meant on a good day, wound her arms around Nyla's neck and pressed the perfect length of her body against hers. It triggered an instant flood of warmth to all of Nyla's secret places, making her ache and ache. Nyla instinctively pressed her breasts forward, taut nipples crying for relief.

Sex with Olivia would seal her fate, and it would break her when Olivia left. She couldn't afford that kind of compromise.

They pulled apart, panting and hungry, and Nyla wanted to feast until the moon reappeared.

But she had a shred of self-preservation still left in her. When the wind had cooled her body and soothed her desire, she took Olivia's hand and firmly turned them toward the plaza. Olivia was quiet during the walk, allowing Nyla to sink into her thoughts. She kissed her again when they arrived at the resort, a kiss that lingered long after Olivia had gone to her bungalow. Her thoughts, together with that kiss, would continue to plague her into the wee hours of the night.

Chapter Fifteen

Olivia

On the first day after their date of their barely exchanging greetings, Olivia chalked it up to being busy. Flyers for the Lights Out Gala and the Arts by the Sea event had already gone up around town, and businesses called constantly to either procure a table or offer sponsorship. After the second day, they still had barely spoken. The only time Olivia had seen Nyla was during their daily debriefs to discuss the status of the code decryption, not even to say hello.

By the third day, Olivia was convinced that the lack of contact was deliberate. She managed to be productive—the part of her brain that was working on file recovery never really rested. It wasn't allowed to. But images of Nyla, soft in the lamplight, eyes bright, her clear, bell-like laughter weaving between them like an unspoken secret, kept tugging at her. Every moment they'd shared the night of their date looped through her head like a song she couldn't turn off.

Olivia knew this was all temporary. It was work, and work was sacred. It was important to keep things clean and professional. That would be the explanation for why Olivia hadn't seen Nyla except in the context of work for the last three days. She had her number and had thanked her for the wonderful night, but Nyla's response—a *You're welcome* with a wave at the end—was equal parts dismissive and childish.

It served Olivia right. This was a work contract and Nyla was trying to get her center back to functionality. She had gone out with Olivia, enough to give in to their mutual attraction, but in the end, this was her priority. She got it. It didn't take a genius to look at Nyla and know exactly where her priorities lay.

None of that, however, had prepared her for the way Nyla smiled when she let her guard down, the way her voice softened when she talked about her turtles or the quiet vulnerability that slipped out when she thought no one was paying attention.

Olivia ran a hand through her hair. *I'm in so much trouble*, Olivia told herself grimly. *Big, stupid, sea-turtle-sized trouble.*

Now turtles had even taken over her metaphors.

And yet… When she'd said good-night, and walked away from Nyla's lingering gaze, Olivia hadn't regretted a single moment.

Olivia stood suddenly from her chair. The Good Lord had not made her the kind of woman who could sit in a chair and wait for anyone.

The hum of the Nest hit Olivia like a jolt the second she stepped inside, so different from her work environment, which banged on with bright lights, ringing phones and the muted click of keyboards filling the space.

Here, the lighting was natural, the smell was not of cooked circuits and heated motherboards, but salt water and vegetation. The Nest was clinical, yes, but also vibrant and rich and alive.

Much like Nyla.

And yet she hadn't followed up after their…date? Could

she even call it that now? Whatever it was, it had left her feeling raw and wired, too wound up to sleep, too self-aware to keep pretending this was all business. And so damned disappointed that Nyla hadn't felt the same electricity that had kept her eyes wide-open and awake when she'd gotten home.

She'd stared at the ceiling half the night, replaying every smile, every soft word, every glance that lingered too long. And Nyla's eyes—God, those eyes—looking at her like she was both a question and an answer all at once.

What the hell was that all about?

Her heart was hammering as she crossed the room, scanning every corner for *her*.

But Nyla wasn't there. Because of course she wasn't.

After pacing the Nest for twenty minutes, she gave up hope and sank into Nyla's chair. Screw it. If she was going to sit here stewing in her own humiliation, she might as well be comfortable.

Her fingers tapped absently on the keys of the unused computer in Nyla's office, some half-hearted effort to make it look like she had a reason to be there besides her need to find some dignity again. But the truth was, she didn't care about the firewall right now. Not really. Not when Nyla had spent three days dodging her like she'd caught something contagious.

Three days. Seventy-two hours of radio silence when it wasn't work related after *that* kiss. After *that* date. Olivia's brain had twisted itself into knots trying to logic it out between professionalism, emotional overload and Nyla's obsessive work ethic, but none of it explained the cold shoulder. None of it made it sting less.

She was really getting tired of being tried on like a fashionable outfit by everyone in the world, and then getting left on the dressing room floor, with no explanation as to why she wasn't good enough.

She leaned back in the chair, stared up at the ceiling. "This is so dumb," she muttered. She should've just let it go, acted like it was no big deal. But she wasn't built that way. Nyla kissed her like she *meant* it, like her world had tilted a little off its axis, and Olivia was the only thing that could right it. And then she ghosted on her?

Olivia wasn't having that.

The outside doors opened, followed by the shuffle of footsteps. Olivia sat bolt upright.

Nyla appeared in the doorway.

Her eyes locked on Olivia's instantly, gear bag falling unceremoniously to the floor. For a beat, neither of them moved or said anything.

After an unbearable silence, Nyla said, "You're in my chair." Her voice was flat but unmistakably edged.

Olivia wanted to throw something at the wall.

Her stomach did a weird flip. She straightened, playing it cool even though her pulse was wrecked. "Oh, hey. Sorry. I, uh, was pushing a patch to the firewall. Faster to do it directly on the device."

God, girl, your game is so weak.

Nyla arched an eyebrow. "Faster…on my computer? It's been off since the malware hit."

Olivia forced a smile, the kind that barely stayed on her face. "It misses me."

Deflection. Classic. Her one reliable move.

But Nyla wasn't buying it. Olivia could see the walls go up in real time, her guard slamming into place like reinforced steel. It made her fingertips burn and her palms itch. She wasn't going down like that.

"You're acting weird," Nyla finally said.

"Am not."

"Yeah. I mean, you're always weird, but now you're being weird and jumpy."

That made Olivia's blood boil. "I might be weird, but at least I'm consistent." She was starting to hear the blood rush in her ears. She stood up, but it didn't help. The air between them was thick, buzzing with everything unsaid.

She could've chickened out. But she was too far in now. The words, bitter and remonstrative, clawed up her throat.

"You kissed me. You asked me out, and then *you* kissed *me*."

It came out harder than she meant it to, like an accusation. But it was the truth, and she wasn't going to back down now. Olivia was a lot of things, but she was nobody's doormat. She hadn't been one with her ex and she wasn't going to start now.

Nyla's eyes narrowed. "You kissed me first."

Olivia's breath hitched. "Yeah, then you kissed me back. *And* you asked me out. So how about it?"

There. Take that. Where was she going to go with this now?

She saw her words hit Nyla almost bodily, the way her posture went rigid, her heartbeat probably pounding as loud and as deafening as Olivia's.

"I shouldn't have started anything," Nyla said quickly, voice tight, defensive. "It was impulsive."

Olivia nodded, her throat dry. "Yeah. It was. But it was also good. Like, really good. I liked it, and I was sure you liked it, too."

She saw it land in the way Nyla's breath hitched, like the air had turned heavy.

"That's not the point," Nyla said.

"No, I know." Olivia blew out a breath, dragging a hand

through her hair. "Believe me, I've had the full internal monologue about why this is a terrible idea. There were even charts involved. Venn diagrams. A whole-ass PowerPoint." Nyla's lips twitched but she managed to keep her smile on lock. "Everything is telling me the same thing. Not the best professional move. And you know what? I still don't give a damn."

That earned her a tiny crack of a smile, reluctant but real.

"You made a kiss PowerPoint?" Nyla asked.

"I did. It included subcategories like 'bad puns' and 'excessive turtle-based metaphors.'"

That made Nyla's laugh come sharp and surprised, and the sound made Olivia's heart clench. God, she'd missed that laugh.

For a second, the tension broke like light filtering through the Spanish moss on the oak trees along Shoreline Drive.

But then the quiet came back, heavier than before. The date wasn't just hanging between them; it loomed like a tidal wave. And Olivia, for all her bravado, felt the razor's edge of fear at standing under something so momentous.

"I'm not great at this," Nyla said suddenly, voice low, as if it ached to reveal anything. "Letting people in. Trusting them. I've been badly burned in the past. I'm all about my life's work, this center and turtle rescue. Sometimes it gives me tunnel vision."

Olivia exhaled. They were talking. This was so important. She softened her voice, trying to meet Nyla where she was. "I noticed. And fun fact, I'm all about my business, to the point of micromanagement. But I'm not asking you to sprint into anything. Just…don't pretend that it didn't happen. And don't pretend it didn't matter. Unless you hated everything about that date, it meant something."

It had. She knew it. She *felt* it, in every nerve. And she would have bet her business that Nyla had felt something, too.

Nyla's eyes dropped, her shoulders tense. "It did mean something. I just don't know what to do about it."

Olivia smiled, the relief real and aching. "Good. Me, too. So how about we take it easy, roll with it and see where it takes us, without getting weird and evasive about it? You don't have to figure everything out at once. Surely, as a scientist, you know that."

Nyla huffed out a short laugh. "I do know something about it."

"Good." Olivia stood and approached Nyla, taking her hand. Nyla hesitated before surrendering, holding Olivia's hand. "Let's not overthink it."

Nyla's eyes lifted from where their hands were locked between them. "I just don't want either of us to get hurt by starting something that might not go anywhere," she breathed out.

"It's a risk I don't mind taking." Olivia's lips itched to kiss her, but Nyla had chosen wraparound windows for the office and there was nothing Olivia could do but curse past-Nyla's lack of foresight.

They swayed toward each other, but Olivia held herself in place. "The only thing keeping me from kissing you right now is professional courtesy." She caught Nyla's eyes, blown wide with heat and hunger, and wanted to throw caution to the wind. "I'll do what's right, but don't think for a minute that this isn't everything I want. I promise you—" she inhaled deeply "—the next time we're together, I won't show the same restraint."

Nyla licked her lips, putting Olivia in a proper existential crisis. "That doesn't sound like rolling with it."

"You think?" Olivia asked, inhaling Nyla's scent like it

was the last thing she would ever smell. "Let's hear what you think the next time we go out together."

Nyla shivered and Olivia knew she had her. This phenomenal woman was not getting away from her. "You act like I said yes."

Olivia threw caution to the wind and ran her nose up Nyla's neck, featherlike, quick and incredibly provocative. "Then say it out loud. Say yes, Nyla."

Her exhale was a shaky warmth against Olivia's skin. She breathed again, and on the next exhale, said, "Yes, you pest."

Olivia pulled back, letting her hands go. "Good. Tonight. This time, I'll pick you up."

Nyla nodded dazedly. "Okay."

Olivia rolled her head, feeling the satisfying crack of something echo inside her. "Have a good day, Dr. Dávila."

She turned on her heel, and on an exit that even she had to admit was pretty dramatic, left Nyla's office.

Olivia wanted to do a victory lap around the center.

Instead, she managed to walk a straight line from the Nest back to her work area. She found Yasmin, Al, Dareen and Jack clustered around their workstations, heads bent over screens. The atmosphere was tense, focused but panicked. More like the electric buzz of a team inching closer to something big. Yasmin looked up first, catching Olivia's eye with a flash of something fiercely intense.

"Don't ruin my mood with bad news, Yas," Olivia said, ambling over to her laptop, the sound of Nyla's *yes* still ringing in her ears. "I'm not having it today."

"*Finalmente*, you're back," Yasmin said, waving her over. "Perfect timing. We've been grinding on that code fragment you decrypted all morning."

Olivia's attention went on high alert, sliding her smoothly into work mode. "What do you have?"

Yasmin's fingers flew across the keys, her eyes bright despite the dark circles underneath them. No one on their team had worked as hard as Yasmin, guilt and a possessiveness toward the center fueling her. Olivia was tempted to offer her a job with her company. "We isolated the payload segment with the embedded email. Started a deeper scan on associated files, looking for any buried communication strings or hooks. It's slow going, but—"

"We're seeing patterns," Al cut in, adjusting his glasses as he pointed at his monitor. "Similar encryption keys on the backup servers."

Olivia nodded, stepping closer to study the lines of code cascading down the screen. "Good. Any progress on tracing the email with the link Anuar clicked on?"

Yasmin's lips pressed into a thin line. "A few dark web hits, but nothing concrete yet."

From the corner, Jack's voice cut through. "I think we're close. Isn't that right, Yasmin?"

Yasmin nodded but didn't say anything, turning her focus back to her monitor with laser intensity. The closer they got to uncovering the source of the malware, the closer they got to landing on a full decryption key to free up the remaining backup systems. For now, it would be one file at a time.

"Dionne is on the schedule for debriefing today?" Olivia asked, eyes scanning the room again.

"Scheduled in person for her daily check-in," Dareen replied, glancing at her watch. "Should be here soon."

"And Nyla?" Olivia asked before she could stop herself, trying to keep her voice light.

Dareen's eyes sparkled with a knowing look. "Oh, you

know, Nyla's been pretty busy lately. But she'll be updated as always during debriefing."

Olivia coughed, covering her embarrassment. "Right. Okay. Let's keep the focus here. Yasmin, keep that scan running. Deep-dive every server tree connected to the backup systems. I want to know if we're sitting on another vulnerability."

Yasmin saluted with two fingers. "Already on it."

Jack moved back to his laptop. "It's smart work. This level of detail? But we'll crack it soon."

"I think you missed your calling in computer science," Dareen said, patting him on the shoulder.

The door opened then, and the temperature in the room seemed to shift.

Dionne stepped in first, all business in a crisp suit, right down to the striped button-down underneath. Her eyes swept the room like she could assess exactly what they were doing with a glance. And true to Dareen's prediction came Nyla, bringing up the rear.

Olivia's heart stuttered at the sight of her. Nyla looked tired but focused, her braids held back at the nape of her neck. Her aviators sat perched on the top of her head, her sharp eyes scanning the room until they landed on Olivia.

For the briefest of moments, everything else fell away, and Olivia wanted to stay in the space that opened up between them.

"Status update," Dionne said briskly, moving toward the center of the room.

Yasmin jumped in first. "We've isolated the payload segment, tracked an embedded email, and we're mid-scan of the backup servers. We've flagged matching encryption signatures and are monitoring for anomalies."

Dionne nodded, her gaze steady. "Progress?"

"Slow but steady," Olivia added. "It's just a matter of time."

Jack chimed in. "We're all hopeful, of course, but nothing confirmed yet."

Dionne's eyes flicked to him, before turning back to Olivia. "Looking forward to hearing all the details during today's debrief."

"Understood," Olivia said, her pulse picking up again as Nyla moved to stand just a little closer, her warmth a quiet presence by her side.

As Dionne turned to speak with Al and Dareen, Yasmin's screen lit up with new scrolling code, the feed accelerating in real time.

"Wait," Yasmin said, her voice taut, her hands freezing over the keyboard. "Something's happening."

"What is it?" Olivia stepped forward, her eyes locked on the screen.

"The scan's hitting something." Yasmin clapped loudly. "Olivia, I'm going to need confirmation, but it looks like we might have cracked an encryption layer on the secondary server."

Olivia leaned in: "You're saying…"

Yasmin smiled. "That decryption patch you wrote seems to have worked. The secondary server is opening up."

It took a moment for everyone to absorb what that meant. It was an important step in data recovery and though their work wasn't done, it was a start.

"Verify everything," Olivia said, taking a seat in front of her computer and beginning a pattern search on other servers.

Nyla stepped forward, placing a hand on Olivia's shoulder. "What does this mean?"

Olivia looked up, her face softening. "Think of it like one

of your turtles. It's been tangled up in a net, barely moving. We just cut the first knot loose. There's more work to do, but at least it can breathe again. With a little work, it will get free."

Dareen, who looked like she was about to float away, continued. "It's a good first step, but the full system has to be rebuilt."

Al, who was tapping happily away at his computer, added, "Then we'll lock it down tighter than Fort Knox so this never happens again."

"Exactly," Olivia interjected. "It's an important first step, but it's only the beginning. We have a few servers to go and we won't hand it back over to you until your system is bulletproof."

"But until then?" Feliz asked, rubbing her hands in anticipation.

"Until then," Olivia said, knowing she sounded dramatic and actually not giving a damn. "Until then, we work…and tonight, we celebrate."

Chapter Sixteen

Nyla

Nyla stood just inside the door of La Taqueria Garcia, blinking at the string lights that crisscrossed the ceiling, throwing warm yellow over the pressed-tin tables. The place always smelled the same, like cilantro, lime and fried masa, making it both comforting and familiar. Outside, the sun had only just set, leaving the large windows streaked with the light of sunset, but inside it already felt like a party.

Nyla felt Olivia step beside her, just close enough that their arms brushed. "You okay?" Olivia asked, voice pitched low, a smile tugging at the corner of her lips.

"I'm beyond okay," Nyla said and meant it. Her body was still humming from the adrenaline rush of the last few days, the pure elation of seeing that first server finally unlock. Nyla was starting to believe that there was a light at the end of the tunnel.

The team streamed in behind them: Anuar making a beeline to the reserved tables at the back of the restaurant, possibly to secure a seat next to Al; Yasmin and Dareen, heads close together, laughing while Jack looked on; Feliz, bouncing on their toes, eager to grab a margarita.

Doña Garcia appeared from the kitchen, wiping her hands on her apron, eyes brightening when she saw the crowd.

"*Ay, mira esta fiesta*! Nyla, *mija*, I'm so glad you brought the whole crew tonight!"

Nyla blinked, catching the way the owner's gaze flicked between her and Olivia, her smile sharpening. "You brought your new friend back too, hmm?"

A flush crept up Nyla's neck. Olivia, for once, looked like she didn't have a ready comeback, her eyes darting to Nyla's and then away, a rare tenderness in them that made Nyla's pulse skip several beats. Nyla glanced around, but she had no idea if anyone had heard.

"We're celebrating," Nyla said with a shaky voice. "We made our first progress against the virus."

Doña Garcia laughed and waved them toward the long table where the others were already figuring out seating. "I don't know too much about computers and viruses, but I know how to make the perfect margarita. *Ven, ven*. Double rounds? Tonight is a party night!"

Olivia flashed Nyla a grin and it felt better than any double shot of tequila Nyla had ever had.

They settled in, the din of conversation rising fast. Dionne slid into the seat across from Nyla and clinked her glass against hers as soon as the margaritas arrived. "Here's to clean servers." Dionne smiled with fond eyes, her usual cool veneer relaxed tonight.

"And to the badass team and their leader who made tonight possible." Nyla turned to Olivia, clinking glasses with her.

"You're pretty incredible too, Dr. Dávila," Olivia retorted, her eyes shining with more than just professional admiration. The table broke into cheers and claps, and Nyla caught Olivia's gaze full of a steady, bright warmth that Nyla wanted to bathe in.

Plates of tacos, sizzling fajitas, burritos and *mariscos*

began arriving, the table crowded with color and scent. Nyla found herself laughing more easily than she had in weeks, letting the tension bleed out with every joke she shared. Anuar told some wild story from his undergrad days in Universidad Nacional Autónoma de Mexicos in Mexico City; Yasmin and Dareen argued good-naturedly over which salsa was the spiciest; Feliz tried to get Dionne to agree to karaoke after dinner; and Jack joined in Al and Anuar's conversation about the ocean deoxygenation in the northern gulf, and its visible impact on sea turtle migration patterns.

Somewhere between the second and third round of drinks, Nyla slipped away to the restroom. When she came back out, she paused in the dim hallway, watching the group of people who had once been two distinct teams but were now her people. Professionals who had worked their asses off, who had shown up for each other and had each other's backs throughout this whole ordeal.

And Olivia.

Olivia was leaning back in her chair, laughing at something Yasmin had said, eyes crinkled at the corners, completely at ease in a way Nyla rarely saw her. Nyla's chest ached with the desire to see her like that always, to have access to the quieter parts of such a large personality, to be able to see the things she didn't often show to others.

She moved back to the table, sliding into her seat just as Doña Garcia appeared with a tray of churros and little cups of thick chocolate. "A little sweetness to finish," Doña Garcia said, eyes twinkling. "For all of you, but maybe especially for these two." She gestured between Nyla and Olivia with a wink.

The table erupted in good-natured laughter and teasing, even as Dionne observed them quietly. Olivia actually blushed, ducking her head, and Nyla felt her own face heat, as well. But this time, she didn't pull back. She let herself lean into the warmth of it, meeting Olivia's eyes across the table, something sparking bright and undeniable between them.

The night wound down gently after that. Everyone was yawning and stretching, with promises of meeting up again at the weekend. They drifted out in pairs and small groups until it was just Nyla and Olivia left, lingering by the table while Doña Garcia wiped down the counter.

"You want to walk a bit?" Olivia asked, voice low and hopeful.

"Funny how someone who doesn't like sand always wants to walk in it," Nyla teased, her heart thudding hard in her chest.

"I'm a complex creature, full of contradictions." Olivia offered her hand. "Walk with me?"

Nyla took her hand. "How can I resist when you ask me so sweetly?"

They stepped out into the warm night, the quiet rush of the sea enveloping them. For a long moment, they just walked side by side toward the boardwalk in comfortable silence, the glow from the low lamps along the path casting soft-amber shadows across Olivia's cheekbones.

"I remember the first time I met you on this beach," Olivia began with an exaggerated somberness that pulled a laugh from Nyla. "And you threatened to report me for using my cell phone's flashlight on the sand. I always say to myself, romance really does exist."

"I think the best part was you acting like snakes were going to sprout from the sand and bite you. Oh, and not realizing that monitor lizards are not native to any place on this side of the hemisphere."

Olivia dropped her head, her shoulders shaking with laughter. "I knew that. Terror made me forget."

Nyla's pulse was still ticking unevenly from Olivia's laughter, and from the way the moon silvered her hair where it fell loose around her shoulders. God, she was always beautiful, but tonight, something was different. She was softer, less guarded. Maybe it was the victory, maybe the tequila, maybe just them, stripped down after so many weeks of circling each other.

Their hands brushed again, and this time, Nyla's captured Olivia's. She tried to keep her eyes on the boardwalk ahead, on the soft, worn planks beneath their feet. But Olivia's nearness was impossible to ignore. Every movement, every breath seemed magnified by the quiet of the night.

"I meant what I said." Olivia broke the silence, voice low and serious now. "Back there, at the restaurant. You… You're incredible. The way you've handled all of this… I've worked with a lot of people, but never anyone like you."

Nyla swallowed, the words catching on the raw edges of her heart. "It wasn't just me."

"I know." Olivia stopped walking, tugging lightly on Nyla's hand to make her turn. "I just needed you to know that."

Nyla's breath hitched. Olivia was looking at her the way she had at the table earlier, like she was the only thing in the world worth watching. Nyla felt every nerve ending in her body come alive, humming with possibility.

She stepped closer, her hand still in Olivia's, her free hand brushing a stray strand of hair from Olivia's temple before she could think better of it. "You're not so bad yourself," she whispered, her throat tight.

Olivia's breath hitched, her eyes flicking from Nyla's mouth to her eyes and back again. "Nyla…"

And that was it. The dam broke. Nyla leaned in, her lips

brushing softly over Olivia's, once, twice, testing and savoring before Olivia's arms came up around her, pulling her closer, deepening the kiss. It was slow at first, reverent almost, but quickly tipped into something hotter, more urgent. Nyla's hands tangled in Olivia's hair, her body pressing flush against hers, both of them breathing hard now.

When they finally broke apart, foreheads pressed together, Nyla felt like she was standing at the edge of something vast and terrifying, and utterly inevitable.

Olivia's voice was ragged when she spoke. "Come home with me."

Nyla shook her head slightly, her thumb tracing along Olivia's jaw. "No." She laughed softly, meeting Olivia's eyes, her own heart thundering. "You live with a football team. Come home with me instead."

Olivia's smile was slow and deep, her eyes dark with heat. "Yeah. Okay."

Hand in hand, they turned away from the beach, the night stretching wide and breathless around them.

Chapter Seventeen

Olivia

Nyla held Olivia's hand the entire drive to her house on the canal when she wasn't changing gears. The soft-top windows were partially rolled down, Olivia's hair raised by the wind but not reduced to a rat's nest by the time they arrived at Nyla's house.

Olivia wasn't sure what to expect—a tiny house away from Beachfront Avenue, or perhaps a bungalow on the beach not so different from the one Olivia was staying in now.

Turned out it was none of the above. Nyla drove them to an adorable stilt house on the canal, complete with a dock and boat ramp. Olivia studied the cheerful green-and-yellow building, reconciling her expectations with reality.

Nyla caught her befuddled expression when she parked the car and shut off the engine. *"¿Que?"*

"Nothing. I just thought you would be in a very high-tech, ultramodern living situation. This is more like somewhere I'd live."

Nyla stepped out of the driver's side, unrolling the window and sealing it in place. "But it is modern. It's a solar-powered building. Panels located on the roof handle most of my energy needs. I asked the designers to go all in on carbon offsetting, too. I planted gardens on every side, and a native plant courtyard that actually improves air quality."

Olivia couldn't help being impressed. She had never given too much thought to carbon footprints, despite the fact that she worked in a profession that contributed significantly to emitting carbon. "A house like this would cost a fortune where I live."

Nyla shrugged. "The house was a fixer-upper, so I just added modifications over the years. It's always been my dream to live sustainably. Look." She rounded the parking lot to a line of giant tanks partitioned off by fencing. "I installed rainwater collection tanks and high-efficiency plumbing.

"Honestly, there are very few places that take sustainability seriously, so I put the work in myself. Even the windows are designed to maximize airflow and natural light, so I only use the AC when the temperature is extreme."

"That's worth its weight in gold in a state that can get as hot as Florida."

"It is." Nyla stood quietly, lost in thought, and it endeared her to Olivia more. She was this wonderful combination of brilliant, outspoken, nerdy and introverted that drove Olivia out of her mind.

Olivia stepped close to Nyla, taking both of her hands. She was seized with a powerful urge to press her nose against her cheek and inhale the intoxicating smell of the sea and whatever elixir could be called Nyla's scent. "Want to invite me inside, or do I have to seduce you out here?"

Nyla's eyes fluttered shut. "You already seduced me." She opened them again, and the smoky expression in her hazel eyes sent a powerful flood of heat though Olivia. "But I agree. This is not the place."

They held hands as they crossed the gravel and climbed up the stairs. Nyla entered a code in the security pad.

"And these plants?" Olivia pointed to potted plants on the landing before her door.

"Oh, they're just there for the vibe," Nyla said, pushing her door open. She turned when the door shut behind them, and by some magnetic agreement that went beyond conscious understanding, Olivia was pressed up against the wall of the corridor, Nyla's firm body crushed into every curve and indentation of Olivia's skin. The kiss—bruising and hot—exploded like an unpredictable summer storm, bathing them both in the heat of desperation. When they came up for air, Olivia looked wildly around her, drunk on need and want. Nyla barely let her catch her breath before she was kissing her again.

"Door…left," Nyla said between kisses.

Olivia let herself be pulled down the hallway by Nyla, whose hands were buried deep in Olivia's hair, Olivia's hands already making quick work of her clothes. Olivia pulled her head away to catch her breath, her lips soft and bruised. "Do you want to talk about this?" she asked.

"Now?" Nyla asked, almost incredulously, then visibly pulled herself together. "I mean, if you want…"

"No. I don't. I don't want to talk." Olivia took Nyla's head in both hands and kissed her, the soft texture of her braids burning against her fingers. Olivia itched to get her naked, to kiss her soft places and lick her tender spots. She wanted to carry the taste and feel of Nyla everywhere she went.

"Later," Nyla gasped out.

"Got it. Later."

Nyla pressed her in the direction of her bedroom, each step an endless eternity of clothes being pulled off and tossed aside. They were in their underwear when they reached the edge of Nyla's bed. Olivia paused, briefly registering the greens, blues and browns of Nyla's bedroom. But that thought slipped away before the statuesque beauty of Nyla's physique—her swimmer's body sculpted by the physicality of her work, the soft brown skin that glowed, reflecting her exposure to the sun and surf of her corner of the sea. Her long fingers and unpainted nails were chipped from the hard labor of her passion. Olivia wanted them on her.

"You're stunning," Olivia said, running her hands over her shoulders, down her arms, up her hips until they rested on the hefty weight of Nyla's bra-covered breasts. Olivia curled a finger around one strap.

"Can I take this off?"

In answer, Nyla reached behind and undid the clasp, the material falling to her feet.

Olivia shook with her need to taste and touch the firm swell of her breasts and the tight dark nipples that seemed to reach for her. To bury herself in pleasure and shower Nyla with it in turn. She tugged her onto the bed and kissed her tenderly. Olivia let her hands dance along Nyla's skin, feel the silky firmness of it beneath her fingertips. She kissed the long column of her neck, hummed her name into the space of her collarbone and licked the goose bumps that spread across her chest in reaction to her touch. Nyla's long, powerful legs cradled Olivia on each side as she kissed a path down her glorious body and dived into her pleasure, using her tongue and her mouth to bring her closer to her climax. Sarcastic to the point of misanthropy, Olivia had finally found someone to worship and she abandoned herself, wholly and completely, to her mission to wreck Nyla with all the joy she could give her.

Olivia crawled over her body and kissed her deeply, Nyla's flavor flooding their kiss. "I want to watch you come apart," she murmured against Nyla's lips.

Nyla whined, writhing under Olivia's touch, and gripped her shoulders as she arched into Olivia's hand. Olivia's fingers worked their way into Nyla's heat, and she watched ecstasy spread across Nyla's face. She read each sign of abandon and sped up or slowed down according to the moans that spilled from Nyla's full lips. Olivia took one dark nipple between her lips and flicked it with her tongue and was rewarded with her name on Nyla's lips. She did it again and again to each one until the only sound was Nyla's breathless voice repeating her name, *Olivia, Olivia, Olivia* over and over like a song.

"Finish me," Nyla begged, and Olivia answered, her hand moving quickly now until Nyla shattered like the crashing of the sea against the shore. The release went on and on, the currents eddying into the flats that ran over the sandbanks.

Olivia gathered Nyla's trembling body into her arms and held her close as she recovered from her release. "Are you okay?" Olivia asked.

Nyla purred in pleasure. "I don't remember the last time I came that hard." She nuzzled into Olivia's neck, and Olivia savored it. She was strumming with desire, and with a need for release as well, but holding Nyla like this was a pleasure that she had not enjoyed in a long time, a pleasure she was not ready to give up.

"What about you?" Nyla asked, running a hand over Olivia's hip and across the flat of her stomach, and lower, bringing to the surface the mindless heat of Olivia's own need.

Olivia kissed her, pressing the length of her body against Nyla's and shifted so that their still-burning desire pressed relentlessly against each other. Nyla pulled her hand away,

Olivia's core wet and shivery from the contact. "It's okay." Olivia's words fell from her lips, broken with hunger and heat. "I'm nowhere near done with you, yet."

She rocked her hips against Nyla's, shifting until the contact seared through them. Nyla's head fell back, the long column of her throat an irresistible temptation for Olivia's fingertips, which she dragged over the tender skin. Nyla reached up to cup Olivia's breasts, cradling their heft in her hands, twisting and teasing their tips between her forefingers and thumbs as Olivia braced her arms on either side of Nyla. The insistence of their movements made Olivia's thoughts go hazy as pleasure built and built in a relentless wave that crested and crescendoed. Olivia moved faster, watching Nyla keep pace with breathless abandon, her hips rising and bucking with the steady insistence of high tide.

"Baby, I'm so close," Olivia breathed, sliding her hand under Nyla's bottom to lift her close and hook her leg high over her waist. "This time, I don't want to come without you."

Nyla mewed, the gift of language having abandoned her so that all she could do was moan and gasp. After several more determined thrusts, Olivia came, Nyla's cries of release following closely behind.

Olivia's heart raced as she sank down onto the pillow beside Nyla, keeping her arm wrapped tightly around her waist. She kissed Nyla's open mouth, wet, sloppy kisses that Nyla was too uncoordinated to return properly. Olivia buried her lips into Nyla's shoulder, lazily licking the skin there.

"You're not…you're not tired yet, are you?" Olivia asked, unable to conceive of leaving her. Already, her desire for Nyla was building again in throbbing pulses between her thighs.

Nyla laughed before pushing Olivia onto her back, sliding a knee between her legs until Olivia gasped from the contact.

"*Ay, bombón*," Nyla purred. "The night's barely getting started."

Chapter Eighteen

Nyla

Nyla woke to the slow rise and fall of Olivia's breathing, her body curled warm against her side, her hair a dark spill across the pillow. For one long, impossible moment, the world outside her stilt house felt very far away—the servers, the deadlines, the hatchlings—none of it existed. Just this: the weight of an arm slung carelessly across her waist, the faint scent of salt and shampoo clinging to Olivia's skin, the quiet satisfaction humming in Nyla's bones.

And yet, she could already feel her thoughts tightening. She wasn't used to sharing mornings. She wasn't used to the kind of tenderness that made her want to stay in bed instead of making her rounds. She brushed a strand of hair from Olivia's face, watching the woman who had crashed into her ordered life with the force of a hurricane, and wondered, not for the first time, where this would go when this project was over.

When Olivia stirred, blinking awake with a lazy smile that made Nyla's stomach flip, Nyla smiled in return. "Morning," she said softly, pressing a kiss to Olivia's temple. "You're going to be late for work."

"Worth it," Olivia murmured, pulling her closer.

"And I have a mini turtle walk this morning." She giggled

when Olivia buried her nose under the elastic of her bonnet, which she used to protect her braids at night.

"That hot pink looks good on you," Olivia purred, leaving small kisses on Nyla's neck.

"You like my bonnet, huh? I have every color to match my pajamas."

Olivia leaned back, lifting the blanket that covered Nyla's naked body. "So you match this Barbie pink with your birthday suit? That's quite a fashion choice, ma'am."

Nyla reached up to lightly slap her on the shoulder. "Smart-ass."

Olivia dodged the blow. Looking under the blanket at herself, she added, "I think green would match well with me. What do you think?"

"I think you are the silliest person I have ever met."

Olivia kissed her, this time on the nose, then her cheeks, then her chin, before wrapping herself around her, effectively trapping her.

Nyla melted into her embrace for longer than was wise before they finally reached for the rhythm of their day. Because if she lingered any longer, she might never find the strength to let go. And it was virtually assured that someday, she would have to.

The folding chairs on the bluff were dusty from the sea breeze picking up and tossing sand, but the local elementary students didn't seem to mind. They crouched along them, eyes wide and curious as Anuar held up a small model of a turtle nest and explained how to tell if the eggs had hatched.

Nyla tried to focus. The coastal breeze should've helped, brushing the heat from her skin and tousling curls into her eyes. But she kept glancing toward the back of the crowd where Olivia leaned casually against the dune fence, one booted foot resting on the bottom rail, holding her giant cell phone that doubled as a mini-tablet. Even now, she was wired and ready for work at a moment's notice.

She laughed at something Yasmin muttered beside her, head tilted back just enough to catch the sun. Nyla's stomach flipped. She remembered that delicious husky laugh from last night after she'd made Olivia come. Multiple times. The memory of it filled Nyla with an energy that she hadn't felt since she was a teenager. Even now, sex-fueled exhaustion dogged at her, keeping her from forgetting what they'd shared. She forced her attention to the task at hand.

"Okay, so here's the thing about sea turtles," Anuar began, kneeling down so he was eye level with the group. "They don't send us a message like, 'Hey, we're hatching tonight!' But if you know what to look for, the nest *does* give you little hints."

He wiggled the model, showing a cluster of tiny white eggs buried under layers of sand. One of the younger kids leaned in, practically nose-to-nest.

"First, when a mama turtle lays her eggs, we mark the date," Anuar said, tapping the top of the model. "Most turtles take about forty-five to seventy days to hatch, depending on the species and how warm the sand is. So we keep track, kind of like a countdown."

"What if it rains a lot?" one boy asked, eyes scrunched against the sunlight. Nyla handed him a pair of kid-sized sunglasses with the center's trademark illustrated turtle on each temple that she always kept on hand.

"Good question!" Anuar grinned. "Rain can cool the sand and make hatching a little slower. Hot sand speeds things up. So we pay attention to the weather, too."

He pointed to the top of the model. "About two days before the babies are ready, we start seeing signs. The sand here—" he tapped the surface lightly "—starts to sink a little, like the nest is caving in. That's because the hatchlings are all moving around, getting ready to break out of their eggs."

A girl gasped. "Do they just, like…pop out all at once?"

"Kind of." Anuar's eyes sparkled. "We call it a *boil* because it looks like the sand is bubbling up. The nest dips, then bam! One night, the babies push up and all these tiny turtles come spilling out and race for the ocean."

The kids giggled, imagining it.

"Sometimes, we use special tools to listen for movement, or we dig a little window on the side to peek inside. But mostly, we watch the calendar and the sand. When we see the dip, we know it's almost go-time." He waved them closer. "And this week, we think, might be a go!"

The children squealed in delight. When they'd settled, he set the model down and looked out at the beach beyond. "When the big moment comes, we'll be here to make sure those babies have the best chance of making it home."

A hush fell over the group, their faces turned toward the sea, eyes wide with wonder.

It was Nyla's turn. She gestured to the display board Anuar had made. "And here you can see the migration or travel paths, color-coded by year. This is important information, too, when it comes to planning for hatchlings, because turtles always go back to the same beach to nest."

One of the kids raised a hand. "What's the biggest turtle you've ever seen?"

Nyla smiled, wrinkling her nose for effect. "A leatherback. She was almost seven feet long. I think she was as big as my surfboard."

The children's oohs and aahs rose like a chorus.

More questions came. Nyla answered automatically, her

brain caught between the satisfaction of her work and the warmth that spread every time she thought of waking up next to Olivia. The utter and exquisite perfection of looking over and seeing her face, soft and sweet, on the pillow beside her. The memory was bathed in sunlight. It brought her a joy she wasn't familiar with.

Nyla glanced up again and caught Olivia staring. She waved, and Nyla waved back at her with an unselfconscious smile.

"Nyla," came a quiet voice from behind her.

She turned to see Dionne standing a few feet away, eyes flitting between her and Olivia, her expression unreadable. It quickly changed into an indulgent smile when two children raced by, their teacher calling them to come back to the fold. But there was a set to her eyes and mouth that told Nyla she wanted to talk about the center.

"Kids look like they are having a great time," Dionne said, watching them play in the sand between demonstrations. Two volunteers would take them down along the shoreline to show them the yellow flags the center used to identify turtle nests.

"School visits are one of the best parts of this job. I'm glad, with the slow return of our servers, we can do them again. The way I figure it, my parents didn't have all this technology and schools still managed field trips, so why can't we?"

"That's what I love about you," Dionne said, smiling proudly. "You are the most can-do person I have ever met. Nothing holds you down."

Nyla felt heat rush to her cheeks. "You know, this hack really knocked me off my groove, but I'm finding it again. I know CyberHunters will get us fully online soon."

"Honey, can I borrow you for a minute? Promise I'll return you to your babies soon enough."

Nyla looked at Anuar, who was fielding questions, and her group of volunteers providing instructions for the mini turtle walk. "They've got a handle on this. Let's head up the beach a little."

Dionne and Nyla walked until they were well out of earshot of the tour group. "I'll keep this short," she said. "You know I admire how you run this place. But I have to tell you—Olivia's work has impressed more than just me. Word's spreading. People higher up are already talking about how quickly she's turned things around."

Nyla smiled, her chest tight with pride. "She's good and she brings out the best in everyone else."

"I can see it in the way she's been able to position Yasmin and even Jack in ways that maximize their strengths," Dionne agreed without hesitation. "The progress she and her team made this week? I've never seen anything like it. At this pace, you'll be fully operational long before the contract even ends. Exactly what she promised."

That cocky brag that she would get the work done in half the estimated time hadn't been just bluster. She'd pulled it off and proved yet again that she was a professional force to be reckoned with.

Olivia had promised results, and she was delivering. Which meant, true to her word, she'd leave when the work was done.

She'd go back to the home she loved so much, leaving Nyla in the place *she* loved so much. Where would that leave them?

Was Olivia even thinking that far ahead, or was Nyla building sandcastles in the sky?

Dionne's gaze softened. "I know this hack knocked you sideways. But you've done an amazing job collaborating with Olivia, making space in your office, but also in your confidence. You blended two groups that could have easily turned antagonistic, and now you're seeing the payoff. This is what leadership looks like."

Nyla gave a shy smile. She loved to praise others, but often didn't know what to do with it when it came her way. "Thank you."

Dionne touched her arm, warm and steady. "I'm saying this as your friend, now. Never lose sight of the bigger picture. This center is your life's work. It'll be here long after contractors come and go. It was never going anywhere. I hope you understand that, now."

Nyla nodded, but inside, her chest felt hollow. Dionne was right—Olivia, like every other contractor who had come before, would eventually leave. She was proving it every day with her brilliance, with how fast she was solving the problem.

And when it was over, she'd walk away. It was never going to end any other way.

That night, Olivia texted.

Olivia: Want to grab a cocktail? I'm wired after today.

Nyla stared at the screen longer than she should have. Her fingers hovered, temptation tugging at her, telling her to just answer her already.

She could picture it too easily: Olivia leaning across a bistro table, her whiskey-deep voice sharing something absurd that Nyla would not resist. A brush of her hands, the smell of her simple but signature perfume, and everything in the world would vanish except for the persistent desire to have Olivia's hands on her.

But the risk was too great. She had the center to think about. Her career. She'd already been reckless. She couldn't have everything she wanted, and she had to accustom herself to that fact. This center, her life in Soledad Bay. Olivia, in her bed, in her life. She wanted it all. And she wanted to curse the universe for showing her the possibility and then yanking it away from her.

She forced her reply to be cool, distant, all the while hating herself and everything in the world.

Nyla: I would love to but I'm swamped tonight.

Olivia: Need help?

Nyla: No thank you. We'll talk soon.

She watched the typing dots flicker on and off...then disappear.

Nyla set her phone face down and exhaled shakily. She'd done the right thing.

This was the right call.

So why did it feel like something inside her was splintering?

The next afternoon, Olivia showed up at the Nest. Because of course she did.

Nyla was at her desk, surrounded by reports and field logs, when she felt the familiar prickle of Olivia's presence before she even looked up. Her pulse kicked up stupidly, then she crushed it down, hard.

"Hey," Olivia said, her voice casual but eyes searching. "Thought I'd check in before this afternoon's debrief. Got a minute?"

Nyla looked up from her screen but didn't allow her gaze to linger on Olivia or she'd give in to whatever Olivia wanted. "Now that you were able to free the secondary servers, I find myself swamped. If it's urgent, Dionne is on-site. I can send her to help you."

Olivia blinked, visibly thrown. "It's...not urgent. I just thought—"

For a long second, neither of them moved. Nyla kept her eyes locked on her screen, pretending to read a paragraph she couldn't actually process. She felt Olivia's gaze and the palpable hurt that radiated like a heat wave across the space that separated them.

"It's like that now?" Olivia said finally, her voice quieter.

Nyla felt the prickle of tears in her eyes but she managed to keep them from sliding out. "You do such good work, Olivia. So good that your contract will be up sooner than expected." Nyla stared at the screen again. "I'm trying to protect myself here."

Olivia made to speak, but what could she say to that? It had been a short burst of wonderful between them, but wonderful would soon be over, and there wasn't much either of them could do about it.

"I get it." Olivia pulled a pink velvet pouch out of her pocket and set it on the desk. "Here, I meant to give this to you. See you at the meeting."

Olivia walked away. Nyla stared at the small pouch as if it would bite. Finally, she picked it up and undid the tie at the top. A solid glass pendant tumbled out, the very same one they'd seen in the glasswork shop they'd visited together. Tears gathered at the corners of her eyes and her throat burned.

What the hell was she doing?

Nyla curled her hand around the pendant until she thought she might crush the glass back to sand again. She sucked in a shuddering breath, wiping furiously at the tears that streamed down her face before shoving the pendant in a side drawer of her desk. She had to stay strong. Nyla wasn't going anywhere ever, and neither was Olivia.

It was for the best.

Chapter Nineteen

Olivia put the finishing touches on the last network protocol. The secondary backups had been instrumental in providing a framework for restoring data systems. The installation of networked and standalone software had been successful. The antivirus was the last step, and she'd handle that in the morning. It was so robust, it would take a figurative tank to break through. Training the staff would be a matter of hours, not days.

Olivia's team would hand over the network, sign off on the forensics and go home.

There were two things still outstanding—first was her suspicion that someone had purposely revised a code and gotten it into the center's network. Anuar had been the poor schmuck who'd clicked the link, but it really irked Olivia that this person would carry on with their lives and never pay the consequences for the mess they made. There were hints in the code, disrupted logs and uneven backups. All of these were easy to dismiss as inconsistencies in protocol or user errors, but they were too strategic, too well placed, to be pure coincidences.

But all Olivia had were messy logs that made sense to her and her team, but ultimately they could do nothing about.

And then there was Nyla.

Olivia stood and walked to the conference room window, arms folded tight across her chest and her forehead pressed lightly against the cool glass. Outside, the day was sliding into evening, the sun spilling yellow and gold across the sand.

Her gaze shifted, zeroing in on the line of offices across the forested path, where she had a direct line of sight to the Nest. Nyla's lights were off, the blinds drawn all the way down. The same wall she'd erected all week stood in recalcitrant glory against Olivia's gaze.

The salty flavor of heartbreak squeezed her throat shut. God, she hated how familiar this felt.

It was the same crap over and over. Let someone in, give them your time and energy, your body and your affection, then wait for the moment when they realize you weren't worth the effort after all. First her mother, who'd loved Olivia as much as her nature could allow until she reached some kind of natural limit and had to leave. Because love, in her mother's worldview, meant sacrifice, and she'd run that battery down when Olivia turned sixteen.

Then there was Aleysha, who had promised to give things a try until giving things a try had turned inconvenient. There were sacrifices she had been willing to make, but not one of them was reserved for Olivia.

And now Nyla.

Olivia's fingers dug into her arms. She squeezed her eyes shut, breathing through the ache in her chest. For the first time, Olivia felt like she'd found someone who wouldn't let her carry the relationship alone. She had found someone who was willing to go halves on everything, and it had felt so different from anything she'd experienced before.

And then came the withdrawal. The way Nyla wouldn't

even meet her eyes now. All that soft, tentative connection that had flourished between them, brick by careful brick, had been knocked over like a pile of Jenga blocks. Olivia understood where Nyla was coming from—it was reckless for them to go deeper into something that had to end.

Her instincts screamed at her to fix it. To march right down that hallway, bang on Nyla's door and demand answers. She was worth an explanation. But that desire to have answers—first from Aleysha, then Nyla, had evaporated. She no longer wanted to know. Not wanting to be with her was all the knowledge she needed from anyone. She would never go to see Aleysha, and she would never chase after Nyla and beg for her love. She'd been cured of both impulses.

What did I do? Tell me how to make it right. Please don't leave.

Her jaw clenched hard, her nails biting into her skin. No. Not this time. Olivia would never say those words again. Her groveling days were over. She wasn't about to twist herself into knots to prove her worth to someone who'd already decided she wasn't enough.

She walked away from her place near the window, slammed her laptop shut and stuffed it into her bag. The sudden noise startled her, but no one came to check. She'd sent her team home and had been trying to tie up the last reports on other, smaller projects that were taking place in tandem with this one. This wasn't her only gig, even if it was the biggest one.

She had a whole company to run. She didn't have time for these emotional shenanigans.

She slung her bag over her shoulder, her movements brisk and determined, even as her heart thudded dully in her chest. She was *done* letting other people decide her worth. If Nyla wanted distance, she could have all the space she wanted, more space than the width of the Gulf of Mexico. Olivia wasn't going to break herself in half to try to hold on to something that didn't want to be held.

She didn't need anyone. She'd be just fine.

A flickering of overhead lights caught her attention. She looked at the time—it was almost nine o'clock. The lights above the conference room table flickered again, once, twice, then blinked out completely.

Her stomach dropped. "Something's wrong," she said to no one in particular. She was already spinning toward the monitors that were always left on, and punched in several commands.

The main network screen flashed red, error logs cascading like water through a breached dam. Out in the hallway, Yasmin swore under her breath as she walked through the door, yanking off her headphones.

"That's not just a power surge," she tossed out as she settled onto a terminal and started punching the keys.

"Do you ever go home?" Olivia muttered.

"Turtle boil," Yasmin said in clipped response. "It's a pretty big deal. Everyone sticks around for it."

Olivia opened her mouth to answer Yasmin but her screen exploded with code. She swore loudly. "I just lost server access. Check the internal grid. I'm calling the team back in."

While Olivia was on the phone with Dareen, she could hear Yasmin talking to herself, and the commentary wasn't promising. "This isn't random. But how? How the hell did they do it?"

Then the room plunged into total blackness, including the monitors and, Olivia feared, the servers themselves. Olivia used the light from the phone she still held to illuminate the room. Several endless seconds of pure darkness passed, and Olivia held her breath the entire time.

"Come on, generators," Yasmin whispered. Almost as if on command, a low, mechanical hum buzzed to life. Lights returned, dim and flickering in pink emergency mode. Olivia paced as she waited for servers to reboot and go online again.

Yasmin hugged herself as systems slowly returned. "This reminds me of the year Hurricane Adaliz hit. Never thought I'd be reliving that again."

"Not something I had on my bingo card for this project, either," Olivia conceded.

Fifteen minutes later, Olivia's team bounded in as if they'd been emptied from a clown car. Everyone was wearing pajamas and Feliz was even wearing her giant elephant slippers. All of them were in place without a word.

"Thanks, guys. I'll make it up to you," Olivia said.

"No problem, boss," Al said. "Are we on generators?"

"Yeah, just got the power back a few minutes ago."

Al nodded. Dareen's voice cut across the room. "Mainframe just dropped. Rebooting now, but it's looking ugly."

Yasmin swore in two languages as her fingers flew over the keyboard. Olivia ran through protocols, launched scans. "Check for time stamp triggers. Anything that might point to where the breach is located." They had been in the middle of rebuilding the network, so how?

She turned, scanning the room, and found Nyla pale and furious, gripping the door jamb.

"Nyla," Olivia said quickly, pushing down the urge to hug her. All the feelings that had been building these last few days needed to be put aside. Business was business, and they both knew how to stand on it. "How is the Nest's smart grid on your end?"

Nyla blinked. "I checked everything—lighting, alarm systems, climate monitors. It's very new, we only just upgraded last year through the state's eco-tech grant," she rambled, and Olivia wished she could just touch her and bring her back from the edge of panic, but Nyla had shut that down between them.

"We need to monitor the smart grid. From what we can tell, the attack is structural and it's going after automated systems," Yasmin said.

"I'm on it," Feliz said.

Nyla's eyes widened. "Automated systems? You mean the pools, too?"

She didn't wait for further clarifications. She was gone in an instant, braids flaring behind her as she bolted down the hallway toward the Nest's eastern wing.

"Dareen," Olivia barked, "kill the uplink to the enclosure node. Hard shutdown."

"I'm trying. It's locked behind a separate protocol."

Olivia hissed through her teeth, already typing in override commands. Of course it was. They kept it isolated for animal safety. Now it was a liability.

The emergency lights briefly dimmed again, but it was enough to raise every pulse in the room. The system buzzed a warning, then Olivia's override failed.

And somewhere down the hall, she heard the unmistakable pitch of a triggered enclosure alarm.

Her heart punched against her ribs.

Nyla.

She looked at Yasmin. "I'm going to access the panel outside the Nest. If we can't shut the automation remotely, we might have to do it manually."

"Got it," Yasmin nodded.

Without another word, Olivia grabbed her phone and

the Nest's tool kit and took off down the corridor. She had promised Nyla she would fix what was wrong with the center. Even if Nyla no longer wanted her, Olivia never made promises she couldn't keep.

Chapter Twenty

Nyla

By the time Nyla reached the Nest's east wing, the hall lights were pulsing on and off as if the building itself was panicking.

She skidded to a halt inside the enclosure room, short of breath, adrenaline pounding in her veins. A figure worked furiously, crouched at the main junction box, elbow-deep in wires and swearing under his breath in rapid-fire Spanish.

"Anuar!"

He looked up, the red glow of the emergency lights carving deep shadows across his strained face.

"I was prepping for the turtle boil when everything shut down," he said without preamble. "Now I've got falling voltage in two tanks and heating coils cutting in and out. I can't regulate temperature, salinity, pH—" He dramatically dropped the wires he was holding. "I am really starting to miss the old days when people didn't have to depend on automation to do their jobs."

Nyla took in the essential information, darting to the central control panel to check for herself. A swarm of alerts lit up the screen like fireflies—temperature fluctuations, light errors, timer overrides. In confirmation of Anuar's assessment, one tank's salinity balance was already dipping below the safe range.

"Settings," she muttered, eyes narrowing. "Why is everything so far off?"

Anuar's voice cracked. "I have no explanation for this. Did we get hacked again?"

Nyla held her head as if she could head off the stress headache that was beginning to build on the top of her head. Data could be recovered. Buildings rebuilt. But each and every sea creature was irreplaceable. Living beings were not chess pieces to be played with, moved around and then discarded. Nyla had no answers; all she could do was take care of her turtles.

Olivia burst into the Nest, her phone's flashlight blazing in one hand, a toolkit slung over her shoulder. Nyla wanted to appreciate the irony of her walking into a turtle rescue center with the very blue light that was so detrimental to the turtle's well-being, but she'd pushed her away and wasn't allowed to have that kind of connection with her anymore.

"I couldn't cut power remotely," Olivia said, her voice terse. Nothing like the tender, funny way she'd spoken to Nyla. "The Nest's smart grid is running on a closed loop and completely off-script."

Jack raced in behind Olivia. "Yasmin told me you were here."

Olivia gave a curt nod before she strode to the wall panel beside Anuar, eyes flying over the breaker index. "Where's your hard kill?"

"There." Anuar pointed with a jerk of his chin. "Corner console."

Olivia's eyes darted over the schematics, taking in the pathways. "We can isolate the bad node if we reroute power from the western solar bank. It'll get those systems off the network. But I have to tap into it directly."

"Then go. We'll regulate environmental systems manually from here," Nyla said.

"I'll come with you," Jack said.

Olivia held Nyla's gaze, nodded once, then ran off. Nyla suddenly wanted to give her a hug, tell her how impressive she was, but forced herself to turn away and mount the ramp to check the incubators.

"I'm useless here. I'll go monitor the smaller tanks," Anuar said, wiping sweat from his forehead.

Nyla's fingers danced across the controls, killing unnecessary feeds, triaging errors, coaxing the system to stabilize. An egg from a batch that had been rescued after being unearthed prematurely jerked beneath the red bulb of an incubator.

"Not now, baby," Nyla whispered, voice thick. "It's a mess out here."

She looked at Anuar. His jaw was tight, his eyes glassy with focus.

"You good?" she asked.

He didn't glance up. "Define *good*." A sudden burst of light flashed outside the windows facing the sea, yanking their attention away from each other.

"What the hell?" Nyla strode to the window and looked out, the bottom falling out of her stomach. Nests that they'd been monitoring all season were expected to hatch sometime tonight. A turtle boil was a big deal. It was the reason the lab was still open and everyone had stayed late. Watching hatchlings race to the water was the highlight of their work. Turtle babies needed access to moonlight and the stars to make it to the ocean, making it essential that no artificial light disturb their journey to the sea.

Now the perimeter floodlights were blazing, bathing the beach in a storm of harsh white. Security lights, rigged for emergencies, were never supposed to activate during nesting season. Someone had overridden the safeguards. The generator's hum deepened as the emergency circuits surged, flooding the enclosure in artificial daylight, turning their sanctuary into a potentially fatal trap for their hatchlings.

"We need to shut those off now!" Nyla shouted as she shoved open the door to the beachfront, a sudden, angry burst of wind slamming into her, electric with threat. The dunes rippled under the security lights, rising and falling like the labored breathing of an ancient beast. Nests that had sunken in preparation for new life dimpled the sands, ready to chase after the light on their journey to the seas.

But it would be the wrong one. Security lights, artificial and wrong, spilled across the sand, casting jagged shadows against the fencing.

This couldn't be happening.

Nyla's sneakers pounded the boardwalk, her heart battering against her ribs like a drum. The outer enclosure gate was ajar, emergency lights blazing as if on fire, fed by the store of energy in the solar rig, energy that should not have been triggered after sundown.

When Nyla arrived on the sand, nests were burbling and surging. Dozens of tiny bodies, each no bigger than her palm, began to spill out from the sand, drawn like moths to the cursed blue-white gleam. The surf, nothing more than a dark ribbon against a horizon weakly illuminated by the moon, was heartbreakingly far.

Nyla's breath fractured in her chest.

"No!" she choked, resisting the urge to chase after the turtles. Everything that mattered was racing in the direction of suicide and she was only one person. One person and so many hatchlings. She'd never get them all. Panic made her desperate.

Glancing up at the buff, she saw Olivia. "Olivia! The lights!" Nyla shouted.

"I'm on it!" Jack's voice came in answer sharp and loud. Nyla scrambled, pushing whichever tiny creature she could get to away from the fence and away from the sure death that waited there for them. Anuar was beside her as well, pushing them back, scrambling and reaching too precious few while nest after nest gave way, spilling their precious little bodies onto the sand. Nyla's tears blinded her before the potential of so much loss.

Finally, all at once, the false lights cut out. Darkness, vast and endless, reclaimed the beach. Above them, the stars blinked back into view, cold and clear and always present. The moon's light reasserted its rightful place, reflecting soft and welcoming off the rolling waves.

The hatchlings froze, stunned by the darkness. Then, almost by common agreement, one turned, then another, sensing the ancient pull of the ocean's true reflection. Nyla exhaled, her whole body sagging in that single, massive release.

"They're reorienting," she whispered.

Anuar, whose own face had grown pale, nodded with solemnity. "Let's help them get home."

Olivia had descended the bluff, followed by Yasmin, Jack and a handful of graduate students, breathlessly hauling tarps and flash shields.

"We saw the flicker from the lab," one of the assistants said, jabbing a thumb at two students. "I rounded up the grad students and grabbed everything we could."

"Perfect," Nyla breathed, wiping tears away with the back of her hand, sand mixing with the moisture. "Cover the dune and any reflective surfaces. We'll form a wall and keep them safe."

In seconds, there was a line of bodies standing guard over the precious contents of those nests. Nyla, Olivia, Yasmin, Jack and the students crouched like sentinels, their bodies forming a living crescent to cradle the path to the sea. Nyla glanced at Olivia, who was so earnest in this unfamiliar work, it cleaved her heart into pieces. Her fierce warrior, giving her all with such relentless determination that Nyla's heart couldn't contain the enormity of what she felt. How could she have given that up?

She reached out a hand and took hers. "Thank you."

Olivia's smile was small and tremulous, as if she'd been waiting for that touch for an age. They turned their attention to the hatchlings as they continued to reorient themselves, their tiny flippers digging into the sand with newfound purpose. They followed each other toward the shimmering tide, answering a promise that had been made to them since the beginning of their existence. They crawled, steady and relentless, toward their destiny in the sea. Birds appeared, predators prepared to feast on their small bodies, but everyone shooed them away. Tonight belonged to these little hatchlings, and no one would interfere with them.

Beside her, Olivia's jacket was coated in sand, her breath ragged, eyes pinned to the moonlit surf.

"Are you okay?" Nyla asked, voice raw with the layers and layers contained in that question.

Olivia looked over, her face illuminated by starlight. "You love them."

"I do. They're ancient," Nyla whispered. "Their ancestors survived the dinosaur extinction, the rise and fall of countless civilizations. But they won't outlive the damage caused by modern humans. Not unless we fight for them."

Olivia nodded at this, her understanding clear. This was a battle Nyla would never turn away from. Anyone who joined their lives to hers had to understand that.

The last hatchling breached the foam line and disappeared into darkness. They walked the fence line, looking for any stragglers who might have gone too far in the wrong direction. Carefully, they redirected the tiny hatchlings so they could clear the sand and reach the sea.

When they were done, Nyla found Olivia, who had not strayed too far from her. She didn't deserve her loyalty. Clasping her hand, she said, "Thank you for staying. Thank you for fighting."

Olivia's smile was small and a little sad. She squeezed Nyla's hand, then let it go, leaving Nyla emptier than a hatchling nest. "I swear," Olivia said, voice fierce and low, "this will *never* happen again. I'm going to figure out what happened and put a stop to it, once and for all."

Chapter Twenty-One

Olivia

Olivia wasn't going to sleep until she got to the bottom of what happened tonight. There had to be a clue somewhere about what had gone down.

Thankfully, her team was on the same wavelength.

Even after walking the perimeter of the Nest twice, even after confirming that every tank, hatchling and power strip was stable, everyone's nerves refused to settle.

The screen in front of Olivia displayed log trails. Thousands of them, each one a potential clue to the culprit of this crime. Yasmin was examining CCTV footage, Feliz and Dareen were studying security logs and Al was rebuilding the Nest's GRID, locking it down for everything except for the most high-level, administrative access.

By 2:00 a.m., the only keyboards still working were Olivia's and Al's. Feliz had put her head down on her closed laptop, and Yasmin had passed out in the rolling chair, hoodie up like a cocoon.

Dareen's head landed on Yasmin's shoulder.

Olivia was laser focused on her screen, getting up every twenty minutes or so to keep from falling asleep. She didn't do her best work when she was exhausted, but rage and indignation were excellent fuel for getting things done. And heartbreak. She couldn't leave that one out.

Nyla's pullback had hurt.

Her gratitude had been annihilating.

It just made Olivia realize what she couldn't have—a tender Nyla made powerful by her relentless love of the ocean and the turtles that made their homes in a land to which she felt bound all the way to her bones.

Olivia wanted that, and she hadn't been enough to have it.

She rested her chin on her hand, scrolling endlessly. She sensed movement and looked up to see Nyla, watching her from the doorway. In her arms, she held a tray of coffees, a plastic bag and a blanket.

Olivia lifted her head, her hand falling to the keyboard in front of her. Without a word, Nyla set the coffee down, setting one next to Olivia's computer. She reached inside the bag and took out frosted cinnamon rolls, miraculously still warm and fresh, arranging two on a plate and setting it next to the coffee, as well.

"Nyla?" Olivia said, completely befuddled by this turn of events.

Nyla smiled, shaking out the blanket. "You're supposed to be asleep."

"So are you."

She reached over and draped the blanket across Olivia's shoulders, arranging the folds so it wouldn't slide off. Olivia blinked up at her, too tired to be witty. Al looked up from his screen, took in the tableau and gave a soft smile before determinedly returning to work.

Nyla tucked a strand of hair behind Olivia's ear. "I brought the good coffee," Nyla added. "Bustello, from my office stash."

"I almost feel special," Olivia quipped, emphasis on the

word *almost*. Because Nyla had made her feel like the center of the universe, but had still let her go. Olivia lifted the cup, sipped and closed her eyes like it physically healed her.

"You know, I'll forgive anything for good coffee," she whispered.

Nyla laughed, just once, soft and surprised. "You should demand more than coffee. You're worth it."

Olivia took another sip, paused to consider her words, then said, "You're right, I am worth more than that. And so are you."

Yasmin snorted in her sleep. Olivia jumped from the unexpected—and loud—sound. She snuggled back into her chair, warm beneath the blanket, steam curling from her coffee cup and Nyla looking at her like she'd hung the moon.

If only it was real.

Yasmin murmured something unintelligible in her sleep.

"I'm glad you're here," Nyla said suddenly.

Olivia's heart gave a fierce beat that sent pain and longing racing through her veins.

Ask me to stay and I will.

"Me, too," she said, instead.

At around four in the morning, Yasmin sat straight up out of her seat, knocking Dareen awake.

"Of course!" she exclaimed, wrestling out from under her hoodie to open her computer.

"Wha-what happened?" Dareen murmured, sleep slurring every syllable.

Olivia lifted her weary head. Al had given up and put his head on his arms, while Feliz had come back from the dead. Nyla had gone back to the Nest, where she and Anuar were cleaning up the mess after tonight's breach.

Yasmin leaned in. "I just remembered something."

Olivia blinked back into focus. "Go on."

"Here." Yasmin highlighted a line of log entries. "Just before the second breach, someone accessed the enclosure node from a remote console, one that hasn't been used since the last firmware update."

"You mean an unused terminal located in the center?"

"Yeah. Secondary admin console. It's basically a dusty backup. They keep it offline except for maintenance."

Yasmin clicked through a few layers of security logs. "Someone turned it on, accessed the system, ran a masking script and logged out. All within a few minutes."

"Trying to make it invisible," Olivia murmured. "Digital camouflage."

"Exactly! We scoured every log for every active networked console in the center. Who would have thought that pulling the logs for a twenty-year-old dinosaur sitting on a desk in the equivalent of a storage closet would yield anything useful?"

Olivia's pulse surged with the possibilities. "Do we have badge swipes? Login access that might coincide with breaches, especially the one from tonight? Any CCTV footage?"

Feliz rubbed her eyes. "There's no way they could have unleashed that level of chaos on a siloed system with its own protocols without manual access."

"I've got the CCTV right here." Yasmin raced through the footage until she found what she was looking for. "You've got to be kidding me." She spun her laptop around for Olivia to see. Al, Feliz and Dareen jumped up to look over Olivia's shoulder. Dareen covered her mouth, Feliz squealed and Al dropped an f-bomb so loud, it ricocheted off the walls.

A grainy still frame loaded from the hall cam. Low-res, time-stamped, unmistakable.

"The little rat," Olivia hissed. "He helped out so much tonight." She was beyond pissed, but there was a light at the end of a long, dark tunnel. She was going to nail this guy, and it was going to feel better than a cold El Presidente on a hot summer night.

"Alright, team," Olivia announced. "This is how it's going to go down."

Chapter Twenty-Two

Nyla stepped into the Nest's main conference room. The room was fuller than usual, oppressively so. Dionne sat at the head of the table, lips pressed into a hard, thin line that never promised anything good. Beside her was a university compliance officer Nyla had met sometime last year, and a state cybersecurity liaison who worked with Dionne. Everyone who had been present during last night's attack was also seated at the table, including Jack, three graduate students and Anuar. Olivia sat to the left of Dionne, her team seated alongside her. She wanted to be closer to her, but there was no way to do so without disrupting the current seating arrangement, so she contented herself with a seat across from her.

They exchanged a glance, and while Olivia's expression was stony and serious, her features softened imperceptibly when she locked eyes with Nyla.

It lasted only a moment. When everyone was situated, Olivia stood near the projector, laptop tucked under one arm. Yasmin sat beside her, clutching a tablet. Their eyes were hard, resolute, no trace of the usual bantering camaraderie. Something had shifted, not between them, but between them and the world.

Nyla's stomach knotted. She knew something was coming, but she had no idea what.

Dionne cleared her throat. "Let's bring this meeting to order."

Olivia stood with the remote in her hand, steady as a metronome. "We're going to walk through what happened last night," she said. "Yasmin will run point."

Yasmin didn't look at anyone when she rose. She clicked to a log view with time stamps and door swipes.

"9:01 p.m.," she said, voice even. "A dusty old computer console, the backup one in storage, was suddenly turned on. It hasn't been touched in months. Then, a single badge opened the storage closet. No one else went in there yesterday."

Olivia leaned forward, recognition flashing across her face. "That's what caused the access irregularities we found," she murmured. "The ones we couldn't pin down."

Yasmin gave a tight nod, the confirmation landing between them before she returned to her presentation.

The CCTV replay still bloomed across the screen: a narrow hallway, the closet door ajar. A figure in profile, hoodie up, shoulders tense, hand on the monitor's power button.

Everyone inhaled as one.

Jack didn't move. Then, too fast, he pushed a smile that didn't reach his eyes. "I was just doing a walkthrough," he said. "Yasmin asked for help with old files last week. I thought—"

Yasmin's gaze cut to him; the first visible crack. "I asked you to carry boxes, Jack."

Olivia clicked to the next slide. "Minutes later, someone used that console to override the safety settings. That's what knocked the power out and tripped the floodlights on the beach. And then the same console shows the shut-off command, when the lights finally went dark."

She looked at him then. "You turned them on, then you turned them off."

Jack swallowed. The smile died. "I saved them," he said softly.

Anuar's chair screeched backward. "Saved? You were trying to kill them."

"I was there first!" Jack's voice jumped an octave, words tripping over each other. "I got to the lights. I saved them. If I hadn't—"

"You shouldn't have turned them on to begin with," Nyla said with slow finality. To think she'd trusted him.

Jack's eyes slid to her as if hoping for cover, found none, and skittered to Yasmin. "You said you needed a partner. Someone you could count on to think ahead. I can be that partner. I showed you I could move." His face hardened. "You never look at me when she's in the room." He jerked his chin at Olivia.

Yasmin went still, like someone had poured concrete from her hairline to her shoulders. "Don't you dare," she said quietly.

He leaned forward, earnestness bleeding into something brittle. "Listen, the fail-safes were there. The moon was bright. It was the perfect condition for them to hatch. I calculated—"

"You calculated what?" Olivia's tone didn't rise, but the edge could've cut glass. "You gambled with living animals."

Jack's breath stuttered. "I knew I could fix it. I knew where the hard shut-off was. I thought if I could get to it fast enough, and show you I can handle a crisis, you'd—"

"What?" Yasmin asked. Not unkind. Just devastating. "Fall in love with you?"

Silence swallowed the room.

Jack blinked hard. "Not like that," he said, which meant exactly like that. "I just… You said after the hack you needed people who step up. I wanted to be that. Show you I can be your backup when things went wrong." He looked around, desperate for someone to translate his heart. "I only flipped the switch. Nobody got hurt."

Anuar made a sound like a choked sob. Al reached for his hand and squeezed.

"Jack," Nyla said. "Look at me."

He did. And for a breath, he looked like a kid who'd just fed the turtles and beamed when praised.

"You risked hatchlings to build a story in which you star as savior," she said. "That's not love. That's control. It's manipulation dressed up as good intentions."

Jack shook his head hard. "No. I would never hurt them. I grew up here. I've been on this sand since I was five. I thought, if I could prove something, Yasmin would see I'm capable. That I'm enough." His voice thinned to a fraying whisper. "I am enough."

Yasmin's chair scraped back. She stood, hands flat on the table. Each word landed like a blow.

"I needed a partner," she said. "Not a disaster. Not a person who manufactures a crisis to audition for my attention." She swallowed. "I never needed a savior. I needed you not to endanger my work."

He flinched like she'd slapped him. "I helped you," he insisted, plaintive. "I've helped all along. I did the nights. I watched the logs. I learned your code. I—"

"And then you used what you learned to hurt the person you love," Dareen interjected, voice stern, but gentle. "That's the part you can't charm your way past."

Dionne rose, smoothing down her blazer like armor. Her

tone was all business now. "Here's what happens next. Jack, you are suspended, effective immediately. Security will escort you to clear your locker. Your access, both physical and digital, will be revoked. You will not return to the Nest or any center property without my authorization."

He opened his mouth. She lifted a hand. "Then, a full report will be sent to the board and our insurers. Tampering with wildlife protection is not a mistake. It is a crime. The authorities will be notified, and the extensive evidence against you will be handed over."

He stared past Dionne, straight at Yasmin. "Tell them I didn't mean to hurt them."

"Intent won't bring a dead hatchling back," Nyla said. The tremor in her jaw was the only hint at the earthquake underneath. "Jack, I will always be grateful for the times you showed up. But this? This makes you unsafe here."

For a heartbeat, all the fight leaked out of him. He looked very young. "I'm sorry," he said, to the floor.

"Be sorry to the turtles," Anuar muttered. "Be sorry to the sea."

Dionne nodded to the two facility guards waiting at the door. Jack didn't resist when they stepped to his side. As they turned him toward the hall, he twisted once more to Yasmin. "I could've taken care of you," he said, soft, like a promise and a plea.

Yasmin's answer was a gift she didn't owe him. "Take care, Jack. Fulfill those promises to yourself now."

The door closed behind them.

Olivia set the remote down. "Operations," she said, voice back to business. "We'll lock down every spare console in this building. No more hidden weak spots. Dareen, draft the internal comms. Feliz, check every emergency circuit tied to the Nest. Nothing runs without a key and a human present."

She turned to Nyla, tone gentling. "We'll seal every gap. This won't happen again."

Nyla nodded once, eyes bright but clear. "Thank you."

Yasmin sat slowly, hands folded, knuckles white. For a moment, she seemed very small. Then she drew in a breath and lifted her chin. "I could really use a nap about now."

Nyla remained rooted to her spot in the chair as people filed out, her hands braced on the table, the adrenaline thrumming through her like a current she couldn't shut off.

She looked up and found Olivia leaving the conference room. Nyla was awash with equal parts guilt, relief and something so tender and fragile, it flooded her with a longing that pulsed like a fresh wound.

She rose to her feet, crossed the room and followed her to the observation point, a place visitors could go to gain an uninterrupted view of the sea. There, Nyla found her leaning her forehead against the glass. She approached slowly until she was standing before her.

"I would have never guessed he would sabotage the center like that after everything the hack put us through," Nyla whispered, her voice rough with unexpressed emotion.

Olivia sighed. "It's wild what a person will do for love." She scoffed. "I can't believe I missed that console. I'm sorry."

Nyla was taken aback. "You're sorry? You have nothing to apologize for. You saved us."

"I didn't save you. I assure you, it was a team effort." Olivia's smile was tired, but real. "Thank Yasmin for the CCTV video and for remembering the old dinosaur computer. It was the breakthrough we were looking for."

"But your leadership gave her the space to do what she needed to do. I've never seen her so happy than when she was working with your team." Nyla's gaze flicked down to

Olivia's hands, then back up, her heart cracking wider. "I have never been so happy."

Olivia huffed out a disbelieving laugh. "Your center makes you happy…as it should."

Nyla withered from the dejection in her voice. "I did everything wrong. I've lived for this center for so long, I forgot that there's room for other things—or people—to live for." Nyla took her hand, and thankfully, Olivia didn't pull away. "I was so fixated on you leaving, on losing you, that I didn't think that maybe I should try fighting for you."

Olivia's face flashed with pain but she shook it away. "You were protecting yourself, your home. I get it."

"Yeah, but who was protecting you?"

Olivia's sudden inhale told Nyla that her words had landed. Nyla squeezed her hand, not giving a hot damn that Dionne was in the building and there was a full staff of people who could walk in on them at any moment. Everyone in that space had sacrificed time, energy and sleep for this center over the last month. Whatever pretense had brought them here, they were her people now.

Olivia was her person.

She stepped closer to Olivia, until their clasped hands pressed between them.

"*Perdóname*," Nyla said quietly. "Forgive me for not showing you the same loyalty and dedication that you have shown me. You deserve so much better. You deserve the world."

Olivia turned her face toward the window, hiding the tears that now trickled down her face. Nyla knew what it must cost a woman as proud and strong as Olivia to shed tears, and her heart broke with the need to wipe them away and to never give her cause to spill tears for her again.

Nyla wiped her face with her thumbs. "Olivia, I'm in love

with you. I want to make this work. Two people as brilliant and capable as we are can surely figure out a way."

Olivia turned her gaze toward Nyla, something unspeakably soft in her tear-reddened eyes, like the gentle shadows that moonlight casts on sand dunes.

"You're in love with me?"

"Yes, *corazón, te amo*. I love you. I'm in love with you, and I want to see where this takes us."

Olivia blinked a few times, as if she were afraid she might not understand her words.

Her silence started to scare her. "Are you okay?" Nyla insisted.

Olivia straightened from where she leaned against the window, wiping the tears from her cheeks. "I think…no, I know I'm in love with you, too."

Nyla nodded, relief overwhelming her ability to think. She lifted Olivia's chin, her face as perfect as starlight. Nyla pressed her lips to Olivia's, who surrendered a miracle that she would never get used to. Olivia opened to her, inviting her in, cradling her in her arms, Nyla pressed into her, the lengths of their bodies molding and yielding to each other. Relief, joy, want, hunger all rose to choke Nyla as she kissed and kissed Olivia. This was something she could live for, something that could give her life shape and purpose as much as the turtles she'd dedicated her career to.

"Does this mean you'll be my date to the Lights Out Gala?" Nyla said when they pulled apart.

"I'll be your date to wherever you want to go." Olivia smiled before offering her a hand. "Will you walk with me on the beach?"

Nyla smiled. "And here I thought you hated sand."

"I do," Olivia said, her lips curling into her signature, devilish expression. "But I think we can come to an agreement on that."

Epilogue

One Year Later

They called it Turtle Tide.

The name of the event for the release of recovered turtles had started as a joke years ago when the center first hosted a community beach day and one of the interns spelled "Team Turtle" wrong on the flyer. To this day, Nyla could not understand how Team Turtle had turned into Turtle Tide in the intern's mind, but like the people who found their way to this town, the name had stuck around.

They'd made it a part of the second annual Lights Out Gala and Arts on the Sea events, until the entire weekend was now known as Turtle Tide, the way these things always seemed to evolve in Soledad Bay.

Nyla stood at the edge of the dunes, clipboard in hand, watching volunteers finish setting up collapsible tents and handwashing stations. Kids were already darting between booths, squealing over the life-size turtle replica. La Isla set up a stand to sell *pastelillos* and guava *empanadas* along with stands from a host of other local restaurants. In particular, the Garcias styled up the beach with a rainbow-colored food truck serving the wonderful tacos, burritos and tamales that could set a person on fire. The ocean stretched behind the boardwalk, silver-blue and aquamarine all the way to the horizon.

The Sea Turtle Research and Education Center had gotten a rebrand after Olivia took one long look at the name and said, "It needs to emphasize rescue, because everything we do here is in the service of protecting and rescuing sea turtles from human encroachment."

The *we* always sent a thrill of pleasure up Nyla's spine. Her hand flew reflexively to the pendant Olivia had given her a year ago, the smooth glass holding the colors of the rainbow, a reminder that there was beauty in the art of fitting disparate bits of glass together into one whole. The way Olivia and Nyla had found a way to fit the pieces of themselves together into a life they shared.

Olivia had given herself over to the way of the turtle with a dedication that made Nyla fall in love with her over and over again.

So here they were, giving out T-shirts with the new title, Sea Turtle Research and Rescue.

"It's shorter, too," Olivia had said when Nyla had agreed to the name change.

She caught sight of Olivia in a special-edition Turtle Warriors T-shirt that was slightly too big for her. She was hanging out near the outreach tent, talking to Gia Marie, Indya's daughter, and her best friend, Miriam. They both wore Sea Turtle Research and Rescue caps with perfectly coiffed ponytails tucked into the gap at the back and T-shirts of the same color and logo. When Nyla walked up, the girls were gesturing animatedly to a clipboard in Olivia's hands.

"So wait," Gia Marie asked, voice cracking slightly with enthusiasm, "you're saying Kayuga's finally getting released today?"

"Yep, she's finally ready to go. Took her a long time after

a nasty infection and two surgeries, but she's gone through every stage of recovery," Olivia said.

"The club kids name them after anime characters," her best friend, Miriam, added. "It's a whole thing."

Olivia huffed a soft laugh. "Nyla told me." She smiled at Nyla, the sun having turned the bridge of Olivia's nose a soft pink. Nyla took out a tube of sunblock and pointed at her before handing it to Olivia.

"Remember Kakashi?" Miriam went on while Olivia applied the cream. "Coolest sea turtle ever. Had a busted fin but still made it back to the water like a boss."

"I remember Kakashi. He was one of my first releases. A real ninja, almost broke my nose with his flipper," Olivia said, impressed despite the injury.

"Dr. Dávila has the coolest field trips," Gia Marie said with deep affection. "She knows how to make science fun."

Olivia handed the tube of sunblock back to Nyla, holding it a few beats longer than necessary when Nyla went to take it. "I agree. She makes everything fun."

Nyla returned her smile, her chest aching with a tender longing for Olivia that accompanied her day and night, even when she was with her. Olivia had been the first person to teach her what it meant to miss a person even when they were present. They'd been doing the long-distance thing for the last year, but a certain pressure had been building in Nyla after the last time she had to say goodbye to Olivia. Nyla was so used to dedicating almost all her time to the center, and Olivia traveled for work more often than not.

Olivia had reminded her that there were more things than the center that she couldn't live without. Olivia was now at the top of that very short list.

Nyla was ready to bridge the two most important things in her life, but she wasn't quite sure how to do it yet.

"Hey," Nyla said when the students left.

Olivia looked up at her, shielding her eyes against the sun. "Hi."

Nyla took the sunglasses Olivia had clipped onto her T-shirt and slid them on for her. "You always forget to put these on."

Olivia threw an arm around Nyla's waist and pulled her in close. "It's my excuse for getting into your personal space."

"Oh, is it?" Nyla teased, her body responding instantly to Olivia's touch. She had to force herself to remember that this was neither the time nor the place.

"Behave," Nyla hissed, gently extricating Olivia's arm from her waist. "Later," she whispered in her ear. "If you're very good."

Olivia crossed her arms and actually pouted. "I don't want to be good."

Nyla chuckled. "You have no choice."

"Fine," Olivia said with exaggerated emphasis. "Ready to release a turtle?"

Nyla glanced out to the sandbar where Anuar was preparing the temporary enclosure they'd set up closer to the shore. "I can't wait."

Olivia followed her to the partially submerged pen, where Kayuga waited in the shallows, swimming with lazy deliberation. Beyond the enclosure, Al popped up out of the water, surprising Nyla.

"Are you here to help us?" Nyla said, rounding the enclosure to give him a hug.

"This cute guy over here invited me, and you know I can't say no to a party," Al answered. His relationship with Anuar had also progressed to the point that they were traveling twice a month to see each other. Al had frequently been Olivia's travel partner when she flew down to see Nyla between projects.

Anuar chuckled, and his cheeks, already pink from the sun and wind, turned bright red. "I'm still cute to you, baby?"

Al waggled his eyebrows. "The cutest. Hey, Olivia, how long are we in town for this time?"

She pushed the sunglasses up her nose. "A week, then we have to get back to headquarters."

Nyla's stomach twisted. She wanted Olivia to stay. She was tired of this back-and-forth, the constant coordination of schedules, the expense of it all. They'd been together long enough to have this conversation. She just had to find the perfect moment to bring it up to her.

She turned to her interns. "Can you press the students back so they don't crowd Kayuga?"

"Yes, ma'am!" they chimed together.

They ran off to do as she asked. Nyla turned to Olivia, Al and Anuar. "Ready to lift the gate?"

Olivia kissed her cheek. This was one of her favorite parts of their work—the turtle release and the turtle boil. She rounded the enclosure to monitor as Al and Anuar undid the latch. On the count of three, they lifted the gate.

Kayuga circled several times before registering the gate opening. His number, 0447, was painted in creamy beige on his shell, a soft shade that blended with this coloring. Together, everyone watched him slip through the opening and slowly swim his way through the waves, his giant shell undulating in the surf until he disappeared under the water.

The crowd of students who had gathered around for the release cheered. Anuar and Al hugged each other, and Olivia pulled Nyla into a hug of her own.

Nyla's heart was so full, she thought all her love for Olivia would burst out like the water that had escaped Kayuga's enclosure. As Anuar fielded student questions, Olivia and Nyla shut the gate and prepared the portable enclosure for inspection in preparation for the next turtle release.

The event lasted into the evening. Kayuga was long gone, a beautiful shadow swallowed by a silver wave. The sand was trampled flat, the *pastelillos* and tacos mostly gone, and the volunteers went home buzzing with that particular kind of joy that only comes from doing good work under the sun.

Once they'd returned to the center and had packed away the equipment, Nyla handed Olivia a beer from her office and they both sat out on the picnic benches that faced the sea.

"You know, Kayuga was one of the turtles I was taking care of when the center was first hacked," she began.

Olivia smiled. "I remember that."

"I'm going to miss him," Nyla continued. "He is a part of our history now, like all the turtles you've helped me care for this year."

Olivia turned to face Nyla, her dark bob lifting with the breeze. Amber lights illuminated the picnic area and even that was infused with the memory of first seeing Olivia on the beach with her cell phone in hand.

"I want to make more memories with you. I'm tired of saying goodbye to you, *mi amor*," Nyla said.

Olivia reached out, threading her fingers through Nyla's. "What are you asking me for?"

Nyla felt her mouth flood with salt. If she wasn't careful, she would cry. "I'm asking to make this permanent. I don't want you to give up anything, but I want to build something with you that lasts."

Olivia grinned, which lit up her face brighter than the moon. "You know, I was discussing things with my team.

We agreed that I could set up another branch here in Soledad Bay. That way, I can stay here with you without abandoning my home, either."

"I know it's an enormous undertaking," Nyla said, almost ashamed to ask her to yet again do so much for her.

Olivia chuckled and Nyla was utterly confused by the reaction. "Why are you laughing?"

Olivia flipped her leg over the bench and pulled Nyla toward her. "Because I already asked about a property about a mile away from the center." She brushed Nyla's hair out of the way. "I wanted to surprise you for your birthday, but you went and anticipated me first."

"Are you serious?" Nyla shouted. "I can't believe it! I'm so happy." She flung her arms around Olivia's neck and held her tight. The excitement had her practically bouncing off the bench.

"I can help you set up. We could get some of my interns to help you. You have to bring Feliz and Dareen. Al won't have to travel between East Ward and Soledad Bay anymore. I know they will love living here!"

"Slow down and catch your breath," Olivia exclaimed. "I'll offer them a transfer." She laughed quietly, then pulled Nyla toward her. "I've wanted to be here with you full-time since the day my contract ended with the center. I just didn't want to rush things. I love you, *mi alma*, and I never want to be where you are not."

"I love you too, *corazón*," Nyla answered, showering Olivia with kisses until their lips met and Nyla couldn't stop herself from giving in to the warm heat of mouth and body. Nyla's hands raced over Olivia, enjoying the magical interplay of soft curves and hard muscles beneath her fingers.

When they pulled apart, Nyla had to catch her breath. "I love you, my fierce, beautiful woman."

"I love you too, Nyla," Olivia said with a sincerity that blasted away any remaining insecurities Nyla might entertain. She was a well-loved woman and she couldn't ask for anything more.

A soft swishing sound caught their attention, and Nyla was moved to see a giant sea turtle digging in the sand dunes before them, throwing sand high up into the air like confetti. She was a beautiful, giant loggerhead with a carapace as large as a snow sled.

"Thank you for showing me this life," Olivia said. "I love you, but I also love the way you enrich my life every day that we're together."

Tears sprang to Nyla's eyes. "Thank you, *cariño*, for the gift of your love and loyalty. No one is stronger or better than you and I'm so grateful to have you every day of my life."

Olivia beamed, as if she'd been waiting her whole life to hear those words. They watched the beautiful turtle dig out the home she would make for her children, the one that would keep them warm and safe until it was time for them to strike out in the world. When she left them to the tides of fate, Nyla and Olivia would be there, watching over them, guiding them home.

* * * * *

 Harlequin® PRESENTS™

Recycling programs for this product may not exist in your area.

ISBN-13: 978-1-335-21396-9

Her Forbidden Royal Boss

 Harlequin Enterprises ULC
22 Adelaide St. West, 41st Floor
Toronto, Ontario M5H 4E3, Canada
www.Harlequin.com

HarperCollins Publishers
Macken House, 39/40 Mayor Street Upper,
Dublin 1, D01 C9W8, Ireland
www.HarperCollins.com

Printed in Lithuania

1 2 3 4 5 6 7 8 9 10 LIT 28 27 26 25

HER FORBIDDEN ROYAL BOSS

JADESOLA JAMES

PRESENTS

Jadesola James loves summer thunderstorms, Barbara Cartland novels, long train rides, hot buttered toast, and copious amounts of cake and tea. She writes glamorous escapist tales designed to sweep you away. When she isn't writing, she's a university reference librarian. Her hobbies include collecting vintage romance paperbacks and fantasy shopping online for summer cottages in the north of England. Jadesola currently lives in the UAE. Check out what she's up to at Facebook.com/jadesolajameswriter!

Books by Jadesola James

Harlequin Presents

Redeemed by His New York Cinderella
Billion-Dollar Ring Ruse

Jet-Set Billionaires

The Royal Baby He Must Claim

Passionately Ever After...

The Princess He Must Marry

Carina Press

The Sweetest Charade

Visit the Author Profile page at Harlequin.com.

"I thank you," said Ikem after a moment, his voice rumbling low in his chest, "for coming. I care very much for my nephew, and you do Kadir and myself a great favor."

Adama was so surprised by his words she nearly dropped her mug. "I am glad to serve the Crown," she finally said.

"Indeed you are." His eyes flickered down; Adama felt that same heaviness in her breasts that had come at the banquet, except this time, thank God, they were restrained by the very tight bra she wore for training. Her nipples were swelling, pushing against the thick fabric in a way that absolutely distressed her, but at least he couldn't see. Not this time. She sat up a little straighter, ensuring that her back did not touch a single one of the absurdly tasseled pillows. She could in no way, shape or form appear to be lounging.

Lust, she told herself. She'd dealt with that before; it wasn't new. This should not be a big deal.